GOOD CATCH

CARLIE JEAN

Printed in the United States of America
First Printing, 2023
ISBN 9798372614239
Kindle Direct Publishing

Editor: Salma R.
Cover Designer: Cat Imb at TRC Designs
Formatting: Qamber Designs & Media W.L.L.
PR: Greys promotions

To my mom, who took me to the library all the time as a kid and inspired my love for books. Now you may want to take me to church after reading this.
Love you.

PLAYLIST

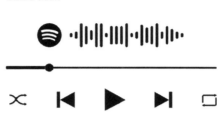

Good Catch
Carlie Jean

Springsteen - Eric Church

Cover Me Up - Morgan Wallen

2002 - Anna Marie

Thinkin Bout You - Frank Ocean

Dilemma - Nelly ft. Kelly Rowland

Say You Won't Let Go - James Arthur

ocean eyes - Billie Ellish

Still into You - Paramore

When We Were Young - Adele

Cruel Summer - Taylor Swift

Starving - Hailee Steinfield

Collide - Justine Skye ft. Tyga

Seein' Red - Dustin Lynch

Dirty Little Secret - The Weekend

Acquainted - The All-American Rejects

Jealous - Nick Jonas

Everywhere - Michelle Branch

Tequila On A Boat - Dustin Lynch ft. Chris Lane

CHAPTER ONE

Rylee

I t's funny how life works sometimes. At least that's what an
infamous quote said, right? But I'm failing to find humour in
the situation I'm in. My brother's best friend, Miles, returned
home after being gone for the past six years.

Miles Anderson was, and I'm sure still is, cocky, hot-headed, and domineering. But growing up, he'd been different with
me. Miles and I had a bond like no other friendships of mine.
He never was solely my brother's friend. We all started hanging
out ever since the day we moved in beside him. But my special
treatment ran out long ago, leaving me in the dust along with
our friendship.

We haven't spoken or seen one another in six years, and
our friendship has ceased to exist since that night eight years
ago. And I'm about to come face to face with him within the
next half hour. How *wonderful* is that?

I quickly glance at my reflection in the rear-view mirror
only to find irritated gray-blue eyes staring back at me. I puff
out a breath of air, sending a loose wave of chocolate brown
hair out of my sight. I take another deep, calming breath and

try to refocus my mind for the upcoming game. Miles is only playing one game with us. I'll barely even have to see him, let alone talk to him. He will play out in center field, and I will be far away at first base.

I'm about to spiral into a cloud of anxiety when my best friend Ava knocks on my trunk, signaling her presence. I jump from the startle and turn my car off.

It's showtime.

Before I even have both feet out of my jeep, Ava starts rambling at a hundred miles a minute.

"Okay, I know this is stressing you out, but look, it's only one game! Your brother is sorry for inviting him, but you know we needed a player with Jaxon gone on vacation, so we're really sorry-"

I cut her off. "Ava, it's not your fault, and you don't have to speak for the both of you. It's weird." Ava and my brother Ryan started dating last year, which most people would think sucks, but honestly, having my best friend date my brother has not changed a thing. If anything, it's made us closer, especially since Ryan and I live together.

"Right, sorry." She smiles shyly, then continues as I head toward my trunk to take my ball bag out, "Can I ask you something?"

Slamming the trunk shut, I throw my bag over my shoulder and turn to face her. "Sure," I say. My stomach is now doing somersaults and preventing me from saying anything else.

Ava stops walking beside me and pulls my arm to face her. Her brown eyes scan mine, and I can see she's nervous to say what she's about to say, which only makes the pool of anxiety in my gut deepen.

"Jesus, Ava, what is it?" I ask, clearly exasperated.

"Ok, fine. Why do you even hate him anyways? It's been

so long that I truly don't even remember why you don't like him," she says hurriedly, as her grip on my arm tenses.

My heart twinges at her words, memories of the past flashing in my mind because of them. I put my hand softly over hers, "First of all, ow," I laugh, and she quickly eases her grip, relaxing a bit.

I don't really want to have this conversation before our game when I should be warming up. But I know she's not letting me move an inch from this spot without an answer. That's Ava for you. She's headstrong, wild, and blunt, but I adore her regardless.

"Miles used to be my best friend. We met when I was 7, and he used to hang out all the time with Ryan and I since he lived next door. But once I got to high school, everything changed. He just stopped talking to me while he and Ryan kept going out but without me. I never knew why," I explain somewhat truthfully, deciding to leave out the major event that was the catalyst for that change. Although I'm 23 now, the memories from what feels like a lifetime ago float through my mind.

Our parents were best friends, and the proximity of our houses meant we did everything together. I don't think there was a day we didn't see one another.

Ava shifts from side to side as she weighs her next words before curling her lips up into a devious smile. "Maybe once he got to high school and his raging hormones kicked in, he realized how in love with you he was and just stopped talking to you to avoid an awkward situation with Ryan?"

My stomach plummets. Where the fuck did that come from? I realize I must have said it out loud when I look at Ava's horror-struck face.

"Woah, calm down. I was just trying to lighten the mood. But," she pauses, and I eye her closely before she blurts out the rest. "It's not totally impossible, you know. Boys are idiots and do stupid things, remember?"

"Do *you* remember? Because right about now, all 8 of your exes are popping into mind when I hear the words idiot and stupid, and you for dating them," I tease, elbowing her in the arm. Diverting conversations is my second language. Although I have thought of her theory once, I quickly dismissed it. I was far from the type of girl Miles was usually interested in.

"Hey, look. I made some bad choices, but it all worked out because now I have my honey bun." She smiles as we start walking toward diamond 3.

"Gross," I snicker.

We put our bags in the dugout before putting our shoes on to warm up. I look around and notice we're not the first ones here. The whole team is, except for our captain, which also happens to be my brother. Oh, and Miles. He's also not here yet. Thank god.

Our coed softball team consists of me, Ava, Ryan, Jaxon, Claire, Brandon, Eric, Katie, Sean, and Lindsay. We have great chemistry, on and off the field. When we're not playing a game, you can usually find us all in one spot or at least a few of us. Simply put, we're like a family.

The best thing about our group is how well-rounded our careers are. Need an electrician? Brandon has you covered. An accountant? Ava is studying to be one. A nurse? Ryan is at your service. If you need a teacher? Well, that's me. A lawyer? Talk to Katie. Ever need your teeth cleaned? Claire would be happy to. That's exactly why Miles will not fit in with our team. Our bond is already set, leaving no room for newcomers. Plus, I already filled the teacher spot. We don't need another one on the team. And before you ask, no, I didn't follow in his footsteps, but that's a story for another day.

Thinking about him has my nerves kicking into high gear and my leg bouncing against the bench. They should be here any minute now. I try to picture what he looks like now, but I draw a blank. I haven't kept up with anything about him over the years. Oh god, I wonder what he'll think of me now? The last time he saw me, I was in grade 10. Let's just say high school me and present me, are two very different people.

I shake my entire body to rid myself of these worries. Why the hell do I even care what he's going to think? Screw him and his stupid thoughts. That's my motto for the day.

"Hey beautiful, let's go stretch," Claire says as she walks into the dugout after throwing with Sean.

Claire is the opposite of Ava. She is softer, sweeter, and the mom of the group. As we reach the grass of the outfield, we begin stretching our arms, and I know she's seconds away from giving me a pep talk.

"How are you holding up?" she asks, stretching her legs into a lunge.

I cross my other arm over my head and feel a crack in my neck as I take a minute to think her question over. I slide my arm back over my head and down to rest at my side as I attempt my signature smile and say, "Honestly, I'm about as nervous as Hannah Montana probably was when she revealed she was Miley. But other than that, I'm just peachy."

We both break out into a fit of laughter. Once we come down from it, Claire steps forward and pulls me in for a hug. I squeeze her back tightly.

"Rylee, I love you, but I hate seeing you so worried over him. He's not worth it. Don't let him control another second of your brain, got it?" she commands.

"I won't, I promise. I'm even going to do my best to be

nice." I spit out the last word because I know it'll be a difficult task. How else am I supposed to act when he decided to vanish from my life with no explanation? It's not on brand for me, as I'm usually the cheerful, peppy one of the group, but I'm willing to make an exception here.

We pull apart from the hug, and I spread my legs wide and forward to stretch my hamstrings. Claire mimics my actions. With my head upside down, my whole world seems to spin when I open my eyes and see none other than Miles Anderson for the first time in six years, approaching the field with my brother.

Our eyes lock and my breathing halts, my heart racing out of my chest. Even upside down, I can tell he's aged well. Too well, dammit.

He waves at us and my conversation from thirty seconds ago is long forgotten as I shoot him my middle finger. Then, I fling my entire body back up before seeing his reaction.

"I thought you were going to be nice, Rylee?" Claire admonishes me as she waves at him and smiles.

"So did I, but actually seeing him in front of me required a change of plans," I huff. My heart continues to pound so loudly that I'm sure he can probably hear it. "Shit, what do I do now? Why did I do that?"

"I wouldn't worry too much. That man is smiling from ear to ear, even after you flipped him off," she reassures me.

Confusion floods my system before transforming into irritation. Why would he smile about that? He must not understand my dislike toward him, but he will find out soon enough. I can feel his presence behind me, and I have the strong urge to run away while I can.

Just like he did.

Instead, I harness all the confidence I can muster and turn

to face him before he approaches me first. My rapid breathing suddenly halts as I take in the man in front of me.

Miles towers over me by a few inches, just enough that he actually makes me feel small. Instead of letting my gaze linger on his body, my eyes fly up to his. Staring right into the green and blue shades I spent my entire childhood looking at fills me with a nostalgic ache for the people we once were to each other. The familiar feeling is instantly gone when I take in his face. A beard covers his sharp jaw where I once thought one would never grow, and his brown hair is neatly brushed to the side.

It's hot as hell. I can still be annoyed with him and appreciate his good looks at the same time, right? God, I don't even know what I'm thinking right now.

My brain is working overtime to account for all the changes to this new version of Miles. But as I bring my eyes back up to meet his, I realize he is doing the same thing.

"Nice to meet you. I'm Rylee Right. In case you forgot," I say sarcastically. A fake smile spreads across my face and I cross my arms over my chest.

"I could never forget you Riles," he says so softly I barely hear him. Riles is what he started calling me when we first met, a mash-up of both our names. No one calls me that except for him, and hearing it for the first time in so long stings.

"You don't get to call me that anymore," I lash out at him.

Fuck his nice guy act. It's only pissing me off more. Is he really going to pretend like the last eight years didn't happen?

"Look Ry, I'm just here to play baseball for one night," he says, sounding defeated.

"And then you'll disappear again for another six years? Thanks for the heads up this time." The words tumble out of my lips harshly, my shoulders squaring up as I prepare for a battle.

"I'm actually staying in town for a bit until my sister has

her babies," he replies blankly, and I get the feeling that he's trying to hide some other emotion. I just don't know what it is yet.

"Great, just keep doing what you've been doing for the last few years, and we won't have any issues," I quip, my eyebrows raised as I shove past him and head toward the dugout.

My body is pumping with so much adrenaline that I have to clasp my hands together as I walk to keep them from shaking at my sides. I need to get a handle on what his presence is doing to me. On one hand, I hate him, but on the other, there's a relief. A relief that has been waiting six years to be wrung out washes over me.

I've missed our banter, and now I'm second-guessing about being so mean to him.

No, my mind fights back. *Stand your ground. Your feelings are valid.*

But the problem is that my feelings are mixed in a tangle I can't clearly see my way through.

I feel a rush of wind at my back right before I notice Ryan walking beside me. He runs a hand through his blonde waves and sighs, "Ry, quit this shit. Put your feelings aside for the game, and maybe try talking to him at some point. He's your friend. Since when do you treat your friends like that?"

Typical Ryan, controlling and chastising me.

I sit on the picnic bench beside the dugout while he sits opposite me, waiting for a reply.

I slide the scrunchie off of my wrist and begin to tie my hair into a ponytail. "Don't worry about the game. I'll do what I need to do. As for Miles, we're not friends, remember? So yes, this is how I treat people who hurt me."

Ryan leans forward on the table, and his tone turns. "Look, we were young. Boys do stupid things. Friends grow apart. It wasn't personal Ry."

As much as I want to call bullshit on that, I bite my tongue. I know it's useless to argue with my brother. Besides, the game is about to start, so instead, I muster up a smile and say, "Perfect, everything is solved then. Guys are idiots, noted."

I stand and ruffle his hair as I walk past him to get my glove. He playfully swats me away in return. My telltale way to know whether he's truly mad about a situation is to ruffle his hair. If he swats my hand playfully, we're okay, but if he catches it mid-air, we're not.

Once I make it to our team's bench, I open my bag and reach for my glove when Ava and Claire appear at my side.

Can I get any peace before this game starts?

"Ry, are you even trying to be nice?" Claire asks, disappointment clear as day on her features. It actually makes me feel a bit guilty, but the adrenaline from my conversation with Miles is still coursing through my veins.

Ava chimes in before I can answer Claire. "Forget about that. Did you not see how he was looking at you?"

Heat rushes to my cheeks involuntarily, and my stomach sinks once again.

"If you mean like someone who's pretending to be nice, but in reality is an asshole who owes me an apology, then yes, I did see that," I say a little too loudly, as the anger takes over. He's the only person to make me feel this way, and I hate it because it's the complete opposite of how I usually am with everyone else.

Claire and Ava's mouths fall open, and their eyes widen. Shit, he must've heard me since there's no other reason for their expressions besides Miles being right behind me.

"Rylee…" Claire half whispers.

I hold my glove tight against my chest and turn to face

15

him. My breath whooshes out of my lungs once again at the sight of him because of the hurt I can see painted all over his face. His eyebrows are drawn in, and the blue in his eyes is softer. His jaw clenches. I don't like that he's hurting, but his feelings aren't my problem anymore.

He swallows down what I think he really wants to say before finally speaking. "Don't drop anything at first."

Just when I started feeling bad for hurting his feelings, he goes ahead and says that. I can't even form words to throw back at him, so I simply roll my eyes and walk past him toward first base. I begin our warmup on the bases by rolling the ball to Eric who's at third base. He scoops it up and whips it over his head directly to my glove.

Ow, that one stung.

I would have continued this with Ryan at shortstop, but of course Miles has to interrupt our perfect flow by stopping to do their handshake on his way to the outfield.

From this distance, I feel like I can put my guard down and take him in a bit more. His tall, athletic frame is not hard on the eyes in the slightest. He's laughing now, a beautiful widespread smile on his face. He always had the best smile, and if I'm honest, I'm happy to see that hasn't changed. His arms and back fill out the navy-blue jersey so well that I have to peel my eyes away and throw the ball to Katie at second base before anyone catches me staring for too long.

Before I can toss it to Ryan, the ump calls the start of the game, "It's time to play ball."

I toss my ball back to Eric who places it on our bench. Nerves start to creep back into my stomach, but I'm used to these ones. The moment before the game begins, I always get jitters, no matter how many years I've been playing.

It's thrilling.

I've always loved sports due to being with Ryan and Miles 24/7, who were obsessed with them, and from generally always being outdoors. Growing up, we always had scars on our knees and dirt on our hands. I miss it, but I push the thought away with a breath and focus on the batter that just walked up to home plate.

Brandon throws the first pitch and the batter swings but misses. The blonde shakes his head at his miss and shifts his feet to prepare for the next pitch. Brandon throws another and this time the bat connects, sending the ball rolling through the dirt toward Eric. Eric runs forward and scoops the ball.

I'm quickly adjusting my stance to have one foot on the base, ready to catch the ball and get the out. Eric's throw is short, unlike our practice throw, so I have to extend my front leg and lunge forward to catch the ball. It might seem complex to some, but to me, it's a split-second decision.

I catch the ball mere seconds before blondie touches the bag. I swing my glove up into the air to show the ump I got it while remaining in an overstretched-out lunge. My teammates always laugh at this, but it's my way of showing them I got it, because there have been some bullshit calls in the past.

"Out," the ump calls out.

Our team cheers and slaps their gloves, not just because it's the game's first play but because we do it after every play. We like to keep the game fun and upbeat, which some teams tend not to appreciate, as they often tell us to turn our music down.

"Nice catch," the blond guy says with a genuine smile on his face as he walks past me and back to his team's dugout.

I smile to myself like an idiot, not knowing how to take a compliment well.

The next batter who steps up to the plate is left-handed. We all shift our positions slightly, knowing the ball is more likely to be hit into the right side of the field. I slightly back up because I really don't want a ball to the face.

The first pitch is thrown, and she makes contact on the first swing, sending a whooshing ball right at me. I barely even have to move since the ball is heading straight for my chest, right where my glove rests, so I simply open it and catch it.

The intensity of the ball takes me by surprise as it slams into my glove and knocks me back a few steps.

Damn, that girl can hit.

Being the overprotective brother that he is, Ryan shouts, "Ry, are you good?"

I shake my head, "Yeah, I'm good."

I swear Miles put something in the air when he said not to drop anything because now, the universe is testing me with two tough plays in the first three minutes of the game. That, or he's my bad luck charm.

The third batter comes up to the plate, and he's ready. His team has two outs, and you can tell he's coming out swinging. Brandon lobs the ball, and the batter makes contact, but pops it up too high. The ball is popped up between Katie and I at second, and the competitive part of me wants to catch this ball and get all three outs to show Miles that I can do my damn job.

"Mine," I shout and run to put myself in position to catch the ball.

The ball hits my glove and I close my hand around it. I hear the ump call the out, and sweet victory fills my body.

Take that Miles.

CHAPTER TWO

Miles

"**M**an, that out you got today was crazy. I didn't think you had it," Ryan exclaims before taking a sip from his beer at our post-game tailgate in the parking lot. The sun is about to set, casting orange and pink hazes across the sky. I take a moment to admire it before answering because sunsets are a guilty pleasure of mine.

"Thanks for inviting me out. I had fun," I admit, taking a sip from my water because I offered to drive us both. It feels strange to be here, drinking and chatting with Ryan like no time has passed. The rush of being back on the field with my best friend in the town I grew up in is like no other. Sure, I played on my university's baseball team in Arizona, but it never felt as good as it did today. I might not have the right words to explain the feelings blooming in my chest, but I know who a large portion of this feeling belongs to.

She's about six feet tall with wavy chocolate hair, deep blue eyes that have hues of grey on the inner part, and a smile that leaves me breathless whenever I'm granted the privilege of seeing it. Which was seldom to none today.

Rylee has given me hints that she's pissed. I pretty much dropped her from my life eight years ago. It's understandable, but I'd rather her hate me than forget about our past. At least with anger, feelings are involved. I think her not being affected by my presence at all would hurt a hell of a lot more.

Do you know what hurt more though? Realizing you were into your best friend's little sister, and you couldn't do a damn thing about it.

Rule number one in the best friend code is the strictly prohibited act of dating one's sibling. I was 16 when I started looking at Rylee differently before I fucked it up shortly after that. No matter how much it pained me to walk away from her, I felt like I had to do it for Ryan. But Rylee was just as much my best friend as Ryan was which made the whole situation a cluster fuck.

I started ignoring her messages, asked Ryan to go out and do things without her, and kept any interaction we had to blunt, short conversations. It felt fucking awful and ate me up inside, but I had to do it because you can't break the 'bro code.' Now, I'm wondering what the point even was because here I am eight years later, after living away for six of them, and she's still all I think about. Day in and day out.

And seeing her for the first time today? Holy fuck, I nearly had to ask Ryan to make sure I wasn't having a heart attack because my entire body felt like it was bursting at the seams with the joy her presence brought me.

Everything around me faded when our eyes connected. Her blue-gray eyes were still as pretty in person as they were in my dreams. She was so goddamn beautiful, and those legs? I was a goner.

Ryan interrupts my train of thought, and thankfully so because the image of Rylee's long, tan, and defined legs in her knee-high socks and near booty shorts are about to give me a semi-hard on. "Nothing against Jaxon, but I kind of want you to come back every week."

"Me too, but I think that idea might only have two supporters," I say. The corners of my lip turn up slightly as I imagine the scowl on Rylee's face if that were to happen. She confuses me. One minute she's shooting me the finger and the next, she's eyeing me up like she wants to memorize every inch of me before going back to hating me all over again. Maybe she had or has feelings for me too...

No, not going to entertain that dream.

Ryan ruffles a hand through his hair before he says, "Yeah, sorry about my sister. I knew she was pissed about the whole high school thing, but I didn't think she'd drag it out like this."

I chuckle to ease the tightness in my chest. "Don't worry man, I deserve it. I was a complete dick to her." I adjust my hat to avoid looking him in the eye, in case he detects anything.

It's so goddamn hard to lie to him because of how much I respect and love him and his family. Which brings me back to why I chose to attend a university out of the state in the first place.

To put as much space between Rylee and I as possible, and to stop myself from doing something stupid.

Ryan swipes a hand in the air, dismissing my comment. "If I really thought you were a dick to her, my fist would've become well acquainted with your face."

I can't help but laugh, and Ryan joins in too. He may be controlling and sometimes too serious, but he is the furthest thing from a fighter. That's why he became a nurse because deep down, underneath it all, he's a giant, caring, teddy bear.

I, on the other hand, have wanted to punch out every guy I've seen her post pictures with on social media for the last few years. According to Ryan, none of them were her boyfriend. I only know this because I'd always find ways to bring it up in our conversations over the years.

"It was probably a good thing we did that. You know how girls are at that age. She probably would've fallen in love with you or something. Could you imagine all that drama?"

Ryan huffs and rolls his eyes before taking another swig of his beer.

I've always let Ryan think it was a mutual decision, that we both wanted some space from Rylee to experience high school as "guys." It was a bullshit excuse, but it helped ease the guilt I felt for the real reason why. The same guilt is easing its way into my system because I'm imagining his words coming to life.

Her being in love with me, running into my arms with that smile and wrapping her legs around my waist–

"I love Ry, but let's talk about something else," he suggests, chugging the remainder of his drink. "I literally see her all the time because we live together."

I knew they lived together in the same house they grew up in because I kept in contact with him over the years. Their parents moved two hours away to Northern Michigan into a spacious cottage overlooking a lake while my parents moved out into a bigger house here just twenty minutes away. I'm aware of the exact distance because I looked up how much space would be between Rylee and I once I came home.

"Although I was excited to get your text yesterday, why the hell did you randomly come back in the first place?" Ryan asks, perplexed. His eyebrow raises in curiosity.

"I came back for Syd. She's almost due and I want to be there for her," I answer truthfully, a small smile forming on my face. "I got back yesterday since school ended last week, and I had to tie up some things before I left."

"Oh right, I should've known. You wouldn't miss that for the world," he remarks sincerely. "I wish you would've visited sooner though, I've missed you man."

I scratch my beard and chuckle. "I've missed you too. Coming back made me realize how much I have missed all these years, you know?"

"Makes sense, so what's your next move?" he asks, getting up and off the tailgate.

I take a closer look at Ryan and thank whatever is above that they don't look alike. Ryan is the complete opposite of Rylee, with blonde hair, green eyes, and an angular face. The only thing they have in common is their height. Basically, you wouldn't even know they were related unless they told you.

His question is one I don't know the answer to. I planned to come home for two months to help Sydney and go back to Arizona before the new school year began. But that plan got shot to hell the moment my eyes landed on Rylee. I don't think I can do it again - leaving her behind. I need her in my life even if it's just as friends because the last eight years of my life have been filled with a void that only she can fill. No matter what I did or how happy it made me, I always wanted to share it with someone.

Her.

Sure, I slept around a few times to relieve stress, but I could never bring myself to commit to anyone because they weren't Rylee. I wonder if Rylee has...*fuck*. I don't even want to imagine her with someone else. Jealousy is a bitch. One that's causing me to curl my fist in an attempt to control the anger threatening to spread throughout my entire body.

"Uhhh, Miles?" Ryan asks awkwardly.

I shake my head. "Sorry, I just truly don't know my next move. I was thinking, and I…" I pause, because I know if I say what I want to, it'll be a permanent decision I can't go back on.

Fuck it.

"I think I'm going to stay here. I already looked into some schools in the area, and there's an opening for a grade 8 teacher position at Westchester Public School."

Ryan's face lights up. "Are you serious?! That is awesome man, I hope you get it. In the meantime, we could seriously use another player. What do you say?"

"Hell yeah, count me in." I grin and hold my hand out for our signature handshake.

Ryan smirks and follows through with the motions of our ritual.

"This is so great, I can't wait to tell Ava. Speaking of her, mind if you drive me home now? She's at the house with Ry, and I miss her," he says, his cheeks reddening at his admission.

"Wow, I didn't know you were 25 and married already," I tease.

"Shut up. You'll understand it once you find your person," he remarks as he heads to the passenger side of my truck.

Little does he know, I already found mine. It just happens to be his little sister. I've done my best to push it away and ignore it, but I'm done fighting it. I knew it the second I saw her tonight. I can't stay away anymore. I don't even know if she feels the same way, and that possibility sends a shiver down my spine despite the eighty-five-degree summer night. But I'm going to give it all I got, starting with getting her to talk to me without her sending me daggers with her eyes.

That should be interesting.

I slide into my truck, close the door, and buckle in. Ryan turns on a country playlist, and I roll the windows down. It's a beautiful summer night, and we plan to enjoy it the right way. With the windows down, country music playing in the background, and the sun slowly fading in the horizon.

I pull out of the parking lot, and we don't say a word for the entire ride home, except for our singing. Ryan and I should never quit our day jobs, let's just say that.

Twenty-five minutes later, I'm turning onto Felix Avenue, the street where I grew up. Suddenly, flashes of memories hit me, and it's bittersweet. We pass the park wedged between two houses, and I'm reminded of the day we tried teaching Rylee how to rollerblade.

Back then we only had rollerblades and helmets, but not the necessary protection for our knees and elbows. Rylee ended up taking a hard hit on the cement, and her left elbow took most of the blow. Ryan ran back to the house to get their parents while I stayed with her.

I remember her eyes were so wide and scared, and I was scared too. I had no idea what to do. I was only 11, and she was 9. The only thing I could think of doing was to hold her hand like I'd seen my dad do with my mom and squeeze it tightly.

I remember how she smiled down at our joined hands and how it made my heart smile. I started reciting SpongeBob lines I knew she always laughed at, and it did make her laugh, even though I could tell she wanted to cry from the pain. Ryan came running back shortly after with their parents and they took her to the ER.

It turned out to be a simple fracture and only required a sling. I think that's also what urged Ryan to be a nurse because he hated seeing his sister in pain with no idea of what to do to help.

I felt a similar fear today as I did then when that wickedly fastball was aimed right at her. I didn't realize I was holding my breath until it released seconds after hearing she was okay. I knew she could catch it since we taught her how to. But it still didn't ease the tension I felt coursing through my body whenever the ball was hit or thrown at her. Any mistake could lead to an injury.

How she makes me feel scares the shit out of me. She's not even mine. *Yet*.

I pull into their driveway, and nostalgia hits in full force as I take in their house. It still looks exactly the same on the outside while my old home has been completely renovated. It seems like no one ever lived there replaced by some new shiny house. I knew my parents had to fix it up to sell it, but I liked the charm of our old place.

"Thanks for the lift. Do you want to come in for a bit?" Ryan asks, his hand on the door, as eagerness sets in to see his girl.

On the one hand, I want a chance to see Rylee again, but on the other hand, I know today was a lot for me, and her. So, I don't want to push it any more than I have.

"Let's catch up tomorrow? I'm a teacher, which means I'll be free for the next eight weeks."

"Yeah, and I work at the hospital, which means I'm never free," he jokes, then continues, "Tomorrow actually works though. I have an early shift, so come over anytime after four."

"Sounds good. See you then man," I say, waving him off as he hops out of the truck.

"Drive safe," he yells over his shoulder as he runs up the porch steps to get into the house. The blinds are drawn so I can't see anything inside the house. God, I sound like a stalker, but you'd be the same way if you hadn't seen the girl you like in years.

Girl I like?

Who am I kidding? I love her, and I've known it since I was 16 years old.

CHAPTER
THREE

Rylee

My alarm goes off at six. I groan and roll over to hit the stop button. Tuesdays are the worst, did you know that? I like Mondays because they're a fresh start to the week and because of baseball, but Tuesdays are just a reminder that you still have four more days to go.

I get out of bed and change before heading to my yoga mat. My daily routine throughout the summer consists of: wake up at six, do yoga for 45 mins, shower, eat and be ready to leave for work by eight. Ava and I work at Bob's Marina, which has the best view of Lake Michigan you can find. We run an eight-week volleyball camp through the week, where we teach kids how to play with some fun social skills-building games.

Ava slept over last night, so I don't have to pick her up like usual, which will give us extra time to get Starbucks this morning. Thank goodness, because I need it. I tossed and turned all night as sleep evaded me at every turn. If you think Miles was the reason behind my lack of sleep, then you'd be right.

When Ryan got home last night, he announced Miles is playing with us for the rest of the season. Oh, and the cherry on top? He plans on moving back here and finding a job at Westchester Public. I was called there so many times last year as a substitute teacher, and the last thing I need is to be working with him. Actually, the last thing I need is for him to be around, period.

Why can't he just go back to Arizona after Sydney has the twins? Why does he insist on coming back at all after all these years?

While showering, I realized that the only way I'll get any of the answers to my zillion questions is to talk to him. My body recoils at the idea, and I shudder under the heat of the water. I don't know when or where, but the next time I get the chance, I'll get to the bottom of this. For my peace of mind, I have to, as much as I don't want to.

Hopping out of the shower, I quickly change into gray biker shorts and a yellow t-shirt. One of the best parts of working this job is wearing shorts and T-shirts to work every day. Being able to work on a beach is pretty great too. I love being outdoors.

As I round the stairs to the kitchen, I see Ava has already started making us breakfast. She has yogurt, seeds, and fruit in two separate bowls, and she's currently topping everything with a dollop of peanut butter. We eat in silence because it's too early to talk. Ava is also smart enough to know that a Miles discussion is the last thing I want right now, so she keeps her lips sealed even though I know she's dying to talk about it.

After finishing our breakfast, we quickly cleaned up the kitchen, and head out the door. Fifteen minutes later, our iced coffees are nestled in-between us in the cup holders. I give Ava about two minutes before she cracks. I check the time on the dashboard: it's 8:42 am. To pass the time, I marvel at the sky above us. It's early, but the sun shines brightly, and the sky is clear of clouds. It's a beautiful day already. I peek at the clock again, and it's only 8:43 when Ava cracks.

"Are we just going to ignore the fact that Miles is going to be in your life again?" she points out.

"I would love that, actually. Thank you," I say, twisting her words against her.

"I don't have enough coffee in me to deal with your sarcasm. Put your guard down, and let's talk, Ry," she says, her tone turning more serious.

Fuck, I won't be able to avoid this.

"Fine," I mutter.

"Good. Let's start with how we can fix this problem between you guys so that you can enjoy this baseball season and your life without worrying 24/7," she says softly.

I can tell she genuinely wants to help me work out this issue. Yes, it would be for her and Ryan's sake as well, but mostly for mine.

Her question takes me aback for a minute as I sit in thought, tapping the steering wheel with my index finger. Finally, I say, "I don't know if it can ever truly be fixed, you know? He hurt me pretty badly, and I don't think I can just forget it."

"That's fair, but there must be something you guys can do to at least be civil, right? You can choose not to let someone back into your life while respecting that they will cross your path from time to time," she advises.

I can't argue with her because she's right. We're both adults. I need to grow up and handle this.

I pull into the parking lot and shift the gear into park. I turn in my seat to look at Ava who's expectantly waiting for me to come up with a solid game plan before she lets us get out.

"I guess it would be worth a try to sit down and talk to him. I have so many questions, and maybe if he can answer them and we can talk it out, it would help." I mumble the last bit, "But I have no idea if he would even want to do that."

Ava reaches over and squeezes her hand atop mine, and gives me a reassuring smile. "Look, I honestly have no idea if he would want to either. But try it. If he doesn't want to, I'll punch him in the throat and tell you that you were right for a month straight, okay?"

I laugh and smile back at her. Ava and I met in high school. We were polar opposites but ended up forming a bond like no other. While I was quiet, sporty, and severely lacking in the boy-friend department, she was the wild child, with boyfriends one after the other, sneaking into R-rated movies and hosting all of the parties. I didn't even have my first real kiss until I was in my first year of college, and it was a drunk dare at a frat party.

How romantic.

Looking at her now, I couldn't be prouder of the person she is. Is she a wild cannon who likes to have fun? Yes. But she's also very smart and disciplined when it comes to work. In fact, she chose to be an accountant because she knew she needed a boring job to balance out the adventurism in her day-to-day life.

Being with Ryan has also calmed her down a little, but not completely. I think Ryan loves how full of life she is, and rather than take that spark away from her he just helps her express it differently.

"What would I do without you?" I sigh and take the keys out of the ignition.

"Absolutely nothing," she teases, hopping out of the jeep.

Hours later, we're taking our lunch break with the kids on the sand. The kids bring their own lunch, which was the smartest thing Ava could have thought of when we created this program. It has saved us so much money and time. She handled the business side of things while I took care of the teaching aspects. We make a pretty good team this way.

I take a bite of my pasta salad and revel in the sun reflecting off the water, the smell of the lake wafting off the waves.

My moment is interrupted when one of our students, Carter, randomly says, "Miss Rylee, do you have a boyfriend?"

Ava stifles a giggle at his question while I nearly choke on my pasta. Where in the hell did that come from? There are two things I love about kids: their brutal honesty and creativity. They'll always keep you on your toes.

Once I swallow the food that lodged in my throat for a second, I reply, "Carter, that's none of your business."

"C'mon, Miss, we just want to know. We know Miss Ava is dating your brother," he reminds me.

Goddamn, this twelve-year-old is too clever.

"No, I don't have one," I admit.

"Have you ever even kissed a guy?"

Is this kid for real?

Ava snickers and I know exactly why she is. My first kiss is a story I like to keep buried away. My first makeout happened when I was 19 during a frat party at university. It was a drunk dare, and I remember it being nothing like the movies promised. Instead of fireworks and passion, it tasted like cheap beer and inexperience. A *great* combo really.

Then, this past year I had sex for the first time at 23. I got to a point where I was tired of waiting for some prince charming to sweep me off my feet and please me. So, during our annual baseball cottage trip in May, I gave it away to someone who didn't deserve it.

It started when Eric brought some of his friends along on the trip. I did not go into that weekend thinking I would lose my virginity, but I guess that's what makes life interesting. You never know what the hell is going to happen next.

Anyway, one of his friends, Wes, had been flirting with me all weekend long, behind Ryan's back, of course. A lot of drinks later, and we somehow ended up screwing in the woodshed during our last night there. It wasn't entirely awful, as he made me feel wanted and sexy. But he came within the first two minutes, and I never got the chance to.

I didn't keep in touch to see if it would go anywhere because the whole ten minutes we spent together were nothing spectacular. So, as you can tell, all of my romantic encounters have been very heartwarming thus far, and it only gets worse.

About a month ago, at Ava's birthday party, Jaxon and I somehow hooked up. We didn't have sex because he spent a total of ten minutes going down on me, and it did nothing for me. I tried to feel the pleasure he was so desperately trying to give, but it wouldn't come. So, I didn't come, again.

Needless to say, our friendship has been a little awkward ever since then. Those are the summaries of the three sexual encounters I've had so far which is why Ava is trying her best not to burst out laughing right now.

"Again, that's none of your business, Carter. But I'd be happy to tell your mom the kind of questions you've been asking at camp," I reply professionally because this is really not the kind of conversation you have with a twelve-year-old.

"Yes, Miss, sorry," he apologizes sincerely. Then he shoves the rest of his peanut butter and jelly sandwich down his throat.

"Alright, lunch is over. Let's do a scrimmage before the end of the day," I announce. I stand and begin numbering kids off to each side of the court.

Ava wipes the sand off her legs and packs up our lunches, then comes over to me and says, "I just realized Carter is the male version of me. Should I warn his parents now?"

This makes me giggle. "Nope, allow them the beauty of uncovering that mystery all on their own."

Once work is done, we climb back into my jeep and blast the air conditioning.

"Wow, today was a hot one. Want to grab a smoothie on the way back?" Ava suggests as she fans herself off.

"I have never heard sweeter words leave your mouth," I swoon. A smoothie sounds perfect right now. I drive us out of the parking lot and head back onto the highway. We have the windows down now to let in the natural summer breeze, and I let my left-hand rest outside of it. I love the rush of wind against my hand.

Ten minutes later, we're sitting on the patio of a smoothie shop because even though it's hot as hell outside, the store feels like an icebox. Ava opted for a berry smoothie while I got the pineapple mango.

"Just a heads up, Ryan texted me that Miles came over," Ava blurts.

I nearly spit my smoothie out, "What? Ugh, why?"

"Well, they're friends, so I am guessing it's to hang out and catch up."

I roll my eyes and tuck a strand of hair behind my ear. "Oh, right," I mumble. I push my smoothie away because suddenly, my appetite is gone.

"I thought you said you wanted to talk to him?" she inquires, confusion lacing her features.

"I do, but I didn't mean today," I groan. I cross my arms over my body, feeling the need to protect myself.

Ava scoots closer to the table and places her arms atop it as she leans in closer to me. "Alright, I'm going to be really blunt here because I am getting tired of having the same conversation over and over again."

Truthfully, I am too, but I am also scared shitless as to what words will come out of her mouth next.

"Rylee, you're not going to like hearing this, but you need to. You like him, okay? Not in the general person like, but in the 'I have a crush,' way," she states like a lawyer representing a client.

My eyes nearly pop out of my head. "What in the world are you talking about? Did they put drugs in your smoothie?"

"Stop trying to change the subject, it won't work this time. You blush whenever we talk about him, and it's not just from anger. I saw the way you looked at him at the baseball game. Is there something that happened when you guys were younger that I don't know about? Something is missing to the story," she proposes, which makes me want to throw up.

I can feel tears pricking my eyes, so I sit up straight in my chair and take a sip of my smoothie to try and compose myself.

Taking a breath, I tell her about the summer before I started high school. It was a Thursday night, which meant Ryan was out volunteering at the nursing home.

Those were Riles nights, just Miles and I.

It was raining, so we decided to have a SpongeBob marathon, but only once we got the perfect snacks. We had walked to the corner store despite the rain because, as teens, that kind of thing didn't bother us. Honestly, it made our walk even more fun. Something about not caring and just being out in the rain was so freeing.

We got sour patch kids, sour skittles, and cherry blasters because clearly, we had a thing for sour candy.

Once we were back at the house, we changed into dry

clothes. Miles kept a drawer full of his clothes in Ryan's room because he basically lived at our house. After that, we went into the basement where Miles had the brilliant idea to make a fort to lay in to watch the show.

It took us about ten minutes to build the coziest fort ever. We used four bar stools to hold up our blanket overhead and laid about five different blankets down that we could lay on. We stuffed the inside with numerous pillows, my pineapple lamp, and of course, all of our snacks. We watched about two hours of SpongeBob and devoured every piece of candy within our reach. And then the power went out.

The only light we had was coming from the pineapple. To top it off, we were home alone. I remember being so terrified because I hate storms. Miles knew this, so he started asking me random questions to keep my mind off it. He had asked what I wanted to be when I grew up, and I told him I wanted to be a teacher because of our impact on the future since I believed our lessons lived on through the generations.

He told me that was beautiful and that I was making him consider becoming a teacher too. He wanted to do something that went beyond making a mere dollar. That moment was the first time I realized how deep and thoughtful he really was for a sixteen-year-old.

It was also the first time I felt like I wanted to kiss him.

The rain was rapidly hitting the glass patio door and echoed against the basement walls, the only other sound being my rapid breathing from fear. Miles then gently reached under the blanket and grabbed my hand, intertwining our fingers.

My chest went from heaving up and down to barely moving within seconds. I couldn't form words because my brain was split. One half was panicking over the storm, while the other was blaring sirens because of the butterflies that erupted in my stomach for the first time ever.

His thumb gently stroked the top of my hand, wiping away the fear. My body relaxed, and I was able to calm down, well at least where the storm was concerned. My heart was still freaking out about holding hands with Miles Anderson, my brother's best friend.

Miles cleared his throat and called me Riles in a tone I'd never heard him use before. I looked over at him as we lay side by side, and I could see a mixture of fear and softness in them. He leaned in, and suddenly his soft lips were on mine. It was my first kiss, and it was perfect, despite it being just our lips pressed together for a few seconds.

When he pulled back, his mouth parted in an attempt to tell me something. But it was cut short because we heard the front door open and my parents walking into the house.

Miles pulled back even more, eyes wide, like he awoke from a dream and realized what he'd just done. He snatched his hand away from mine and told me, "This was a mistake."

My body went from being on a high, from having my first kiss to it crashing down hard the second he left the warmth of the moment he created. He went upstairs, had a small chat with my parents, and left.

That was the last time Miles was himself with me. Which is how I came to resent him because who does that? Who comforts, holds, and soothes someone like that, only to tell them it was a mistake, and never talk to them again?

As I finish telling Ava the story, I can feel relief flood me for finally getting it out of my system. I've never told a single soul about that night, and it feels good to let it out. Admitting that it happened and that the sadness and happiness it still brings me is okay to feel.

I can't tell if Ava is seriously pissed off, upset, or shocked.

Her face is a party mix of emotions right now.

"What the fuck, Ry? Why didn't you ever tell me? That is seriously so messed up. I don't even blame you for feeling the way you do. I am so sorry I ever bugged you to talk to him, truly," she admits, her eyes sincerely apologetic.

"I'm sorry, I just was… I don't know, slightly embarrassed? I hate talking about my feelings, and admitting how he made me feel something, then took it away just as fast. It hurts," I admit.

"Please don't be embarrassed Ry. It's okay to have feelings for someone. What's not okay is what he did to you." She pauses and sips her smoothie. "Do you still have feelings for him? Did they ever go away?"

I sigh and take a moment to think over her question. I can't lie, seeing Miles does something to me that I can't explain, but I think I've narrowed it down to anger now.

"I … I was 14 and just starting to look at boys that way. So, I developed a crush because, how could I not? Even at sixteen he was handsome, but we also were so close. So, after he held my hand, looked at me in a way that no one had before, and kissed me, I realized I had feelings for him. But I was also furious with him, obviously. It was weird, and it still is."

I take a sip of my smoothie, then give her the answer I know she's still waiting for, "To answer your question more clearly, no, I don't have feelings for him anymore. Do I still find him attractive? Well, I have eyes?"

Ava chuckles, and I smile faintly. "So, yeah, it's hard not to find him attractive. But despite that, I think the hate over the years dissipated any feelings I had for him."

As I say it though, I know in my heart that that's not *entirely* true.

"That's fair, and there's nothing wrong with that. I just want you to know I am so sorry for what happened. You deserve the whole fucking world Ry. You're truly one of the best there is," she says warmly, her eyes brimming with tears.

Crap, now I can feel my eyes start to fill too. "Thank you," I say with a shaky voice.

Ava scoots her chair back, stands, and pulls me up to wrap me into a tight hug.

"Let's have a girl's night tonight? I know Miles is at the house with Ryan, so we could stop and grab what you need before going to my house. I'll even go in for you," she offers, pulling back but holding my shoulders with her outstretched arms.

"Ava, I appreciate the offer, truly. But I'm not some injured dog who can't walk himself. It's just an old wound, and it's time I heal it for good. I'm still going to talk to him," I confess, surprising myself.

She eyes me up for a moment, then curls her lips into a devilish grin. "Give him hell, Ry."

CHAPTER FOUR

Miles

I've been at Ryan's house for about two hours now, and my head is spinning with the memories that randomly keep popping into my head. I glance over at Ryan sitting on the couch, shoving slice after slice of pizza into his mouth as we watch the Detroit Panthers play against the Toronto Beavers.

The staircase behind him reminds me of a time when all three of us slid down them on our winter sleds. God, this house was my entire childhood. Even though I didn't live here, all of my memories center back to this house.

It's making it harder and harder to keep my mind off Rylee. Not just from the flashbacks but because I can't help but notice everything in this house that's hers. The yellow mug sitting under the coffee machine? Hers. The jar filled with sour gummy worms in the cupboard? Hers. The white lilies on the dining room table? Her favorite flowers. Hell, even her scent of vanilla and cherries is all over the couch. I faintly smile at the fact that she still uses the same shampoo.

As if on cue, Rylee and Ava come through the door, and damn it, she looks good. Her hair is in a low bun, her legs have that out in the sun all day glow, and her face is fucking perfection as usual. I nearly have to grab a pillow to hide my semi-boner. What the hell is wrong with me? I'm acting like a fifteen-year-old who's never seen a girl before. But Ry's not like any girl I've seen before. Her beauty is unmatched, along with those long fucking legs of hers. And now I'm pissed at all the men who probably ogled her all day long.

Ryan hops off the couch and meets Ava halfway as he picks her up and kisses her. They're so in love, I don't know whether to be happy for them, annoyed or jealous. I think I'm a bit of all three.

Rylee finally makes eye contact with me, while I've been staring since she walked in. This time she doesn't roll her eyes or give me a death stare. But her eyes are still distant, and her body is guarded as she folds her arms across her chest. I hold her stare, waiting for one of us to break the silence.

"Are you just going to stare, or did the math teacher forget how language works?" she shoots out, her sarcasm locked and loaded, ready to fire off.

"I didn't know whether I should poke the bear," I try, testing my ability to joke with her.

Wrong choice of words, apparently, because she shoots me the finger, and stalks down the hallway to the stairs that lead into the basement without another word. Part of me is slightly turned on because she's the only girl who's not intimidated by me to do that, while the other part feels like an ass.

I run my hands through my hair and curse myself quietly. I want to follow her and demand that she talks to me, but knowing her that would only push her away more.

"What's up her ass today?" Ryan asks Ava, who's still wrapped in his arms.

She squirms her way out of them, and I can tell she's

about to give it to him.

"Let them figure it out, and stop being such a dick to your sister. I know he's your friend, but he was hers too. Just stay out of it and be nice to her," she demands, her tone steady and strong. She knows how to put him in his place.

I expected Ryan to argue back or question her, but he simply shrugs his shoulders and says, "I'm sorry. I'll talk to her and apologize."

He must really love her.

Ava moves in closer, leans up on her tiptoes to kiss him on the cheek, then whispers something in his ear. I can tell by the look on his face it was something dirty because his eyes widen and his teeth sink into his bottom lip in restraint.

I'm starting to feel slightly uncomfortable, so I stand and begin to thank Ryan for having me over when Ava cuts me off.

"No. Go downstairs and talk to her," she orders.

"I don't think that's a good idea," I say, even though deep down, that's all I want to do.

Ava sits beside me on the couch, quickly looking over her shoulder at the staircase, before focusing her attention back on me. "Keep this between us, or I swear I will rip your balls off, got it?"

"I wouldn't test her," Ryan pipes up.

"Got it," I swallow because she's honestly scaring me for someone so little.

"I am only telling you this because I want all of this shit to be over with, and the sooner, the better," she whispers.

I nod in response because I agree. I want this awkward, hating phase to be over.

"We talked about you today, and all I'm going to say is that she wants to talk to you about this whole thing. So, go downstairs and do that."

"Wait, what did she say?" I can't help but ask because my mind is now running a thousand miles a minute trying to imagine what they talked about.

"I can't tell you. Only she can. You're lucky I even told you she's open to talking, be happy with that," she whispers, stealing another glance at the stairs.

"Can you at least give me any advice?" I pry, looking for any crumbs I can get.

"Miles, you're what, twenty-five? Figure it out." She stands up, then saunters over to Ryan. "I promised my boyfriend something, so we're going to be upstairs for a very, very long time."

Ryan shoots me a look of apology. "Sorry, man, do you mind?"

"Not at all, don't worry about it. I'm back now, we can hang out whenever," I remind him.

"Sounds good," he says before turning his attention back to Ava. He picks her up bridal style and carries her up the stairs.

God, I want that. I don't think I'll ever be able to have it with Rylee, and it really won't happen if we never have this conversation. I take a moment to compose myself, but I don't think I'll ever be ready. So, I whisper to myself *fuck it* and stand to make my way to the staircase.

I slowly walk down the stairs and see that the small basement hasn't changed since I was last down here. The same TV hangs on the wall, and the worn black leather couches are against the opposite wall, while the mini bar still holds space in the back corner. It takes me two seconds to realize she's not down here. I glance outside the patio door to see a glow in the backyard.

I step outside and turn to see that she's sitting around the propane fire, her gaze focused on the flames. I click the door shut, and her eyes shoot up to mine. If looks could kill, let's just say I would be gone.

"Hi," I say with a small smile on my face as I stand frozen in my spot. I don't want to do anything that would set her off in any way.

"Ah, so he does speak," she laughs, but her tone has no humour.

"Not well, apparently, because I always seem to say the wrong thing," I say, taking a step forward, testing the waters.

She doesn't flinch or scowl, so I continue until I sit across from her, the flames burning between us. We stare at each other for a bit, and it feels like those ten seconds at baseball when I got a bit of the Rylee I used to know before something clicked and she shut down.

Our staring match is intense and we never break contact, trying to read each other the way we used to. I can tell she's angry, but she's also willing to talk. The silence becomes unbearable, our breathing and the flickering flames the only sounds filling the space.

"Ry, I don't even know where to start. I don't think sorry even covers it, but I need you to hear it. I am so sorry for what I did." I release a breath.

"And what exactly did you do that was wrong, Miles?" she prompts, wanting me to acknowledge what happened.

But I'm not ready for that yet, so I beat around the bush.

"I pushed you out of my life and was a complete ass to you when you did nothing to deserve that," I admit, still holding her gaze intensely.

"You're right, Miles. I didn't. We were best friends," she chokes, her words cracking with emotion.

I break our stare down because seeing her get emotional is tearing me up. I want to break down right with her and punch my fist through a wall at the same time. I was such an idiot back then, and I'm paying for it now tenfold.

"Why, why did you do it? Don't bullshit me either, please. If we're going to have this conversation, just be honest," she pleads, her tone steadier now.

Fuck, I guess it's now or never.

I run a frustrated hand over my beard and bring my eyes back up to meet hers. "Because Rylee, I was sixteen and was starting to look at you in a way that no guy who's best friends with your brother should."

Rylee looks like she stopped breathing altogether as my revelation sets in. Her brows crease in confusion, so I continue, "That night in the fort, I let those feelings get the best of me, and it was wrong. Your parents coming home was the reality check I needed-"

"What were you going to tell me that night before my parents showed up?" she interrupts me, her eyes curious but cautious.

I sigh, not wanting to tell her the truth, but hell, we're already this far in. And if I'm being honest, it feels fucking amazing to get it off of my chest.

"I was going to tell you that I thought, still think, you're the most beautiful girl in the world who I can be weird and have fun with and that you were really cool too," I admit, my lips turning up slightly. Sixteen-year-old me was not smooth at all. I have had those words etched in my memory ever since that day.

Rylee gives me her infamous smile, and I'm damn near breathless now, knowing I made it happen. She bursts out into laughter, and I can't help but join her. It wasn't the most romantic thing to say, but I meant it then, and I still do.

"That was really cheesy," she says with a chuckle.

I grin, "Yeah, it wasn't my best line."

"Neither was telling me it was a mistake," she says, her tone serious now.

I feel a slight tension in my chest because I knew this was coming. I can't tell her how I partly only said that in hopes of convincing myself it was because as soon as our lips met, I knew with hundred percent certainty that she was it for me.

"I... I'm sorry I said that. I was worried about Ryan finding out, and I know if I said that, it'd piss you off. To make it easier for you to let me go. I had to distance myself because we couldn't be more than friends. I couldn't do that to Ryan, or to our families."

"Ouch," she says, but she also seems to understand, her head nodding. "But I get it. I wish we could've stayed friends at least. Losing our friendship stung more than anything."

Not being around you, not being able to talk to you and kiss you stung just as much, I think to myself.

"I was young and dumb. Forgive me, please. Do you think you can let me try to be your friend again?"

She takes a second to think it over. "Yeah, I'd like that."

I smile at that, my entire body wanting to sag with relief. This may be a stepping stone that will hopefully lead to her becoming mine.

"Can I ask you something?" she prompts, her voice barely audible.

I can tell she's nervous about whatever it is that she wants to know, and that makes me equally as nervous.

"Anything, you know that," I say softly, despite the hard and rapid beating of my heart.

She sits up and leans forward, her arms resting across her knees. "Why did you really go to Arizona?"

I feel my heart sink. I did not expect her to ask about that, nor do I want to explain why, but we're already this far gone. Why not go all the way and tell her that I love her too? *Not now,* I remind myself. She will freak out, and I'll lose her for good just as I'm starting to get her back into my life.

I take a deep breath. "You really want to know why?"

"I mean, obviously, I asked for a reason," she jabs sarcastically, her brows raised.

I smirk and roll my eyes. God, I forgot how much she drives me insane with her smart mouth. The things I would like to do with that mouth… Fuck I need to stop this train of thought by answering her question, or I'm going to get uncomfortable in my pants real quick.

I shift in my seat. "I got an amazing scholarship in the sunniest state in the country, and I couldn't turn it down,"

"Because you hate the cold," she finishes for me, proving she knows me better than anyone.

"Exactly, and when I looked into the education system in Arizona, I found out how easy it was to get a full-time position. We both know that teachers here stay on the supply list for at least three years," I say, giving her only half the truth, hoping it's enough for her not to dig further.

She scoffs. "Tell me about it, I'm going into my second year of supplying, and I cannot wait to have my own classroom."

I want to tell her about my interview tomorrow for a full-time position as a grade 8 teacher at Westchester, but I refrain. Instead, I offer her some encouragement, "You will, I don't have any doubts. I bet you're a phenomenal teacher."

The corner of her lips tugs up as she rolls her eyes, murmuring, "Thanks."

My heart breaks at the fact that she still struggles to accept compliments. I'm making it a goal of mine to change that. The crackle of the fake fire fills the silence between us for a moment, and I look up to admire the night sky.

There may be no stars visible, but I don't care because the brightest thing to ever come into my life is sitting right across from me. I lower my head back to look at her only to find her staring intensely at the fire.

"Rylee, you okay?" I pry because I can practically see the wheels running in her head.

She snaps back to reality. She shakes her head, and it causes her bun to come undone, her waves falling across her sun-kissed shoulders. My fingers itch to run through her hair, tucking some behind her ears to fully open up her face to me.

"Yeah, just tired," she says, her eyes averting mine which is a dead giveaway that she's lying, but I'm not going to dig deeper after tonight's revelations.

"I should get going anyways," I suggest, standing up from my seat. There's an awkward pause between us because I'm not sure if I should hug her or just walk away. I'm going with the latter.

"Thank you for finally telling me," she calls after me.

I pause and look over my shoulder. "It was long overdue, but thanks for talking to me without dagger eyes for at least ten minutes."

Another smile erupts on her face. God, I love today.

"Oh, I am sure they will come back, don't get ahead of yourself," she teases.

I can't help but smile, because Rylee does that to me. She makes me smile over something so simple like teasing me.

Fuck me, I am in so much trouble with this girl.

CHAPTER FIVE

Rylee

I t's currently two am, and I have to be up in four hours. Thanks to my overactive brain, sleep is not on the menu tonight. But you know what is? Overanalyzing every piece of information I learned from Miles tonight. Just when I think I understand it all and get to relax, my brain picks apart something else he said, and I go down another loophole.

He liked me? What the *hell*? He thought I was beautiful? The 14-year-old me who had a mouth full of braces and was overall, awkward?

Did I somehow jump into a parallel universe? I can't wrap my head around it. Miles, the most attractive person I've ever laid eyes on, had a crush on me?

When I asked why he went to Arizona, I could tell he was holding something back. I know he was telling the truth about the scholarship, but there has to be more to it because I know Miles. Or at least I knew him. He would never purposely move that far away from his family unless something else pushed him to go.

Did I have something to do with it? Who am I kidding?

There's no way his little crush on me made him move across the country. I need to stop daydreaming. But why is there a part of me that hopes that could be true?

Not in the 'I'm proud I made him leave kind of way,' but in the 'Miles freaking Anderson had such a crush on me that it affected him.' My brain will send me into cardiac arrest with the way it's running laps.

I huff into my pillow and reach over to my side table, grabbing my phone. The 2:12 am stares back at me, but what catches my eye is the unread notification.

I haven't posted anything in a while, so my heart stops when I open the app and see that Miles liked a photo from eight months ago. Was he stalking, and liked it by accident? Or did he want me to know that he was looking? But why? He said he *had* feelings for me, not that he *has* them. We did agree to be friends, so that could be why.

I decide to look through his profile since it's public and I don't follow him. I find three pictures. One of him and Ryan playing baseball as kids. The other is a Christmas family photo, and the most recent one is of a sunset in Arizona, with mountains and palm trees in the background.

I decide to like it, and follow him because our friendship has to start somewhere right? I'm about to put my phone back down when a message pops up.

MilesA13

Online friends? What an honor.

I groan. I hate the way his message makes me smile this much.

RyleeIsRight

I don't spend much time here, so don't get too excited.

He replies instantly.

MilesA13

I'd rather see you in person anyways.

He could mean that in a friendly way, right? Right. Since I don't know what to say back, I leave the message open and exit the app. I set my phone down for good this time and roll over. I drift off to sleep as exhaustion finally hits me.

"Baby," he huffs into my ear.

I straddle him on the dugout bench and he moves his hips, making his growing erection rub against my pussy. His lips suck on my neck and my fingers dig into his back in response. I let out a moan and suddenly his lips are on mine, swallowing up every sound I make.

His lips are full and soft against mine, but the way he kisses me isn't. His mouth moves unforgivingly against mine, taking all I have to give to him. I can feel my core heating up, and it's sad to admit this might make me cum.

Jaxon going down on me for ten minutes couldn't do it, but us dry-humping definitely would.

I grind and move against him because I'm desperate for more friction. His tongue slips into my mouth. I swallow his moan this time and the vibration scatters chills down my body.

"That's a good girl, riding me like you've been needing my cock inside you," he says roughly against my mouth.

I feel a pool of wetness in my panties. Who knew dirty talk was something I'd enjoy? Actually, I just think Miles has this effect on me.

"Miles," I moan, his name falling off my lips in a plea for more. His hand leaves my ass and comes up to grip my chin. "Come for me, baby. Now."

My body does as he says and comes so hard it wakes me up from my dream. My breath pumps rapidly as I try to come down from the high. I sit up, run my fingers through my hair and rest them on my forehead. I shake my head and try to pretend that this did not just happen.

I just had a sexual dream about Miles, and I had an orgasm without having to use my vibrator. Two new things in one night?

Go me, I think sarcastically, trying to find humor in the situation because I'm trying not to freak out.

I check the time, and realize I have two minutes before my alarm goes off. I sigh and trudge myself out of bed so I can get ready for the day.

The next three days are the same. I wake up hot and bothered from dreams involving Miles, go to work, and come home to read in my backyard to avoid thinking about him. Ryan's been working afternoons all week because of a random shift switch, so there's no reason for Miles to come around the house which has been nice.

Until Friday morning. I'm at the marina, reading on my parent's boat, when Miles appears on his parent's docked right next to ours.

"Whatcha reading, sunshine?" he calls out.

I startle not only because of his sudden presence, which I wasn't expecting, but because of the nickname. It's stirring things in me and I don't like it.

I instantly shoot up. "Jesus, Miles."

I press my hand over my chest, willing my heart rate to settle.

"You're reading about Jesus? Interesting," he jokes, a panty-dropping smile on his face.

"No, I'm reading about a princess who's in love with her bodyguard," I retort. I unexpectedly feel hotter than I was before when Miles's eyes roam all over my scantily clad body, my yellow triangle bikini top and bottoms suddenly feeling smaller.

"Now that's interesting. Any explicit scenes?"

"Oh yeah, this book is thoroughly detailed," I say, instantly regretting it.

Why would I willingly talk about sex with Miles? We just became friends again. I quickly change the subject before he can respond. "What brings you here?"

"I wanted to clean the boat for my parents since they haven't been out yet," he responds. His arms flex as he removes the cover off the boat. My eyes are glued to every minuscule movement he makes.

I've always loved that Miles was a family man, ready to do anything for his parents or sister. It's nice to see that it hasn't changed.

"And what are *you* doing here?" he asks.

I drag my eyes away from his muscular arms only to find a sly smirk on his face. He knows I was checking him out. *Fuck.* I glance away, holding my book up before shoving it in my tote bag.

"I came here to read for a bit and tan. It's relaxing out here, you know?" I say, knowing he knows exactly what I mean since we both grew up around this lake.

"Yeah I do. It's nice to be h-" His words die on his tongue when I stand. His mouth parts and our eyes lock on one another's, the space between us heating. My breathing stills at the sight of his jaw ticking.

I blush, unaware of what's happening, but it feels like it shouldn't be. I reach into my bag and throw my cover-up on, ending the moment.

Miles frowns. "I'm sorry if I made you uncomfortable. It's just wow, you uh, you look really good Rylee."

My face turns beet red, the light sway of the waves rocking the boat lulling my body as his words weaken my knees. "Thanks." I pause. "So do you," I finish awkwardly, returning the compliment.

He smiles widely before ducking his head under the boat's bow, giving me a minute to gather myself. What just happened wasn't super flirty. It was just two friends acknowledging that we had both grown up nicely since the last time we'd seen each other. That's all.

I make my way to the back of the boat and plop down on one of the seats. Miles returns to the deck of his boat with cleaning supplies in hand.

"Is this what it's like to be a freeloader all summer?" I tease him.

He glares at me playfully. "Funny."

"You're stating the obvious, Anderson," I chuckle, loving that we can easily fall back into our friendship.

"I stay very busy actually," he muses, wiping down the seats on his parent's boat.

"Yeah, doing what?" I challenge.

"Wouldn't you like to know." He winks and returns to his task so casually as if the simple action doesn't make my thighs clench.

What the hell is wrong with my body?

"Did you see that the Lynx went down a place in their

division?" I bring up, unsure why I'm looking for ways to continue our conversation.

"Don't remind me. They need to get their shit together. I'm tired of losing money in my fantasy league." He groans. "I wouldn't count on it anytime soon. Their pitcher's out for shoulder surgery. You may as well be a Panthers fan now."

Miles doesn't hate our state's baseball team, but he's also not their biggest fan. He claims the New York Lynx are the elite baseball team.

Miles stands up straight, pointing a finger at me. "Over my dead body."

"Don't be so dramatic, Miles." I chuckle, loving how serious he gets whenever I tease him about it.

"Don't you have a book to read about a bodyguard railing his princess?" he says, returning to cleaning.

My mouth gaps at his bluntness, but I quickly close it. "I think I like bugging you more."

"So do I," he says, catching me off guard.

Alright, it's time to go.

I stand and pull out the tarp to cover the boat before I leave. "I forgot I have to meet Ava soon. We're going shopping for snacks for our movie marathon night."

"Movie marathon, huh? Reminds me of our Riles nights. I miss those," his voice is so sincere that it stills my movements.

There's a slight pain at the memory of what happened that night, but I push it away, trying to convince myself that we're moving past it now. "Yeah, me too," I admit shyly.

Miles clears his throat. "You can go. I'll lock up for you."

"No, you don't need to do that."

"Rylee, I'll be here for another few hours. Besides you just said you needed to get going so let me help you," he pleads, catching me off guard again because I forgot how kind he can be.

When I think of Miles, my mind usually reverts to the side of him that he presents to everyone else -cocky, intimidating, hot-headed. I sometimes forget how he truly was with me which is a giant teddy bear.

"Okay, thank you. I owe you one," I say, holding onto the dock as I step onto the pier.

"You never have to owe me anything," he says so low I almost miss it. "Have fun tonight."

We part ways, and I walk toward my Jeep. I can't seem to erase the smile on my face or the giddiness spreading through my body from our conversation.

But once again, I remind myself that this is purely platonic.

CHAPTER SIX

Rylee

L ater that night, Ava and I are having our 2000s rom-com marathon. We stuff our faces with popcorn, sour patch kids, and cookies. When I finally tell her about what Miles said last night and earlier that day, she reacts in a way only Ava would.

She screams and jumps around, her excitement so genuine and pure. I tell her to relax and give her the same pep talk I've been giving myself - that it doesn't mean anything- but she doesn't buy it.

"So, what's the plan again for tomorrow?" Ava says before shoving a mouthful of popcorn into her mouth.

I pop a few sour patch kids in mine and mentally list the events in my mind. "Baseball practice at 10 because Ryan wants Miles to get acquainted with the team."

I think it's just his excuse to play more baseball, but I'm not complaining.

She groans. "Of course I end up with the boyfriend who wants to work out on a weekend." She sighs and reaches into the bag for another handful of popcorn.

"Then, we have the team party here later, remember?" I

remind her.

Ava loves a good party, whereas I prefer smaller gatherings. There are too many people to please when you're in larger groups and that's too much pressure, a stress I'd rather avoid.

"Oh, hell yeah." She beams until she sees my less-than-thrilled expression. "Let's go shopping for a new outfit after practice," she suggests.

Even though I don't care much for parties, Ava knows I love to buy new clothes for any occasion. It's my guilty pleasure. "I could kiss you," I say, winking playfully.

"As much as I love you, dating siblings isn't my thing, but you know what is?" she says, her eyes gleaming with mischief.

I eye her cautiously. "Do I really want to know?"

"Being blindfolded, not knowing where his tongue-"

I throw a pillow at her. "Ew, please stop talking about my brother's tongue thank you very much."

She chuckles and throws it right back at me.

My phone vibrates and I see a message from a number I don't have saved.

Weird.

I open it and read.

Unknown

I have 4 dollars.

I laugh out loud at the random Patrick quote and instantly know who it is.

"Who just made you laugh like that?" Ava asks, her eyebrows piqued in curiosity.

"No one," I lie, holding my phone close to my chest.

Not at all suspicious. Good job Ry.

"I already know it's Miles. He asked Ryan for your number a few days ago," she admits.

I turn to face her, "What? Why am I just hearing this now? What did he say?"

She crosses her legs and stares at me with amusement. I know she enjoys torturing me. "Because I knew you'd react like this, so just be chill. He told Ryan you should have his number in case you ever needed anything when Ryan isn't around."

"Well, I've been fine without him this whole time. Doubt I'll need him now," I say. My fingers hover over the keyboard.

"You might need someone to finally give you an orgasm," she quips.

My mouth drops open. "Not going to happen."

"Yeah, yeah. Keep denying it for now. What are you going to say to him?"

I bite my bottom lip as I think of something to say, before quickly typing out:

> Good, that can buy me some sour patch kids.

Miles

> Anything you want.

My heart stutters for a moment, but before I can reply, he sends another text.

Miles

> What's the plan for tomorrow?

Ava reads over my shoulder and squeaks, "Oh, that Miles. He's so stupid."

I give her a confused look, "What are you talking about?"

"Rylee, he sent that second text because he probably realized how forward he was being, mister 'anything you want.'"

She chuckles to herself, clearly satisfied with her investigation into his words.

"Has anyone ever told you that you look into things too much? He's just being nice because he feels guilty about what happened in the past. That's all," I say, trying to convince myself more than her because deep down, I'd love to believe Ava's version.

She rolls her eyes and turns her attention back to the TV. I look back at my phone and type in a response.

> Baseball practice is at 10, so be there because you need it. If you make one mistake, you're not allowed to come to the party later.

Miles

> I've always loved a good challenge, so you're on. But if you make a mistake though, you'll owe me a favor.

My mind instantly fills with dirty images of him asking me to stroke, lick - no not going there.

I'm tempted to tell Ava what he said, but for some reason, I want to keep it between Miles and I. Ava would freak out, and cause me to overthink it, so I'm just going to play it cool.

For my sanity and hers.

> Deal. See you tomorrow, hot shot.

Miles

I look forward to it.

My heart feels full and I internally chastise myself. I shouldn't be talking to him again, knowing I still have underlying feelings because we both know how it will end - with my heart in pieces, and Miles thousands of miles away again. My brother wouldn't have it any other way.

I lock up the butterflies swarming in my stomach and throw the key away for good. I can't let anything happen between us besides a rekindled friendship.

CHAPTER SEVEN

Rylee

va and I are the first to arrive at the baseball field, partly because we like to show up thirty minutes early to everything but mostly because we wanted to get Starbucks beforehand.

We begin warming up by throwing the ball around for about ten minutes, when the rest of the team starts trickling in. I take a deep calming breath and try not to spiral on how awkward things might be with Jaxon, especially after his failed attempt at going down on me a few weeks ago.

We've seen each other since then and it's been fine, but a part of me always worries that it'll change somehow. This is exactly why you shouldn't hook up with someone on your team.

We all chat and start stretching when Ryan and Miles stroll up together. My core burns at the sight of him, a feeling I've never felt before, and it takes everything in me to try and ignore it.

The way his shirt clings to his biceps as he lifts his bag out of the truck. The dark blue of his shirt accentuating his eyes has desire taking over my brain at the moment.

What is wrong with me?

Ava leans over and whispers, "Are you two just going to eye fuck each other from now on?"

I elbow her side and immediately snap out of it. Before I return to stretching, I allow myself one more glimpse and catch him smiling. The smug bastard knows the effect he has on me.

"Who's that with Ryan?" Jaxon asks, gesturing towards Miles with his head.

When my eyes connect with his, I can swear I see annoyance swimming in them. But what for? He hasn't even met Miles yet.

"That's Miles, one of our childhood friends," I reply, noting how I said 'our' and not Ryan's friend. I guess that's progress in the friendship department.

"He'll be playing with us for the rest of the season. He's amazing," Ava boasts, and I fail to understand why she said that. Knowing Ava, it has some cryptic meaning that only she understands.

"Great," he mumbles low enough for only me to hear. He stands and walks over to Eric to throw the ball around.

"What was that about?" I question Ava.

We follow suit and stand to stretch our arms.

"He's clearly jealous of the attention you gave Miles, so I just had to dig it in a bit more. He deserves that much after failing miserably at making you c-"

"Okay, we're done here," I say, trying to sound annoyed but failing as giggles slip out.

Ryan approaches the pitcher's mound and drops a bag filled with baseball balls. It's batting time, my favorite.

"Some balls you got there," Jaxon shouts to Ryan, who cracks up at his joke.

I'm all for dirty jokes, but hearing it from Jaxon makes

me cringe, especially when they're directed at my brother.

Ryan coughs, getting everyone's attention. "Alright, team. This is my good friend Miles who'll be playing with us for the rest of the season. He's a great ball player and an even better person, so I expect everyone to welcome him to the family."

Everyone nods and introduces themselves one by one. I watch intently as Lindsay stares a little too long after her handshake with Miles. I brush it off and try to ignore the jealousy coursing through my veins because it shouldn't be there in the first place.

I walk by Miles who's talking to Jaxon, when I hear Miles say, "My eyes are up here."

I glance over my shoulder and catch Jaxon's eyes glued to my ass before he looks back to Miles with annoyance.

What the fuck is happening? Why is Jaxon checking me out?

I thought his failed attempt at oral would change his attraction toward me, but I guess not. Also, why did Miles sound annoyed that Jaxon was checking me out? He's said he had feelings, so maybe he's just doing his brother's best friend duty of protecting me.

Yeah, let's go with that.

"Ry, you're up first," Ryan shouts, and I internally thank him for it. He knows I love hitting. Being the captain's little sister sometimes has its perks.

I grab my watermelon bat. It's steel with pink and green mixed around, and of course, a yellow grip pad at the end of it. The rest of the team scatters in the outfield to practice their fielding.

I approach the bag and swing a few times, warming up my body. Ryan nods at me, and I signal I'm ready. The first swing hits the wrong spot on the bat and it falls short in the dirt. The next is the same, with me barely hitting it past second base.

What is wrong with me?

As soon as my inner voice asks the question, I immediately know it's because of the too attractive for his own good man in left field. I can't seem to focus, knowing he's watching me.

"What's going on, Rylee? You're better than this," my brother says, which is his way of giving me a motivational speech. So heartwarming.

I adjust my stance and get ready. This time I hit the ball right, but it's too high, and ends up being a pop fly. Claire catches it in the outfield.

Dammit.

The rest of my hitting goes the same, crappy ground balls and pop flys. My growing irritation with myself doesn't help and only adds to my inability to concentrate. After the fifth pop fly, I give up and trade-off with Brandon.

I whip my gloves off and toss them in my bag before grabbing a yellow scrunchie. I angrily throw my hair into a ponytail. I'm hot and annoyed with myself, on top of being confused with my attraction to Miles.

I close my eyes in an attempt to calm myself when I'm interrupted by one of the main reasons for my frustration.

"Looks like I won the bet," Miles says cockily. He sits down next to me on the bench, beaming. He's sweaty and still looks as gorgeous as ever. How is that even possible? I feel and look disgusting right now.

"Shit, I forgot about that," I say out loud, even though I meant to say it in my head.

"I'll cash in my favor when you least expect it." He grins and my heart stutters. "What happened out there?"

I shake my head and look toward the field where Brandon is hitting because I can't stare into Miles's eyes right now. "I just couldn't focus and then I was getting mad at myself, which didn't help."

I sigh.

"Stand up and come with me," he orders softly, and for some reason, my legs are upright and following his command. No questions asked. He walks toward the fence and retrieves a bat. He then walks back to where I'm standing behind the dugout where no one can see us.

I look at him confused. "Is this the part where you kill me? Because I thought we were becoming friends again," I say sarcastically, taking a step back for dramatic effect.

"I forgot how cute you are when you're trying to be funny," he says, his blue eyes piercing right into mine. He smiles crookedly and my thighs clench at the sight.

God I hope he didn't notice.

"Then what are you doing?" I say, folding my arms across my chest in an attempt to shield the effect he has on my body.

He takes a step forward and sticks the bat out to me. "I'm going to help you fix your swing."

"You're so cocky. You know that, right? You assume I want your help because you're a baseball God?"

He raises an eyebrow. "You're the one who just called me a baseball God, not me. But look, I know you. And I know you like to be the best at everything, so let me help you."

Shit, he got me there. I roll my eyes and accept defeat. I take the bat from him.

"Good girl," he praises, and I'm instantly reminded of the dirty dream I had where he said that in a very different context. "Now raise your arms like you're getting ready to swing and I'll do the rest."

I bring my arms up, and place them in a hitting position.

My breath quickens as I wait for him to do whatever he plans on doing to fix my swing. Is he going to touch me? Where would it be if he did? Shit, did I shave my legs this morning? God, I hope so. The possibilities have all my nerve endings standing on alert. Wait, what am I saying? I should not be feeling this way.

He comes up behind me and my mental chatter halts when his body heat engulfs mine. His chest is *mere* centimeters from my back. If I shifted slightly backward, I could grind on him.

What is happening?

His hand comes to my side and I shiver from the contact. I must be nervous. That should explain it. He then lightly drags his hand up my waist and my entire body feels like it's going to combust.

Okay, so maybe it's not just nerves.

Miles trails his fingers up to my right arm which is bent behind me and he raises it gently. "This arm needs to be higher, so don't let it drop. Hold it high and steady," he whispers against my ear and the sensation causes me to curl my toes.

Has his voice always sounded this good?

His other hand grips my waist and he quickly shifts my entire body so that I'm nearly flush against him now, my ass mere centimeters away from his body. "Your body needs to take a step back like this to give your legs more power," he huffs, his voice sounding strained.

He then takes the hand that was previously on my arm and drags it around the small of my back, around my front leg before sliding it down to grip my thigh. "Speaking of legs," he whispers.

A slight gasp escapes my lips and if he notices, he doesn't say a word.

He twists my leg so that my foot is turned slightly inward, "Twist this front leg a bit if you want to try hitting into the right field for a change-up." Instead of letting my thigh go, his grip tightens. "Are you with me, sunshine?"

Oh, I'm with you alright.

My panties are officially soaked and my heart is racing faster than I can keep up with. "Yes," I say breathlessly like a pathetic idiot, letting him know exactly how much he has me worked up right now.

Miles intakes a sharp breath as the hand on my thigh pulls me even closer to his body. There's absolutely no space between us now. A slight moan escapes my lips when I feel his hard length against my ass. My body instinctively grinds against it, seeking friction, and it feels so damn good despite it being wrong.

His hands rest on my hips, and he clutches me tighter when I move against him once more. "Rylee," he groans.

I open my mouth to say something, but we're interrupted before I can respond.

"Rylee, where are you?" my brother shouts from the other side of the dugout.

We both freeze. I quickly move out of his hold and hand him the bat. I quickly take a look at the bulge in his pants, and my mouth parts while he shoots me a shy smile.

Miles being shy? That's new.

I don't have time to process it because Ryan is now walking towards us and I can't have him seeing the three of us – Miles, me, and the erection that's making itself known between his thighs.

"Thank you for the hitting tips. I appreciate it. But maybe you should practice what you preach. I wouldn't want you to embarrass yourself in front of the team, newbie," I say, patting him on the shoulder. I pass him and walk up to Ryan.

Ryan looks puzzled. "Why don't you worry more about not embarrassing yourself, Ry?"

"You're right. Can we go hit some more while Miles practices his swing?" I nearly beg, trying anything I can to keep Ryan from seeing Miles's boner.

"Miles doesn't need practice. What are you talking about?" he asks, confusion lacing his features.

Miles looks over his shoulder. "It's been a while, give me a couple of minutes to warm the old arm up and I'll be out there."

"I'll be expecting a home run then," Ryan says, before walking back toward the field and waving me on to follow him.

I don't even glance back at Miles. Instead, I follow my brother back to the field. This was a close call.

It suddenly hits me, and I know exactly why Miles did what he did all those years ago. Because I just did it myself to save us both from Ryan finding out and losing his shit, and ruining our relationships.

That's when I also realize that I am so goddamn attracted to Miles and I can't bring myself to deny it anymore. I don't know what it means and its complexity, but I do know that we can never be together, so whatever just happened, can never happen again.

And it never will.

I'm making a promise to myself right now that I will not flirt, kiss, or touch Miles Anderson.

CHAPTER EIGHT

Miles

"**M**iles?" my mom prompts me from the head of the kitchen table.

I shake my head. "Sorry Mom, what did you say?" I'm having a hard time focusing on the conversation because my mind keeps replaying this morning's ball practice. For starters, that prick Jaxon is clearly interested in Rylee, and I don't like it at all. From the moment we met, I didn't like him. Not just for the fact that he couldn't keep his eyes off Rylee, but because he gives off asshole vibes.

I'm honestly not sure why Ryan even likes him. He's the complete opposite of him.

Then, coaching Rylee through her hitting stance got my dick harder than it's been in a long time. I know now that she felt the attraction too. Her little gasps, the way her body was attuned to mine, and her perfect ass grinding against me. I know the signs all too well from my less-than-holy college phase.

Thank god for her quick thinking because I thought I was about to be in a lot of trouble.

This brings me back to another thing plaguing my mind.

What the fuck am I doing? I knew exactly what I was doing when I gripped her thigh and whispered against her neck, but did that stop me?

Nope.

Part of me wants to say fuck it and go after Rylee without caring about Ryan, but the other, better part of me, is fighting against it because that's what I should be doing as her brother's best friend.

My mind is a cluster fuck.

"I asked what your plans were tonight. Your father and I are going to the marina to get drinks with some friends," my mom says as she takes her last bite of lasagna.

"You mean you're drinking tonight while Jim and I take care of you ladies," my dad chimes in, a smirk on his face.

"I'm going to Ryan's place for a baseball get-together," I tell her, the excitement threatening to explode inside my chest.

I can't wait to have the chance to finally hang out with Rylee. And the rest of the team, of course. It's been a while since I've been a part of something like this.

"That sounds like fun, dear, but be safe and spend the night if you drink too much," Mom advises.

"Sara and John are so proud of Ryan and Rylee. Those kids turned out to be something special. Both smart and kind," Dad says as he stacks the empty plates.

Special doesn't even cover how Rylee is. She's so much more than I could ever put into words.

"They're lovely," Mom agrees. She shifts towards me. "Do you know that Rylee came here once during the summer you left for Arizona, and your sister for Europe?"

I nearly spit out my sip of water, but recover and ask, "Why?"

The look on my mom's face is mischievous, and I don't

like it one bit. What is she getting at?

"She brought over some video games you'd left at their place. I invited her to stay for lunch. We had some girl time, that's all. She's a great girl you know."

"What's your point Mom?" I say a little more bluntly than intended because I don't want her to know how I feel about Rylee, not when she's best friends with Rylee's mom.

"Son, my point is that you're a great guy, and she's a great girl…" she trails off.

I cut her off before she could continue.

"I could never do that to Ryan, Mom. It's the first rule of a friendship: never date either person's sibling," I say.

I realize I didn't even deny being into her. Fuck.

My mom smiles because I know she caught it too, but my dad speaks up this time. "That 'bro code' crap doesn't exist past high school. You know what does?"

"What?"

"Love, true love. If you love someone, it shouldn't matter. If they truly are your best friend, they will want you to be happy, no matter who it is. We're talking about that forever kind of love, not some stupid high school fling that's not worth it. So, what you need to ask yourself is if Rylee is worth it?"

My dad pretty much summed up the dilemma I'm facing because I know Rylee's worth it, but I'm also terrified of the damage our relationship could have on the people that mean the most to us. If we dated and it went badly, it wouldn't just affect our relationship with Ryan, but both of our families.

It would all go downhill and I could not deal with being the reason for that.

My attention snaps back to the present when my mom asks me a question out of left field, "How did your interview go at Westchester?"

Shit. I have been so consumed with thoughts about Rylee that I forgot to tell my parents the news. I need to get a grip.

"I got the email last night, and they offered me the job," I say, unable to hide the pride I take in being able to say that.

Becoming a full-time teacher in Michigan is tricky and I got so goddamn lucky. Whether I liked it or not, this was my path now. Here in Michigan, being near Rylee, because I'll be damned if I waste another minute wondering about what-ifs and only being able to love her from afar. I always tell my students you never know until you try, and it was time I take my own advice.

My mom and dad hug me, showering me in congratulations and love as we discuss everything the job entails. They agreed to let me stay at their house until I found a place of my own, which is something I needed to get started on. But I wasn't in a rush because to be honest, I've missed the hell out of my family since I moved away. I also don't mind my mom's infamous blueberry muffins that she bakes every Sunday.

As I get in my truck and drive over to Rylee's place, I debate back and forth over what to do about my growing inability to control myself around her. She brings out this possessive side of me that I don't understand or like.

During our practice today, Ry had on black shorts that displayed her tanned, toned legs in all their glory. Although I was admiring them myself, I couldn't help but want to punch every guy who looked for too long. It took a lot out of me not to tell them to fuck off and keep their eyes off of what's mine. Christ, she's not even actually mine yet, and I feel this way already. I'm in trouble.

Ten minutes later, I walk toward Ryan's backyard gate. The music booms from the backyard, laughter peaking through the mix. I love summer nights like these. When you can hear people enjoying themselves, the crackling of a fire, the faint smell of a late BBQ dinner, and just the perfect weather where it's not too hot, but not too cold either. I already have a good feeling about this night, despite my mind debating whether I'll kiss Rylee, should the opportunity arise.

My debate ends the moment I enter the backyard, and I see her in the crowd. I'm definitely kissing her. *Holy fuck.*

Her usual waves are curled, framing her face. She never wears makeup, and I like that about her. But what sealed the deal for me was the outfit she was rocking. Her long, sexy legs are on display, with white shorts that barely cover her ass. Her skin glowed against her yellow halter top. A lot of her skin is showing, and my body won't make it through the night without my lips on hers, anywhere she'll let me.

Fuck, I need to keep myself in control with her.

I sure as hell am not a saint when it comes to sex. I like it to be spontaneous and rough, neither ideal for my sunshine girl I assume. I start to worry that I may be too much for Rylee when it comes to what I like, but my spiral train is halted when Ryan approaches me.

"Hey man, glad you made it. Ready to party?" Ryan exclaims, clapping me on the back.

I can tell he's already buzzed, and I'll need to catch up fast. I don't care about drinking as much, but it's fun to let loose every now and then.

"You know it. Want to shotgun a beer?" I suggest it because it's the quickest way to start pounding back drinks.

Ryan stares at me with wide eyes before breaking into a smile. "God, I've missed you. Let's do it."

We walk over to the cooler filled with beer and mixed drinks, grab two beers, and head to the grass.

"Woah, woah, you're shotgunning beers without me?" Ava

yells over the music as she and Rylee make their way over to us.

"Sorry, babe, boys only. Can you be our referee?"

Ava thinks for a second, then gives in. "Fine, but Rylee and I are next."

Ryan takes out his keys from his pocket and pokes a hole in each one, quickly passing me one as we keep our fingers on the holes to avoid spilling any.

Ava throws in a last-minute challenge. "Winner has to go against the winner between Rylee and me. Then, whoever wins that round gets to dare the loser to do whatever they choose."

I plan on winning because I know Rylee. She's all smiles on the outside, but deep down, she's extremely competitive and does not like to lose. This means I need to win this so I can face her next and have her complete a dare on top of the favour she owes me.

"1 … 2…. 3… Go," Ava shouts.

Ryan and I release our fingers, then lean our heads back. We tip our cans as high as possible and try to drain our drink before the other. My competitive side loves this, but I'm also reminded how I hate chugging like this.

"Let's go, Ryan." Rylee cheers her brother on, and it's the perfect kick to get my ass into gear.

I swallow even faster and toss my can to the ground a mere second before Ryan does. Sweet victory. Rylee rolls her eyes because now she will actually have to try against Ava, not wanting to give up the opportunity to try and beat me in the final round.

I can't wait to make her eyes roll for a very different reason one day.

Ryan slaps me on the back. "You still got it, man."

"Honey bun, you suck. Watch how it's done," Ava says as she retrieves two beers from the cooler, passing one to Rylee.

Ryan pulls Ava in for a kiss, then quickly releases her to poke holes in their cans. Rylee and Ava stand opposite each other, their knees bent with their smiles now gone. These girls are ready to battle it out.

"Alright ladies, 1….2…3…. Go," Ryan shouts, his hand raising between them like a green flag on a racetrack.

Both girls stand tall. Their heads are tilted back as they try to guzzle their alcohol in record time. My dick threatens to come to life as I watch Rylee's throat bob when she swallows, because I'm imagining her swallowing under very different circumstances.

It's a tight race, but like I knew it would happen, Rylee throws the can down with seconds to spare. She crushed it, and I don't know why, but it adds to my attraction for her.

Ryan pretends to whisper something to Ava, but he says it rather loudly, "Hey babe, we suck."

Ava giggles and shoves his chest away. "Alright, Rylee and Miles you're up. Remember, the winner gets to dare the loser to do anything, as long as it's legal, or at least won't get them caught."

"You're so going down, Miles," Rylee says, her smile wide as she stands across from me.

In my dreams, I do go down on her for as long as I please. *I need to stop with these thoughts.*

"I hope so," I say low enough only for her to hear. My heart pounds in my ears because I have no idea how she'll react, especially since what happened this morning.

Shock registers on her face and her cheeks turn pink. Her bottom lip falls, opening her mouth slightly, and that's how I know she doesn't hate that I'm flirting with her.

I still know this girl all too well and it fills my chest with something warm.

Ava hands us our drinks, and Ryan pokes the holes once we've secured them in our hands. We hold a finger over it and we stare into each other's eyes, waiting for go time.

I take the time to appreciate her face. Her blue eyes are dark on the outside, with tones of grey filling the inner part. She has faint freckles across her cheeks and nose that I find so fucking cute. Her top lip is full, the bottom one even fuller. I want to bite it. I also love that she's not wearing any makeup, but she's beautiful either way. I can't help but lick my lips at the sight of her, and she responds by pressing hers into a thin line. Interesting.

I'm pulled out of my lust when Ryan yells, "Go!"

We lean our heads back and I stand up as straight as I can, trying to drain my drink as quickly as possible. I drown out the sound of Ava cheering Rylee on. Rylee starts coughing and I know it's game over. She starts to spit whatever she choked on as I toss my can to the ground, claiming the win.

She is immediately on the defense. "That's so not fair. I swallowed down the wrong hole. We need a redo!"

"Sorry, babe. You know choking is not grounds for a redo. It's a challenging part of the game," Ava says apologetically.

"Nice job, Miles. You really came to win," Ryan comments.

Yeah, to win your sister over. I shake myself out of my head. "Winning is all I know."

Rylee groans and I shoot her a wink.

"I hate you and your cocky ass grin," she says it as if she means it, but after all of her tell-tale signs today, I know she doesn't.

"Don't be a sore loser, Rylee," Ryan chastises her.

"You, me, dance floor now," Ava demands. She grabs Rylee by her wrists and drags her over to the concrete ground where a dancing crowd has formed.

"Hey, she owes me a dare," I shout over the music.

"Get her later man. She hates to lose so don't let her get off easy," Ryan jokes. He then leans in closer. "But remember, she's my sister, and even though I'm dating her best friend, it's different. You're a great guy, but she's not just some girl you can screw around with, got it?" he whispers before walking over to the crowd to dance with Ava.

No, I don't fucking 'got it.' He gets the green light to date her best friend, but it's wrong when the roles are reversed. Bull. Shit. I don't like how he assumes that I'll discard her after being with her, that I'm not good enough for her. Not that I've particularly proved my willingness to be in a relationship ever in my life, but still.

Does he seriously think that lowly of me, or is he just trying to protect his sister?

I take a moment to think of my sister, and honestly, I have to agree with him. I wouldn't want my best friend, who used to sleep around, to make a pass at my sister. But what if I told him it was more than just sex? That I wanted her, all of her. Her heart, her smiles, and her laughter to cherish.

I fucking hope that's enough for him because I don't know how much longer I can hold back from her.

I follow but remain on the outskirts because I can't dance with Rylee unless I want a fist to my face. But I don't want to dance with anyone else, especially not with Lindsay who keeps throwing me fuck me eyes as she grinds to the beat.

Although she might be pretty, she's not my girl.

I try not to watch Rylee, but it's impossible. Her toned leg strain as she sways making me want to wrap them around my waist. Rylee has no problem dancing alone while Ava and Ryan find their own rhythm. Her confidence is evident as she grinds, shakes, and throws her smile around freely. She's feeling herself and doesn't give a shit about anyone else.

She finally feels my eyes all over her and her head snaps up to meet my gaze. If she notices the lust on my face, she doesn't show it.

Except I notice the way her body moves more sensually as she turns so that her ass is facing me now. Fuck, my dick threatens to come to life because I want her doing that to me right now.

As if the universe received two separate requests at the same time, Jaxon's gets answered first. He comes up behind her and wraps two hands around her waist. I clench my fists at my sides because it's taking everything in me not to tear him away from what's mine.

I internally curse myself. Jealousy isn't something I'm acquainted with and I hate the feeling creeping its way under my skin. My hands twitch at my side and I turn on my heel, heading toward the gate to get in my truck before I do something stupid.

Like beating Jaxon to the ground simply for dancing with her when we're not even together. I need to get a grip, but Rylee makes me feel so possessive.

I don't turn around to see if she's noticed I left or stopped dancing with him. I know if it's not the latter, the jealousy will embed itself in my veins, burning me up from the inside out.

I hop into my truck and smack my steering wheel out of frustration.

I felt something between us earlier today. It wasn't just sexual, it was more than that. It was the soft intimacy we've been tethering with since we were kids. The one that transcends touch and has been stoking the fire burning between us.

So, why the hell is she dancing with Jaxon? I know she can't stand him, I could read it in her body language today at practice, how her body recoiled every time he neared or spoke to her. I know she's had a lot to drink though, so that could explain it. Truthfully, I don't know what the fuck is happening.

All I do know is that I'm not sticking around to watch. I get out of my truck and start walking home because I am not drinking and driving. I text Ryan that I feel sick and that I'll pick up my truck tomorrow.

Then, I do what I apparently do best with Rylee. I leave.

CHAPTER NINE

Rylee

I instantly step away from Jaxon the minute I realize it's him. The alcohol has made me less coherent because, fully sober, I would've felt his presence and rejected him before he even put his hands on me.

Jaxon tugs on my wrist, trying to pull me back onto him. "Come back here."

I snap my wrist free, anger pulsing in my blood. "No."

He rolls his eyes. "Always such a tease Rylee. You had no problem grinding on my dick a few seconds ago."

I narrowed my eyes at him. "I didn't know it was you... I thought it was– "

Miles, I finished in my head.

I look to where he was standing a minute ago, but he's gone. My heart sinks a little, and I hate that I'm letting his presence affect me once again.

Before Jaxon can reply, Ryan cuts in.

"What's going on?" Ryan says, looking between us.

"Ryan," Ava starts, but I cut her off.

"No, Ava, it's fine. You want the truth? Jaxon and I...

messed around once, and we haven't been normal since then," I say, my words slurring a bit.

"Rylee," Ava squeaks, tugging on my arm.

Ryan steps around Ava, and if looks could kill, Jaxon would be dead. "What the fuck, Jaxon?"

Jaxon stutters, "L-look man, it was a one-time thing. I thought tonight we could try again, but–"

"My sister is not a one-time fucking thing. I'd rather you be in love with her because this is so much fucking worse."

Furious, I speak up. "Ryan, you don't control me. I can do whatever I want, with whomever I want." I pause, glaring at Jaxon. "And it won't be Jaxon, I can promise you that."

Ryan stares at me with indifference, then glares at Jaxon. "You're off the team. Don't text me either."

"Seriously? All over some fucking girl?" Jaxon says, shaking his head in disbelief.

"That's the problem, she's not just some girl," Ryan shouts back. "Honestly, Jaxon, it's not just because of this. You've been pissing me off for a while with your shitty behavior. If you weren't good at baseball, I honestly don't think we'd have gotten along for as long as we did."

"Whatever, man," Jaxon says, turning on his heel and not looking back.

When the backyard gate shuts, the rest of the team and a few of our friends stare back at us in awkward silence.

"Sorry," I mutter, feeling guilty for ruining the vibe.

"Rylee stop," Claire starts, her hand squeezing my shoulders with soothing reassurance. "We didn't like him that much anyways. You did us a favor by getting him kicked off the team."

The rest of them nod in agreement.

"Not that we wanted it to happen how it did. I want to punch him in the dick for how he treated you," Ava adds, her ears reddening from anger.

Claire and Ava come to my side, and we hug for a moment. Their love and support fueling me from the inside out.

"I love you both," I whisper into Claire's hair.

"We love you more," Ava says, squeezing my ass.

I yelp and jump away from them.

"Jesus, Ava. What the hell," I try to yell at her, but laughter erupts instead. She knows how to get me to smile and that's just one of the many things I love about her.

The party returns to normal now. People talk, drink, and even swim in our pool. Ava returns to my brother's side, wrapping her arm around his waist as he talks to Sean. Claire and I sit around the fire with the rest of the team, talking and laughing.

But I can't focus enough to join the conversation, because I'm debating whether or not to text Miles. On the one hand, we just became friends again, and it's not weird for friends to text each other. But we also had a… moment earlier and I feel like the line has blurred ever since.

At least for me, it has. I have no idea where his head is at or where *he* is at.

Screw it. I pull out my phone and text him.

> Everything ok? Where did you go?

I wait anxiously for two minutes until he replies.

Miles

> I'm fine. Home.

> Why did you leave? What's wrong?

Miles

Nothing.

That's it? Nothing? He's an awful liar.

I shake my head and reread his message while an ache spreads across my chest. He's never been this short with me, except six years ago when he started pushing me out of his life.

The reminder feels like a slap in the face.

I just got my best friend back, yet here he is, hurting me again. But this time, it's partly my fault. My fault for letting him back in my life again, my fault for thinking there could be something more.

At practice, a truth that I'd been denying myself for so long became loud and clear in my head and heart. I like him, and I'm very, very attracted to him. I think back to how I felt when he came up behind me to help me adjust my hitting stance. When his strong, large arms wrapped around my body, and how it for once felt perfect in his arms.

Stupid, stupid, stupid, I repeat to myself.

A tear threatens to escape, but I quickly pinch my eyes shut and keep them at bay. He left me again, with no answers and an ache in my chest.

Classic Miles Anderson.

CHAPTER TEN

Rylee

I t's a beautiful summer evening tonight at baseball. The breeze is slightly cool, while the day's warmth still lingers in the air. I look at the sky and breathe it all in, taking in the beauty right in front of me. I smile to myself.

My moment is short-lived when Miles appears in my peripheral vision. My eyes avert to his and my stomach flutters up to my chest. But pain immediately accompanies it, a reminder of how mad at him I am.

He's been a dick and hurt me by leaving me with no explanations *again*. He looks rigid, his jaw set tightly and his posture solid. He walks towards the dugout and I'm not sure why he looks so pissed off, but I don't care. I can't.

I turn my attention to Claire, wanting to get out of this dugout before he takes up the space and infiltrates all of my senses. "Claire, want to warm up?" I ask.

"You got it, Ry," she beams.

We walk to the outfield together. We throw the ball around for a few minutes, then take a few more to stretch.

"Alright, spill it. What's wrong?" she asks, her deep brown

eyes staring straight into my soul as we stretch our legs on the ground.

I sigh and explain to her what happened with Miles at practice yesterday, up to our texting debacle. I expect her naturally sweet demeanor to flicker into her overprotective mom mode, but instead, a huge grin fills her face.

What the fuck. You'd think I just told her I made out with Chris Evans last night.

"Claire? Did you hear what I said?" I ask, confused.

She quickly glances around to make sure no one can hear. "Rylee, he's jealous. It's the only thing that makes sense. He got a freaking boner from helping you with your swing. You guys were flirting all night, and then he saw you dancing on Jaxon. What did you expect him to do? What if you saw him dancing with Lindsay?"

Wait, no. That can't be right, can it? Did I misread the whole thing?

My body physically cringes as images of Lindsay with Miles infiltrate my brain. I shake my head and that's when I feel it, the raging jealousy coursing through my body.

If this is a fraction of what he felt, I partly get it. But I don't think I would've left without talking to him first. Not like he did to me.

"But why didn't he text me, and I mean how he usually would've, not with these one-worded replies?" I wonder, more to myself than to her, but she answers anyway.

"He likes you, Ry, but he won't admit it or can't. It's probably making it hard for him to communicate why he's upset. Maybe try talking to him in person?" she suggests.

We both stand and walk back to the dugout. "If he wants to talk, I will, but I'm not initiating it. He can't leave every time he gets upset and expect me to chase after him for answers. I didn't do that before, and I won't do it now."

Claire nods in understanding, and we chat about our days while we sit on the bench before the game starts. After a few minutes, I stand and quickly head to the washroom before the ump calls game time.

Just as I round the corner to head toward the bathrooms at the back of the pavilion, my chest collides with a more solid one. His scent invades my brain, and for a moment, I forget that things between us are bad. But then I glance up at his blank face, and I'm reminded of it all.

"Sorry," I mutter.

He nods, sidesteps me, and walks back toward our dugout.

A nod? Are you fucking kidding me? This is exactly why I should not have accepted his apology. What was the point when he wasn't going to change? Annoyed, I quickly do my business and then walk back to see my team heading out onto the field.

The game is about to start, so I make my way over to first base and begin our usual warm-up routine with my fellow infielders. Eric's throws are a little off today, which makes me a bit worried about the game because I myself am having trouble focusing on the game with everything going on.

The first base coach from the other team makes his way over to my base, and stands off to the side to avoid getting hit by a ball. He's about my age, my height, with blond hair.

"Hey, how's it going?" I ask cheerfully, trying to put myself in a good mood. One of the things I love about playing first base is meeting new people and being able to chat when we have a small break.

When he looks up and makes eye contact, I realize he is the same guy I got out on a stretch during our first game of the season. He had complimented me on it. I've been so absorbed in my mind over Miles that I didn't even realize we were playing a repeat team tonight.

"I'm great now. How about you, gorgeous?" he says confidently, flashing a wide smile.

Is he flirting with me?

I can't help but blush because I'm not used to being called gorgeous often, so I smile. "I'm pretty good too."

Our conversation is cut short when the ump call for us to start.

"Good luck," I add before turning and focusing on the batter in the box.

He doesn't reply, but I can feel his gaze lingering on my body. In that moment, I notice how different it feels from how Miles looks at me, and I feel discomfort rising in my throat.

I watch as the batter hits the ball through the dirt. I get ready to receive the throw, but Eric throws it way off to my right. *Fuck me*. I move off the bag to make the catch, quickly throw my left leg back as far as it can, and somehow, my foot lands on the bag. I nearly did the splits to get it, but I did it.

"Out," the ump calls out.

"Are you kidding me, Kevin? How was that an out?" the batter spits out, fury etched in his features.

Before I can jump in, blondie who I assume is Kevin, responds. "Yeah, sorry, bro. Look at her legs, you're not beating those things."

I want to vomit at the lust in his voice, but I pretend I didn't hear him and wait for the next batter to come. I am unsure if this is how he usually picks up girls, but it's not working for me. Even if I don't get compliments often, it doesn't mean that overly sexual ones from sleaze bags will do me in.

I feel a set of eyes burning at my back, and my gut knows it's Miles, but I shake it off and return my focus to the game. The following two outs are easy outfield flyouts and are caught by Miles and Ava.

Miles is up to bat first, which I'm grateful for. It avoids the potential of having to be near him in the dugout, at least for now.

Ava plops down on the bench next to me, and before I can tell her I don't want to talk about it, she says, "The tension between you two is so thick I feel like I am suffocating in the crossfire."

I glare at her. "What in the hell are you talking about?"

She rolls her eyes. "Seriously, Ry? I've caught you glancing at him all night. I can see the hurt in your eyes, but there's something else too. Look you're staring at him right now."

Shit, I totally am.

I couldn't avert my eyes away from him. He oozes confidence and strength while taking his stance to bat, his muscles filling out his jersey.

"And he can't keep his eyes off you either."

What? I thought I felt his eyes on me, but to hear it be confirmed is different.

She keeps going. "In the outfield, I caught him stealing glances whenever he could. Besides, when that guy at first was arguing over the call, I could see his chest rising faster."

My heart thumps wildly in my chest, but it also aches because what the fuck does all of this mean. I know I have zero experience in the feelings department, but I feel like this is not normal.

"Then why is he staring and wanting to defend me when he can't even bring himself to talk to me?" I ask out loud, wearing my vulnerability on my sleeve. I hate it, but I know I can't keep this frustration in.

The resounding crack of the ball hitting the steel turns our attention. We watch Miles's ball fly past the outfield and bounce off the fence. He lets out a guttural groan that has my insides warming. He crushed that ball, nearly a home run. He clearly seems pissed and I want to know why.

"Only he can give you that answer, babe," she says.

We watch him sprint around the bases, making it to third base. I sigh, knowing she's right. You know what, screw it. He's already hurt me so many times before, what's once more? I make a promise to myself that after the game I'll talk to him.

"By the way, what was up with the first base coach? I was watching from the outfield, and he seemed to talk to you a lot," Ava notes and I can tell she's worried from the crease in her forehead.

"Uh," I stumble over my thoughts, not wanting to start any drama. I don't like people fawning over me or worrying too much.

"Okay, what are you not telling me? Spill or I will tell everyone that all those books you read are pretty much porn."

My mouth drops. "Hey, those books have a good plot too. I'm a sucker for love and detailed sex, is that so wrong?"

Ava glares at me, so I relent. "He's been eye fucking me and has made a few comments here and there that have made me uncomfortable."

"Rylee, what the fuck? I know you didn't put him in his place, which shocks me because you had no problem giving Miles a whole ton of sass when he first came back."

"That's ... true. And I honestly don't know why. If I had to guess, it was probably because, with strangers, you never know what they are capable of, you know? I'd rather just be nice and let it go, but if he tried to touch me, I would defend myself."

She gives me an understanding gaze. "I just wish you would let others help you. Let me go kick his ass right now, please?"

"Save that ass-kicking for the game, okay? And please

don't tell anyone else, Ava," I plead.

She nods and gives my thigh a squeeze before we return our attention to the game.

Lindsay is up to bat, hitting a pop fly that gets easily caught in the outfield. Sean grabs a bat and sets up in the batter's box, taking a few swings. He fouls out, giving us two outs. Claire is up next and hits a ground ball that gets her safely to first base because of a lousy throw. Miles stays at third, not wanting to risk another out.

Ryan is up next, and he hits the opposite way. It takes their outfielder by surprise and they're no match for his speed because he ends up making it all the way home, Miles and Claire included. They clap each other's back at home plate, their faces beaming with smiles. It warms my heart to see my brother and his best friend together like old times.

Ava is up next, and she smacks a ball right down the middle, over the pitcher, and into the outfield, getting her a single. When it's Eric's turn, he pops up, and it's easily caught by their shortstop.

Shit. That means I have to lead off—my least favorite thing to do.

We're back on the field now, and Kevin resumes his place as first base coach once more.

Great.

"So tell me, are you single?" he asks bluntly, his eyebrows raised in curiosity.

"Yes," I reply hesitantly because I have no idea how to respond to his question. I didn't want to tell him that I was single, but I couldn't think of anything else.

"Wow, today really is my lucky day. Think you can make it luckier by going out with me one night?" he asks, his lips curling up into a grin that may work on most girls. But not me. His emphasis on 'one night' tells me all I need to know. He only wants to sleep with me.

"Hold that thought, games on," I say, grateful for the game starting as a way out of that conversation. As much as he's been a sleaze bag, I don't have it in me to be mean to him. There's no batter at the plate, and Brandon throws his hands up in confusion.

"Batter?" Ryan calls out, heavily annoyed at the mix-up.

"Oh, shit, that's me," Kevin says to himself, then he looks back at me. "This one's for you, darling."

God, I hope he strikes out.

Kevin gets up to the plate and misses on his first swing. I have to put my glove over my face so no one can see the big smile on my face. His next swing makes contact and sends the ball flying into Ava's territory. It should be an easy catch for her, but she's suddenly cut off by Miles, who swoops in front of her and makes the catch.

Everyone cheers for the out, but I'm momentarily confused why he did that.

The ball was clearly Ava's, and she had it. Why did he run all the way over there to make the out?

The following two outs are easy pop flies to the infield, one caught by Brandon, and the other by Ryan. As I walk back to the dugout, Ava runs up to walk beside me.

"Did you see that?! He totally caught that ball as a 'fuck you' to that guy," she said, clapping her hands together in excitement. Ava lives for this kind of stuff.

"Wait, you told him? Ava, what the hell." I scowl at her.

"Slow down, I didn't. But I was watching him out there, and he was watching you two. My guess is that he put it together himself and wanted to get the out because, hello he's a guy. Testosterone? You know?" she explains as if my life is out of a romantic comedy.

I don't even have words, so I just shake my head and get my batting gloves because I'm up.

In the batter's box, I take a practice swing and then step up to the plate. The first pitch is nice and high, just how I like them. But, I swing and miss. My focus is not here right now. I shake my head. No, I *won't* let him throw me off my game. Instead, I'll show him how he won't derail me from this.

But, I take a moment to think about the tips he gave me. I fix the position of my legs and readjust to get ready to swing. I nod to the pitcher, and she throws me another beautiful pitch. This time I made a connection, sending the ball into right field and right over Kevin's head.

The adrenaline it gives me is like no other.

I sprint past first and round my way to second when Ryan shouts at me from the foul line. "Come to third base Ry."

I continue running to third, and the ball is coming in hot, so I slide. I can feel the burn of the dirt scratching my legs even through my knee-high socks.

"Safe," the umpire calls out.

I sigh in relief. Ryan helps me stand and gives me a high five, but his smile vanishes the second he looks down at my leg. I look down only to find a tear in my sock, right on my left calf, where there are a few scratches and a cut that's bleeding.

Fuck.

"Ry, are you okay? Do you want a courtesy runner?" Ryan asks as he squats down to check it out, his inner nurse coming out.

"I'll be fine," I say through clenched teeth. Since I know it's there, it's starting to sting a bit.

"When we get off the field, I'm cleaning it up and wrapping it for you, got it?"

"Yes boss," I reply, a smile forming on my lips.

We may bicker a lot, but it's moments like these that I'm reminded of how much he cares for me.

Brandon is up next, and he hits a double that scores me in. Ryan then does as he said, and takes care of my leg, wrapping it to avoid an infection. The rest of the game goes smoothly, I actively avoid interacting with Kevin, and we win the game 7-3.

We're now sitting at the pavilion, enjoying some post-game drinks. I'm already down a cooler and feeling more talkative than usual. Alcohol does this to me.

My irritation with Miles is slowly fading until I see him sit down at the end of the table with Ryan, and I'm reminded of everything. I do need to talk to him at some point, but right now, I don't really feel like it so I stay seated with Ava, Sean, and Claire.

We're chatting and laughing about one of Claire's clients when Ava nudges me with my shoulder, then leans in and whispers, "When you slid into third base and stood, the damage to your calf was visible and Miles was sitting next to me. He shot off the bench next to me and his eyes were trained on you the whole time. I could see his palms twitching to go out there and help you. Oh, and when Ryan was wrapping you up, he ran his hand through his hair like fifteen times. Fifteen times, Ry. I counted."

My stomach bottoms out, and butterflies attempt to fill the space. Why would he react that way only to not talk to me? It's so goddamn frustrating.

"Why are you telling me this?" I whisper back, my fragile heart causing me to feel nauseous.

"To show you that he cares. Despite what he's saying or not saying, he cares. You're both just being stubborn so I'm being your wing woman."

Hating how right she is, I instantly stand up and turn to Sean and Claire, who seem to be getting a bit friendlier tonight.

Does she like him?

While I want the best for Claire, I'm not sure Sean will be that for her. She's always been the mom of the group, sweet, loving, and quiet, while he's a goofball and a commitment-phobe. I'm not judging him, but I know he's the biggest player of the group and I don't want her to get her heart broken by him.

"Anyone wants anything?" I ask.

All three voices chime in at the same time. "Nope."

As I wait at the concession for another drink, I feel a hand snake around my lower waist. I instantly know it's not Miles because we're not talking right now, and the touch doesn't send shivers throughout my body. I glance up to see it's Kevin. I back away from his touch and put some distance between us.

"Let me buy you a drink. It'll be practice for our date," he slurs.

I can smell the alcohol coming off of his breath.

"That's okay, but thank you," I say nicely despite my voice threatening to shake with the uneasiness he brings me.

The vendor hands over my drink, and I quickly pay her so I can get out of here. I turn on my heel to walk away when Kevin grabs hold of my hip and spins me back to him, his fingers digging into my skin.

"So, what is it then? You don't like nice guys? I can be rough too, darling—"

Kevin doesn't get to finish whatever disgusting thing was coming out of his mouth because suddenly, Miles puts himself between us, quickly glancing over his shoulder to make sure he's fully covering me from him.

What is going on?

He whips his head back to face Kevin, and I can feel the anger rippling off his body. "If you touch her again, I will break every single one of your fingers so you can never touch anyone again," he says tightly, his tone furious yet controlled.

"Didn't know she was taken, bro. Sorry." He holds up his hands in self-defense, then looks over Miles's shoulder.

I try to make myself smaller behind him. Sensing my discomfort, Miles extends his hand behind his back in search of mine. I intertwine my fingers with his, and warmth spreads up my arm from the contact. His gesture makes me feel safe and protected. Despite being confused about our relationship, I reel in the present moment and the secure feeling he's providing me.

He snaps at him, and I can tell he's on the edge of losing it. "Don't even fucking look at her. Turn around and go home. Now."

Ryan appears at Miles' side, just as angry as he is. "Yeah, I suggest you leave. *Now.*"

I quickly drop my hand, and instantly feel the loss. My hand feels much cooler than it ever has before.

"I'll walk you to the bus stop. Make sure you get on it," Ryan commands, not leaving room for debate.

"I can drive you idiot," Kevin mumbles, a lot less cocky than he was two minutes ago.

"Not with that much alcohol in your system. I'm a nurse and I'd rather not get called in for a drunk driver call tonight. So, your options are I call the cops and they're your ride, or I can walk you to the bus stop to make sure you don't drive," Ryan says coolly, clearly fed up with his shit.

"Or I can kick your ass and send you home in an ambulance," Miles offers.

I chime in. "I'd pick option two."

Before he gets time to choose, Ryan shoves him backward. "Let's go, jackass. Next bus comes in ten minutes."

Miles remains protectively in front of me until they've left the pavilion and hit the parking lot. He grabs my hand again, takes the drink out of it, and places it on the table.

Suddenly, he's dragging me after him as he rushes us down the stairs and around the back of the building where no one can see us. My pulse spikes, unsure of what's to come. There's a scowl on his face, yet a longing look clouds his eyes.

It's confusing, but it's time we figure out what the hell it is we're doing.

CHAPTER ELEVEN

Rylee

Miles is pacing and tugging on his hair until he snaps and twists to face me. The anger rippling off him reminds me of how pissed I was earlier, pushing me to start the conversation we need to have.

"What the hell was that, Miles? You push me out of your life once again, for God knows why because you won't talk to me anymore. Then you lose your shit for what? To appease my brother by defending his little sister? I already have a big brother, I don't need you to fill that role too."

He runs a hand through his hair, his anger boiling. "Rylee, I've never played the big brother role with you."

I groan, my own anger rising. "What does that even mean? Why did you run away from the party and ignore me *again*? Tell me the truth, Miles. Because I'm done with this whole routine where we're friends one minute, and the next, you shut me out."

He takes a deep breath, his eyes aimed at the ground. He slowly raises his gaze back up and I can tell he's about to confess. "I left the party because I wasn't going to stand around and watch you grind your ass on Jaxon when I have fucking feelings for you that are sure as hell not brotherly."

My world stops for a moment, and I swear I can hear my heart thumping in my chest. He has feelings for me, not out of friendship but... romantic? No fucking way this is happening right now.

"If you'd stayed for ten more seconds, you would have seen that I shoved him off because I thought it was you at first until I realized it wasn't."

I can see the surprise in his eyes. The tension deflates from his body, but not by much. His chest starts pumping rapidly as he charges his way over to me.

"Miles, relax. He's off the team and I don't like him, but I also don't like how you've pushed me away."

Our chests are mere centimeters apart, our breaths mingling in the space between us. "We're going to talk about that later, but that's not what I'm losing it for right now," he swallows and his hand comes up to my cheek.

Without a second thought, my own hand comes up, covering his. My heart is pounding furiously in my chest, making itself heard loud and clear.

Kiss me.

"Oh," I whisper because I don't know what else to say.

He interlaces our hands, then brings them to rest over my heart, making my heart beat even faster. My chest is betraying me and he smiles down at our hands once he feels the truth. He then lifts them off my chest and places them over his heart showing me his is beating as fast as mine, if not faster. How is that possible?

Confused, I lift my gaze to meet his, noticing a dark tint has taken over the normal blue-green he usually has. Miles slowly steps forward until my back is flush against the concrete wall. He drops our hands and brings one of his up to tuck a strand of hair behind my ear.

"Why do you think our hearts are beating so fast?" he finally says, breaking the intensity of the silence surrounding us. His hand travels slowly down the side of my face, and my neck, causing me to shiver, all while his dark eyes stay transfixed on mine.

With a shaky breath, I say, "You tell me."

Miles sucks in a breath before he whispers in the small space between us, "Seeing two men put their hands on what's mine is driving me insane."

My whole body nearly melts at his words. Thank goodness for this wall bearing most of my weight. My lips part in shock, and I bite down my bottom lip to stifle the smile the words 'what's mine' bring me.

"I didn't know I was yours," I breathe out, barely able to keep from launching my lips to his. They are so painfully close to mine already.

His hand travels lightly down my arm, causing a shiver to run through me again.

We shouldn't be this close, shouldn't be talking like this. But I can't pull myself away, it's like there's an invisible force pushing me toward him rather than away.

"Your body just told me it does," he replies, his tone as ragged as mine.

Holy hell.

His nose nudges up against mine, and I suddenly don't remember anything else before this moment. All I can think of is him, the mint and pine scent filling my brain, and the heat his body is creating around us.

"Prove it," I challenge him because if I don't kiss him right now, I feel like I'll explode.

Miles wastes no time and crushes his soft lips against mine. My entire stomach feels like it's getting shocked by lightning with the way it's fluttering.

This is so different from our first kiss in the fort.

This kiss starts soft and curious. Wanting to learn every inch of each other's lips. Once that's covered, Miles kisses me like I'm his. His mouth is possessive on mine, claiming me as his tongue enters my willing mouth. He wraps his hands around the small of my back while mine tug at the strands of hair at the back of his head.

My tongue follows his lead, exploring his mouth hungrily and my leg involuntarily wraps around his hip. Miles picks up on this instantly, bending down to grab my ass and lift me off the ground.

"Go ahead and wrap those sexy legs around me, baby," he orders.

I follow suit. A whimper escapes my mouth as he pushes me against the wall again and devours my lips with his.

"That sound is driving me wild, you know that?" he says breathlessly between kisses.

I bite his bottom lip, then kiss my way along his jawline, and down his neck, sucking and licking as I go. A groan escapes him and I can feel the slickness in my panties. Knowing I'm turning him on, is turning me on. Immensely.

He suddenly lets go of me, and before I can try and stand upright, he quickly catches me and readjusts me lower onto his hips. At first, I'm confused. Until he grinds his hips into mine, and I can feel him hard beneath his baseball pants.

I was right, this is heaven. I grind back against him, trying to gain some friction.

"I knew it," he huffs against my lips.

"Knew what?"

"That you'd be this responsive to my touch," he praises.

Desire pools in my core and I take his lips once more, feeling desperate to have his lips back on mine. Our lips meld like they were meant to, every press of our lips moving in perfection. I grind myself over his hardened length, reveling in the feel of him against me as my hips rock back and forth.

Miles breaks the kiss and I'm left fighting for my life as I try to regain my breath. We're both heavy-breathing messes.

"Not here, and not now," he manages to get out.

"Why not?"

"Because Ry, I have too much respect for you, no matter how bad I want to drag you inside that bathroom," he says, despite his eyes and dick telling me a different story.

"Maybe I like it when you're a little disrespectful." I blush, avoiding his eyes as I marvel at the size of his erection through his pants.

Holy shit. That's never going to fit inside me.

Miles brings his hand up to cup my chin and forces me to look at him, "Don't shy away from me. This whole thing isn't going to work if you don't talk to me, okay?"

How does he go from hot one second, then turn cute and romantic the next? I can't form words so I smile and nod to let him know I understand. "Okay." I lean in for another kiss because my entire body is aching for more.

Miles meets me halfway, his lips sweetly enveloping mine unlike before. I moan into his mouth. I'm on the brink of losing it.

"Riles," he says softly, pulling back from our kiss with a look I hope to never forget. His lips are a bit swollen, and his eyes are bright and relaxed. He looks like he just experienced pure bliss.

Join the club.

"You used my old nickname," I point out because he hasn't attempted to call me that again since I told him he lost that privilege.

"*My* nickname you mean because you're only *my* Riles," he says, possessiveness wrapped around each word.

I've always loved the idea of belonging to someone, wanting that person to want me just as badly. Just enough to be slightly territorial.

I'm not sure what all of this means right now, but I do know that the idea of being his sounds more than good to me. Before I can say anything, I hear Ava's voice come closer.

"I don't know Ryan. I think Rylee and Miles were just calming down back here, away from everyone," she says loudly because deep down she knows exactly what happened and is giving us time to get out of our compromising position.

Our worried eyes lock onto one another, and then we're moving. I quickly jump down his body, while he turns around to adjust himself in his pants. I run my fingers through my hair and try to fan myself off because I feel like a heater. Miles laughs to himself and I can't help but smile widely. I can't believe that even happened.

Ryan and Ava round the corner, having no idea that our lives will be forever changed from this moment on because I don't think I'll ever be able to recover from that kiss. I don't want to kiss anyone but him again. Granted, I've only kissed three guys, but it's never felt like that. Ever.

Ryan comes up to me, scanning my body for a sign of injury. "Are you okay?"

"I'm good. Thank you for getting rid of him," I say gratefully.

"I'm your brother. It's my job to keep jackasses far away from you," he says proudly.

"And Miles's too apparently," Ava adds in, winking at me, knowing Ryan can't see her face right now.

"Right. Thank you for looking out for Ry. I appreciate it,"

Ryan says to Miles, clapping him on the shoulder.

"Yeah, no problem man," Miles says, shifting his weight from side to side.

Ava grimaces. "What a creep. You should've tripped him when he was rounding 1st base."

"Wait, this dick was creeping on you this whole time? Why didn't you say anything?" Ryan groans, running an irritated hand down his face.

"This is exactly why I didn't. I don't need my big brother to swoop in and save me. Besides, it was harmless, nothing I haven't handled before." I sigh.

Miles's fists ball at his sides and his jaw is clenched. Shit. He's pissed, and my gut is doing somersaults at the idea of him regretting everything that just happened between us.

"Ry, you shouldn't be used to guys incessantly hitting on you like that. If you weren't showing interest, he should've stopped. End of story," Ryan retorts, and he's not wrong.

I have a hard time sticking up for myself at times because I hate hurting others. When in truth, I should've told Kevin to fuck off the moment he made me feel uncomfortable.

"I'm sorry," I mumble, my previous bliss gone.

Miles speaks up now, his stern eyes fixed on me. "Don't apologize. Nothing is your fault, you hear me?"

Due to the alcohol and that kiss, I don't think driving is a safe choice for me right now. I need some space and time to think about everything that happened today. "Got it. Ava, can you drive me home? I don't think I can drive."

"Of course, let's get our stuff," she says, then leans up and kisses my brother on his cheek. "I'll see you at the house."

"Drive safe and text me when you guys get there please," he says, then kisses her.

Miles and I take this time to stare at one another, and

he looks strained. He's clearly trying to hold himself back, but from what I don't know. But I hate seeing him like this. I walk over to him and pull him in for a hug, a safe option with Ryan right there.

His arms clutch me to his chest, and his hand squeezes my sides, nearly sucking all the air out of me. He carefully looks to see if they're still making out and takes the opportunity to quickly give me a kiss on my forehead. I melt into him a little more, and relief floods me.

He might be mad, but it's not about what happened. He finally releases me because two friends don't hug like this.

I take a few steps back. "Thanks again for all your help tonight."

He grins crookedly. "The pleasure was all mine."

My eyes widen at his pun, but no one else seemed to have noticed. He winks, and my body instantly responds. What kind of witchcraft power does he have over me?

Ava finally breaks apart from my brother and joins me as we wave the boys goodbye. She surprisingly stays quiet until we get into my jeep.

Then she pounces.

"I am not driving this car a centimeter until you tell me everything," she demands, shoving the keys in her bra for good measure.

I blush at the memory as it plays in my mind. "We kissed."

Ava's face lights up. "I knew it. No man drags a woman away like that without devouring her. I want details, go."

I cover my face from the embarrassment of how turned on I am after one stupid kiss. I give her all of the details I know she's itching to hear.

Ava fans herself. "Okay. wow. Not only was that hot, but it was so sweet too."

I give her a small smile. "I know, but I don't know what to make of it. We still need to talk about everything that happened."

She finally takes the keys out of her bra and starts the jeep. "Stop, don't overthink it. Wait for him to text you first, and go from there."

I nod, and we roll the windows down, letting the perfect summer air drift in. I crank the music to avoid talking about it anymore with her because I don't want to complicate it. I just want to be present, enjoying how I'm feeling at this moment.

And currently, I'm feeling it all. My body is buzzing with adrenaline from our kiss. My lips are tingling at the memory of his lips pressed on mine. My mind is swirling with what happens next. But most of all? My heart feels like it's bursting at the seams, overloaded with so much damn joy and warmth.

CHAPTER TWELVE

Miles

My life will never be the same again after kissing Rylee because holy fuck. She branded me with her intoxicating scent, the feel of her tongue, and how her lips perfectly molded against mine. I know with a hundred percent certainty that no other girl will ever compare to her.

No kiss will ever feel like that, because there is no one else like Rylee.

Our chemistry, our past, the tension from the weekend, everything about us made that kiss feel like the fourth of fucking July going off in my body. I don't just want more of it, hell, I need it. I crave more of her.

After coming at the memory of our kiss earlier, I roll over and grab my phone from the nightstand.

> Riles

She texts back five minutes later.

Rylee

Hi

Is she seriously trying to play it casual after what happened? Fuck that.

I sit up and call her. She picks up after the third ring.

"Are you okay?" she asks, sounding concerned.

I fake laugh. "Me? You're the one acting like I didn't nearly fuck you in the bathroom two hours ago."

She sighs. "Because I need time to process everything. I'm still mad at you."

"I know, and I'm mad at you. So, let's talk."

"What?" she whisper-shouts, and I can picture her eyebrows raising up her forehead.

I groan in frustration at not being able to do this in person. I need to be able to read her. I also need her to be able to read me.

"I know Ryan got called into a midnight shift. He left the ball diamond shortly after you. Mind if I come over so we can talk in person?"

She's quiet for a few seconds. "I-I guess, but you can't spend the night, and we are sitting outside."

I chuckle. "Riles, what's with all the rules? Why do you sound nervous?"

"My lips are sealed, hot shot."

"Please," is all I say, hoping that one word will grant me mercy from her stubborn act.

She huffs, and I know she just rolled her eyes at me. "I'm feeling way too much when it comes to you. It's overwhelming and scary. I need us to have some distance because I don't trust myself to be good when you're around."

My pulse skyrockets at the prospect that she feels even

an inch of how I feel about Rylee. I understand exactly what she means because whenever we're together, there's an electric charge in the air that draws us together. When we're close, it fucking explodes all throughout my body, and hopefully hers too. It's scary what I feel for her, but I believe that a little fear is good now and then.

"I'll be there in twenty, meet you at the back gate," I say, not wanting to continue this conversation on the phone.

"Okay," she responds, then abruptly adds, "Drive safe, Miles," before hanging up.

I smile to myself. My girl is fucking adorable. I dress quickly, throwing a dark green t-shirt on, and black gym shorts, before quietly heading out the door. My parents wouldn't care if I'm leaving at ten at night. They know I'm an adult, but I'm still quiet, making sure not to wake them up out of respect.

Twenty minutes later, I'm at her back gate, but she opens it before I get the chance to knock. My lungs tighten as I take her in, my breath stalling. Her wavy hair falls loosely down her shoulders, and she's in nothing but an oversized t-shirt. I can't even tell if she has panties on.

Jesus. Christ.

"Hi," she squeaks.

I walk past her and into the backyard and as soon as the gate shuts, I'm on her. My hands grip her hips, and I pull her to my chest. A gasp escapes her lips before I sweetly press my lips to hers.

I kiss her lightly because I know she's nervous, and I want her to trust that I won't take it farther than she wants. Her lips are soft when I press mine against hers gently, savoring her unique taste, a mix of vanilla and cherries. Her hands grip my biceps, and my muscles twitch under her touch. I pull back and kiss her forehead, lingering for a moment before stepping away from her.

When I look at her, I can see a mixture of emotions across her face— surprise and longing, mixed with anxiety. I take her hand in mine and lead her to sit on the edge of her in-ground pool. I kick my shoes and socks off and dip my feet into the water. Rylee follows suit.

The cold water is a welcome reprieve from the heat of a June night.

I angle my body to face hers, and once her eyes are on mine, I say, "I have never felt the way I feel around you with anyone else, so believe me when I say I understand exactly what you mean. It's consuming, and sometimes I don't know how to deal with it."

Her eyes soften at my words. "Is that why you left the party?"

I nod. "Yes. I wanted to kick his ass, but I couldn't. Ryan would ask questions, and fuck, I can't have him ruin this before we give it a chance. I'm so sorry for making you feel like I pushed you away again, that wasn't my intention. I was jealous and needed some time to get a handle on it, to control myself. But, regardless of my intention, I hurt you. Again. And I'll make it up to you every day if you let me."

Her lip trembles slightly. "Honestly, if you hadn't kissed me and made me feel all I'm feeling… I would've told you to leave me alone for good. But I can't do that now, not after we crossed the line. All I ask is that you talk to me. Don't ever do that to me again, okay?"

Now that I know she feels the same, I won't. It was just hard to let her know how I felt when I wasn't sure it was mutual. I want to be able to take a chance on us—best friend's sister or not.

"Understood," I reply, bringing her hand up to my lips and pressing light kisses to each finger.

"So, you want to give us a chance? Us, as in you and me? Together, romantically?" she asks, a slight tremor in her voice as she rambles on.

I take her hand in mine, a rush flowing through my body at the contact. "Yes, Riles. Does that scare you?"

"Uh, yeah?" she says as if that's a no-brainer. "You're…you."

I frown at that. "What do you mean?"

She huffs, then waves a hand at my face. "Miles, you're gorgeous. I know you're more experienced than I am. I don't know how to please you, I've never even dated-"

I cut her off. "I've never dated either, so we can figure that out together, okay?"

She nods, her entire demeanor lighter than when I first walked in.

"And Rylee, you being yourself pleases me. The number of times I got hard just watching you exist isn't normal."

Rylee gasps, her mouth parting in shock. Then, she starts laughing. My girl has the sweetest laugh. One I want to listen to for the rest of my life.

"That laughter is great for my ego. Keep it up sunshine," I say, but her joy is infectious and I find myself laughing with her.

Once we've both calmed down, I grab our hands which are still interlocked, and bring them to my lips, kissing the top of her hand. "I'm serious."

She turns our hands over, then brings the top of my hand to her lips, placing a soft kiss there. "Sorry, it's just hard to believe, that's all."

I frown. What the hell does she mean by that? Does she seriously not see how goddamn beautiful she is, inside and out? But before I can ask, she explains.

"Look, I've had four intimate encounters in my entire life. The first was my first kiss, with you. Another was a drunken makeout session in college, which by the way sucked. Then, I lost my virginity at the cottage to one of Eric's loser friends because I wanted to get it over with. And last but not least, Jaxon went down on me once and it was awful. That's it. So I'm not exactly... experienced."

"When did that happen with Jaxon?" My tone is a little sharper than I'd like, but hearing about the three bastards that got to touch her makes my blood boil. Especially Jaxon.

She looks shy, her cheeks turning a pretty pink hue. "Uh, a few weeks ago at Ava's birthday party. I thought I'd let him try because I never had an orgasm when I had sex that one time. He spent ten minutes trying before giving up. I darted out of Ava's room after that from embarrassment. Something's probably wrong with me."

"Nothing's wrong with you, you hear me?" my eyes lock onto hers, waiting for a nod to let me know she understands. But when she doesn't, my blood pumps with a need to make sure this girl knows how perfect she is.

"Riles, you're perfect to me, in every way possible. Those idiots obviously didn't know what they were doing. If I know you like I think I do, then you probably weren't comfortable enough to be present and enjoy it, right?"

Rylee nods in agreement this time.

"I don't care if it takes you an hour to come, as long as I'm the one making it happen. You never have to worry about that with me. I want you to be comfortable, always."

"Okay," she hums thoughtfully, so I don't push her for more, knowing she needs a moment to think.

She kicks her legs in the water, the waves rippling between our legs in the quiet of the night. I can tell she has more to say since she's restless. It's one of her tells.

I patiently wait for her to continue despite the fact that

my mind is reeling at all this information.

"I've avoided him as much as I could since he was still on the team. I know what you're thinking, but I don't like him. It was purely sexual, well not really, since he didn't turn me on at all." She chuckles to herself at her jab, then sighs. "I've only ever come with my vibrator. It's him and I until the end of time."

God help me.

The image of Rylee using a vibrator nearly sends me over the edge, so much so I need to grip the edge of the pool to ground myself.

There's so much to process here, and my dick is throbbing at the prospect. I badly want to be the first to make her come, I want it more than my next fucking breath. I can only hope she holds out for longer than ten minutes because I want all the time in the world between her sweet legs.

Besides, what kind of prick gives up just like that?

I lean in closer to her, lightly grabbing her chin with two fingers to tilt her head toward me. "Sunshine, I could make you come in two minutes, but I hope it takes longer, at least for my own pleasure," I say, licking my lips because I'm nearly salivating at the thought.

Rylee's mouth drops open. "Jesus," she breathes out, looking up to the sky. Her chest moves more rapidly, and I know my words have as much effect on her as she has on me. "This is what I mean, Miles. You say stuff like that, and it stresses me out because I have no idea what I'm doing, and–"

I cut her off. "That doesn't matter to me, Ry. We can take it as slow as you want. I'm in no rush." I lean in and press a kiss to her cheek, reveling in how soft her skin is, and how my simple touch causes her body to react.

I don't tell her it turns me on that she's inexperienced, knowing I'll be the one helping her learn her body.

No one else. Me.

"Also, I am a pretty good teacher. I can coach you through it all," I tease, giving her a knowing grin.

Rylee blushes before she kicks her legs wildly in my direction, soaking me. She shouts over the noise of the water, "You're such a cocky ass-"

She doesn't get to finish her sentence because before she can even react, I reach over, lift her up onto my lap, then toss her into the water, a quick yelp escaping her lips before she goes under. I scoot off the edge and hop in after her.

When she emerges from the water, she spits water directly in my face.

"Thanks, Ry," I chuckle, rubbing my eyes.

She swims closer and shoves my chest. "I don't like you."

Her pool isn't deep enough that we have to tread water, so we can easily stand. I grab hold of her hand and pull her flush against me. Her heart beats erratically against mine, but what I really focus on is her wet shirt, her hard nipples pressing through the fabric against my chest.

I ignore her comment because I know she's teasing, and instead, ask the question I want to be cleared up before moving forward. "Are we okay then? You're not mad anymore?"

She surprises me by leaning up to kiss my cheek. She pulls back to look me in the eyes. "No, we're good. But promise me, you won't walk out on me again, we can't work like that."

I hold my pinky out to her. "I solemnly swear I won't leave you again Rylee."

Rylee hones in on my pinky, her face scrunching up. "A pinky swear? Really?"

I mock gasp. "This is legit stuff, Riles. I haven't broken a pinky promise in my entire life. I would give you an example, but that would cause me to break said promise."

She gives me one of her big smiles, the ones I love the most. My heart bursts at the sight.

"Fine," she chuckles, then wraps her pinky around mine. Before letting go, she adds, "Are *you* still mad at me? What were you even mad for? You never told me."

I rub my thumb over her hand that's still wrapped around my pinky. "I was mad at you for being so casual with me when I texted you, but I now know that we need to take things slowly. So, no, I'm not mad."

She lets go of my pinky, then slowly traces her hands up my body. She starts at my ribs and slides up to my chest before resting them on my shoulders. "I want to talk about that more, but right now I want to try something," she says, her voice low but sweet.

"I'm yours," I say, a truth I've known since I was 16. "What do you want to try?" I ask, my nose nuzzling the side of hers in encouragement.

Rylee takes a deep breath. "I want to learn how to kiss you in different ways. Slow, soft, deep, rough… Each guy that kissed me was sloppy, so I didn't get much practice with all the different ways lips can communicate. Our lips can express so much, and I don't mean with words."

I stare at her in amazement because only Rylee can take the act of kissing and make it sound so artistic as if it's a skill to be practiced and perfected. I love that about her, her ability to make seemingly overlooked things detailed and beautiful. She's a romantic, reading romance novels any chance she could while growing up.

I'll romance the hell out of her if that's what she wants.

Her scent invades my senses, making it harder to keep control of my need for my girl. "My lips are at your service. Kiss away," I whisper.

I watch as she stands a little taller, confidence settling over her. She leans up, and I wrap my arms around the small of her back, holding her tightly. Rylee's lips cover mine so softly, I can barely feel them. She kisses me again, adding a little more pressure this time, and adjusts her lips to kiss me slowly at different angles.

I try to remain still, my hands firm around her back as I let her take control, and I'm enjoying the hell out of it. So is my dick, which is hardening as we speak.

She applies even more pressure this time, deepening the kiss. I groan, unable to control it and she gasps. I'm tempted to explore her mouth with my tongue, but this is her experiment, not mine.

I think my groan spurs her to move on to roughly kissing me because her lips suddenly attack mine with urgency. Her tongue pokes at my lips, demanding entrance, and I readily grant it. Her tongue slides in my mouth, and then her lips suck on my tongue briefly before pulling away and nipping my bottom lip.

God fucking dammit.

"Happy with your experiment?" I ask above the sound of our panting breaths.

"The results are inconclusive. I might need to retest them."

I smirk. "I'll be your willing participant anytime."

Then, I take my turn, bring one hand up to the nape of her neck, and angle her head to kiss her deeply. Her hands rest on my back, digging into my wet shirt. We kiss slowly but with need. I drag my other hand up her waist, digging my fingers in, and I feel her body tremble under my touch.

I bring my hand up just under her breast, teasing a finger along the underside of it. "Is this okay?" I ask, stroking her gently with just one finger.

"Yes," she breathes out before kissing me again, her lips

devouring mine.

Noting the desire in her kiss, and her consent, I take it a step further and bring my hand to cup her breast and give it a light squeeze.

Rylee whimpers in my mouth, and I suck on her bottom lip in response. I flick my thumb over her hardened nipple, causing her body to arch into mine.

"Is this hard for me?" I ask, bringing my mouth to her ear, where I nip it lightly as I pinch her nipple between my fingers.

She moans and the sound is like a calling to my dick. I want her. So. Fucking. Much.

I'm only asking her because even though it's a warm night, her pool is chilly and it could be from her being cold.

"That and..." she trails off.

I instantly pull away, my concern for her taking precedence over anything else. Rylee frowns up at me as a slight shiver wracks her body.

"C'mon, let's get you inside. It's getting cold."

"But I'm... you know," she mumbles under her breath.

I grin. "I'll take care of it once you're nice and warm inside. I can't focus on giving you anything until I know you're okay."

The look she gives me warms my fucking soul.

"Miles... that's really sweet. Who are you, and what have you done with the real Miles?" she teases.

"Funny," I deadpan, and it reminds me of our friendship growing up. Rylee would tease me, and I would reply like that sometimes, a one-liner with no emotion, and she would smile even brighter. It was and still is my favorite thing to do.

As if on cue, her smile brightens before she turns away from me and swims to the edge of the pool. She hoists herself out of the water and my jaw fucking drops when she jumps to lift herself up and her shirt flies up, giving me a glimpse of what was underneath. And guess what? She has no fucking panties on, no shorts, nothing. She's been completely bare this whole time.

I run a hand through my hair, stifling a groan. She's going to be the death of me.

I'm still standing in the middle of the pool, dumbfounded when she turns on her heel to look at me. "You coming?"

Nearly baby, nearly.

"Jesus, Ry. If I knew you were bare this whole time... fuck," I admit, with no shame whatsoever.

"Really?" she says more to herself than me as if in shock at my admission.

I nod, swim to the edge of the pool, and lift myself up. I'm bringing a leg up the edge when Rylee pushes me back into the pool. Seconds later, I surface the water to find her bent over in laughter, and can't help but smile. I deserved it and got to see her smile, which is a win in my book.

When I get to the edge this time, she lets me get up and we head inside to the laundry room in the basement where the towels are.

Rylee bends over to the hamper, pulling out a t-shirt for herself, along with one for me and a pair of shorts from what I am assuming is Ryan's pile, and hands them to me.

"Do you mind turning around? I..." she trails off.

"Not at all. We're going at your pace remember?" I say softly, then turn around and change out of my wet clothes, throwing them into the washer. The urge to turn around is strong, but I also want to respect her boundaries. "You good?" I call out.

"Yep," she squeaks.

I turn around, and she looks just how she did when I first got here, except now her hair is wet, and her cheeks are flushed.

I slowly approach her and stop when I'm right in front of her, my hands gripping her waist gently. "Remember you owe me a dare and a favor, right?" I remind her, to hell with Ryan's warning about not making it dirty. I'm too far in, and I'm not turning around.

"Oh god, I was hoping you forgot," she says, her breaths coming out faster when I pull her against me.

"Not likely," I say, leaning down and kissing her like it might be the last time. My lips are rough against hers—sucking, nipping, devouring. And she matches my energy.

I break away from her and rest my forehead against hers, noticing how swollen her lips are.

My brain screams *mine.*

"I dare you to let me go down on you."

CHAPTER THIRTEEN

Miles

I feel her body jolt against mine, her knees knocking together. "W-what kind of dare is that?"

I feather kisses down her neck and, between them, whisper, "A good one."

I can sense her hesitating, so I pull away and look up to see her lust-ridden eyes. "But it's up to you, Riles. I want to make you come so badly, but I'll wait as long as you want me to."

It's quiet for a moment, our breaths and the washing machine filling the air. I can tell she's struggling internally, but then she finally speaks with the utmost confidence. "I accept your dare."

Fuck. Yes. I'll finally get to claim her first non-battery orgasm and every one after that too.

I bend and pick her up, my hands gripping her ass, and she instantly wraps her legs around my waist. I set her on top of the washing machine and marvel at her for a moment, taking in the depth of her gray-blue eyes, the freckles that pepper her skin, and the fullness of her lips.

My tongue dips out to lick my top lip. "Did you put panties

on this time?"

Her hands grip the edge of the washing machine as she shakes her head no.

I spread her legs around me and step into her space so I can be closer to her. We're eye to eye with her sitting up here, and I reach out to stroke her cheek. "Relax, Riles. Tell me what you like and don't like. If you want me to stop at any time, you tell me, okay?"

"Okay," she says, her shoulders dropping, the tension rolling away. She pulls out her fist to me.

I look at her quizzically. "What is that?" I ask.

She scrunches her nose at me. "A fist bump. I thought we were doing things with our hands to make promises."

I look at my girl in awe. She's so sweet and perfect. Only she could make me laugh right before I devour her pussy. I bring my hand up and we bump fists. She smiles widely, but it's gone once my mouth starts trailing kisses down her neck, her shirt, over her breasts.

I suck on a nipple through the fabric and her back arches, her body asking for more. I give it what it wants. I switch over to her other breast, giving it the same attention while my hand plays with the other, squeezing and rubbing.

Rylee whimpers softly, a reminder that she needs relief and I'm the only one who'll give it to her. I kiss my way down her stomach, and instead of going where she needs me, I turn my head and kiss the inside of each thigh slowly, drawing circles with my tongue, then sucking the skin there.

"Miles, please," she begs, and that's my undoing.

I grab her hips, scooting her right to the edge of the washing machine. She inhales a sharp breath as I lift her shirt high enough to give me the perfect view of her pussy. I kiss the top of it, her skin soft and bare. I trail my hand down and slide two fingers down her slit, noting how wet she is.

I bring one finger to my lips and suck her arousal off, delighting in the way her eyes darken at the sight. I hold the other finger up to her lips. "Taste yourself, baby. I want you to know exactly why I'll enjoy acquainting your pussy with its new owner."

Rylee's lips part, her eyes intent on mine as she grabs my hand and brings my finger to her mouth, tasting herself.

The sight has blood rushing to my cock. "Such a good fucking girl when you listen. Do you like it when I take charge?"

"Mhm," she sighs.

I swipe my fingers over her slit again and she groans.

"But I'd like it more if you went down on me like you said you would."

I grin at her assertiveness, liking it as much as she does when I'm the one in charge. I finally give in to my girl because I know she can't wait any longer, and neither can I.

I bring my lips down to her swollen clit, and give it a light flick with my tongue. Her body jolts forward, so I bring my arm to rest across her stomach, holding her down. I lay my tongue flat against her clit and insert one finger inside her. She's so fucking warm, and tight. Rylee moans and my dick hardens instantly. It's a fucking Pavlovian response now.

"So fucking sweet," I grunt against her pussy as I begin to slowly thrust my finger inside her while my tongue licks her up and down, savoring her taste.

Her legs start to shake, and she tightens around my finger, her body telling me she's close.

I insert another finger, still fucking her slowly with them as my tongue laps around her clit. Her hands fly to my hair, holding me there. She likes that a lot so I do it again, and she grows even wetter around my fingers.

Christ.

I suck her clit into my mouth, soft at first, then release it to lick again, and this time when I give it a hard suck, she comes for the first time. She moans my name and her legs quiver, her pussy clamping down on my fingers, her arousal coating my beard.

I glance up to look at her face Rylee coming is truly a sight to see. Her lips are parted slightly, and, her eyes are nearly shut as she whimpers out the remnants of her orgasm.

Once she's relaxed, I pull my fingers out and suck them into my mouth, licking up every ounce of her.

Delectable.

I look at Rylee, and her eyes widen, not in shock but with a deep desire this time.

She hops off the washing machine, kisses me wildly, then breaks it all too soon. "Thank you," she murmurs.

Rylee thanking me for making her come is adorable but it also doesn't sit right with me.

"You never have to thank me for giving you pleasure," I say, pushing a strand of hair out of her face, my blood pumping with need. "Especially when you taste that good. When you taste like *mine.*"

She narrows her brows at me. "Relax, caveman."

I kiss her nose. "Not sorry about it. I made you come when no other guy has. I'm so fucking happy, sunshine."

She rolls her eyes, then roams them down my body. "Oh my God… You're… hard."

Not what I thought she'd say.

I look down to see my erection straining against the gym shorts she let me borrow. Yeah, there is no hiding that, nor do I want to, but I don't want her feeling pressured to do anything about it.

"I could spend forever with my head between your thighs. It'll become my favorite hobby," I say, trying to turn the conversation so she doesn't feel obligated to return the favor.

Rylee visibly swallows. "You saying that is such a turn-on," she says, her words filled with unbridled lust.

I smirk at her comment. "Yeah?"

She nods. "Yeah, I just wish I knew how to please you..."

I cup her cheeks with both hands, stroking the side of her face. The look on her face tells me she sincerely wants to know, so I give in a fraction. "I could teach you if you want..."

Her eyebrows furrow in confusion. "I didn't expect you to be so gentle with this stuff."

"I'm gentle with you because you're my soft spot," I remind her.

Her eyes crinkle with her smile, and she nods in agreement. I let my hands fall from her face, and she shocks me yet again by gripping me through my shorts.

I stifle a groan. "Rylee, I'll take care of it when I get home."

"Teach me. I want to learn how to make you feel good, please," she whispers, her plea chipping away at my restraint.

"Are you going to listen as a good girl would?"

She nods, and I can see her nipples harden through her shirt.

"Get on your knees, now," I command, knowing now that this kind of talk isn't too much for her.

Rylee responds by eagerly dropping to her knees, a shy smile on her lips and hunger in her eyes.

Both of her hands fall on my flat stomach. I shiver as her fingers slowly trail to the waistband, and yank my shorts down to my ankles with no warning.

An audible gasp emits from Rylee as my lengthy cock springs free. "I...don't think this is going to fit ...anywhere," she says, her voice strained and eyes wide.

While any guy loves to hear how big they are, I also don't want her to fear being intimate with me.

I reach for her hand resting on my thigh and interlock it with mine, giving it a squeeze. "We don't have to do anything you don't want to do, okay?" I wait for her to nod in acknowledgment, and when she does, I continue. "I won't get any pleasure if you're not into it for any reason, get me?"

Her eyes soften, and she looks up at me with a gentleness I haven't seen before. "I'm happy I'm doing this with you. You make me feel safe and desired at the same time."

My heart hammers in my chest at her sentiments. "I'm not afraid, just unsure how this all works. The guy I lost it to was not this big, and I've never done this before – exploring a guy's body, learning how to please it. And I want to please you so badly. Just walk me through it, and if I choke, don't laugh."

I chuckle softly at that. "Trust me, I won't. When you deep throat and choke, your throat tightens, and it feels really good on my end. But don't even worry about that. As for going inside you, your body will adjust when you're turned on. I won't go in unless you're soaked for me, okay Riles?"

"Okay," she says softly, then her gaze becomes hungry again. "Now, lead the way, Mr. Anderson," she coos, her big blue grey-ish eyes pleading.

Fuck. I don't even think she realizes how sexy she is, and she's not even trying.

"Tease me, build me up by stroking me," I tell her.

Rylee reaches out, gently squeezes my tip, and I jolt forward.

Rylee's hand shoots back. "Oh my god, did I hurt you? I'm so sorry-"

"No baby, the tip is just sensitive. I suggest starting at my base with a firm grip, and making your way up."

Her hand returns to my dick, at the base this time, her grip too gentle. It reminds me that I'm in charge, which is how she needs me to be.

"Grip me harder. I'll let you know what feels good," I urge her, running one of my hands over her wet waves.

She keeps her gaze on mine and she grips me a bit harder. When I nod at her in encouragement for more, she finally grips me just right – firm and tight, with just enough pressure.

"Perfect Ry. Such a good girl."

My girl responds to the praise and starts stroking me, up and down, her grip switching from just right, to light, and back to the way I like. She's teasing the fuck out of me, and I have no idea if she even knows it.

"Riles, I'm going to come if you keep that up, so if you want to learn how to take me in your mouth, I suggest we move on with the lesson," I croak, my jaw clamped down to try and get a hold of the pleasure building at the base of my spine.

"No, you keep your shit together. I want to taste you," she demands roughly, her voice laced with lust.

"You keep talking like that, and you won't get to." I bite down on my lip, my control wanting to snap. Hearing those words from her plump, perfect mouth is too much right now. "Wrap one hand around my base, and pump it as you take me in your mouth."

Rylee's hand grips me, and my dick twitches at the warm contact.

"Now, there are different ways you can start… you could be aggressive and take me in deep, or you can build me up by starting with the tip."

Her hand starts to pump my length and she asks, "Which do you prefer?"

"Whatever you're cool with, anything you do will feel good," I tell her, then take charge and continue to guide her knowing the aggressive approach won't be her style. "Lick the tip, swirl your tongue around the crown, then go up and down my length with your tongue. Get a feel for me, and listen to the sounds I make. You'll know when you hit a sensitive spot."

She takes me in for a moment, then leans forward and plants a soft kiss at the tip, our hands still interlocked. I've never held a girl's hand before, but I like that we are. She's vulnerable with me, and I want to make her feel confident as she learns.

Her tongue comes out, and she swipes it over my slit. A groan slips free from my chest. Her tongue swirls around the tip, and she wraps her lips around it, sucking before releasing, the popping sound making my spine shiver.

"Quick learner," I smirk. "Now, you can start taking me in deeper if you're ready. Go slow and wrap your lips around your teeth. Remember to pump me with your hand at the same time. It'll help with getting the rhythm."

Rylee listens, and I watch as her lips sheath her teeth. She then wraps them around the tip again, but this time, she pumps at my base and continues to take more of me in her mouth. She does this for a bit, sucks me in, then releases, taking more each time as she adjusts to my size. She releases me for a moment, licking the tip before making her way down my entire length.

My body inches forward when her tongue crosses a sensitive spot on my underside, and she hums.

"That turns you on, baby? Knowing how much that sweet mouth of yours is driving me crazy?" I rasp, my breathing erratic. I'm so on edge that it's un-fucking believable.

Her lips wrap around my cock and her eyes flit up to mine as she moans her answer. My balls tense up from the vibrations, but I use everything I have to hold back.

"Touch yourself. I want to see how much you love being on your knees for me."

She takes her hand away from mine and reaches between her legs to stroke herself. Her eyelids flutter at her touch, and the sight is almost my undoing. Knowing she enjoys this, turns me on more than anything. She brings her hand up to show me, and I can see them glistening with her arousal.

I reach out and tug her wrist up higher, and I suck them into my mouth, wanting more of her taste on my tongue. She whimpers around my cock, then takes me in deeper, my tip reaching the back of her throat. She chokes and the sensation edges me closer.

"Ry, I'm close. Do that again, then let go so I can come on a shirt or-"

She cuts me off. "Is it okay if you come in my mouth? I want to taste you. I know some girls don't like it, but I want to try it."

My balls fucking feel like exploding at her words, so it's between sporadic breaths that I say, "Jesus...Ry, that's more than okay."

Her left-hand pumps me while her right comes up to lightly squeeze my balls and her mouth sucks me in deeper. I shut my eyes as the pleasure builds at the base of my spine, and everything around me fades except for the sound of her sucking my dick, and the feel of her choking on it. I grunt and forcefully come so fucking hard and I spill myself into her warm mouth.

"That's a good girl, don't miss a single drop," I growl, my hands stroking her hair back as she does exactly as I demanded, swallowing, sucking, and licking me clean.

Rylee stands once she's done, her stance confident, while my knees feel like buckling from the aftermath of my orgasm.

"You okay?" she asks, a small smile on her lips.

I tug her into me, capturing her lips with mine, tasting myself on her tongue. I exhale a deep breath once we part. "You've ruined me. I will never be the same after that."

Her smile disappears, and I immediately backtrack, "In a good way, Riles. I'm very proud of my girl."

Her cheeks flush, and her chin dips down. "I liked it...seeing you come undone like that because of me. I felt powerful."

I smile brightly at her. "Yeah? And how did you like... would you prefer to spit or for me to come elsewhere next time?"

I tip her chin up with my fingers, forcing her to look at me so I can read her eyes to see how she's truly feeling. When they meet mine, I can tell she's being truthful. "I liked that too. You can always come in my mouth."

This. Fucking. Girl. "You are going to be the death of me," I tease, bringing her into my chest, holding her to me tightly.

Rylee's arms wrap around me just as snuggly. "I hope not, I'm just starting to like you again." Her laughter vibrates against my chest and mine follows suit.

I'll take what I can; having her admit she likes me is enough for now.

CHAPTER FOURTEEN

Rylee

My mind is officially blown after last night, no pun intended. For one, I wasn't expecting Miles to be so freaking sweet and gentle when it came to exploring each other. Speaking of which, I was not expecting to have my first non-vibrator-delivered orgasm either.

I never thought there would be a difference… but oh boy is there. The orgasm that ripped through me from Miles's mouth was like nothing I've ever felt, and I'm worried I'll grow addicted to him, for him to become a drug I'll always want to be high on.

I also didn't expect to like giving head as much as I did. It made me feel so confident and powerful, knowing I could pleasure him and help him find his release.

After we held each other, we made out for a little while, and even though we were both ready for round two, Miles found the strength to stop and leave. Part of me wanted him to stay and hold me through the night, which is something I've never experienced, but the other half was grateful that he respected my wishes and wanted to take things slowly.

On our way to work, I recounted last night's events to

Ava and she squealed with joy. It's currently our lunch break and the kids are playing in the lake because it's hot today.

We spent the first half of the day on conditioning because any sport requires workouts and skills training. Ava and I are wiped after being challenged to join them and being a teacher is all about leading, not commanding. So, I gave in, which made Ava do the same.

We're now both enjoying the down-time before we start our skills session this afternoon when Ava covers her mouth and looks at me with wide eyes.

I groan, wiping the sweat off my forehead with my forearm. "I don't even want to know what you're looking at. If the kids are fighting, can you deal with it? I'm tapped out."

She shakes her head and winks. "Nope, this one is all you."

Sighing in defeat and somewhat anxious, I turn to where her gaze is directed and freeze. It's Miles, and he's walking towards us with two smoothies and what looks like a bouquet. My bottom lip drops as he approaches.

What is he doing here?

Ava jumps to her feet and wipes the sand off her legs. "Miles, nice to see you here. Are you looking to take some volleyball lessons? Maybe teach us lessons on how to-"

Oh. My. God.

"Ava," I yell, cutting her off because I know exactly what's coming next out of her no-filter mouth.

She smiles at me, and Miles doesn't seem to mind because he simply laughs at her.

"I only teach those kinds of lessons to Rylee, but I'm sure Ryan wouldn't mind giving you one," he says once he's standing in front of us, his body blocking the sun above.

"Hmm, that's a fun role-play option. Thanks for that," she says playfully.

I want to vomit. Having your best friend date your brother is weird because Ava and I always share intimate details, but now I'd rather not.

I stay seated on the sand and watch this interaction between my best friend and my... I don't even know since we never put a label on it.

Miles hands her one of the smoothies. "I brought you both a smoothie since it's hot as fuck today. I just guessed the flavors, so I'm sorry in advance if I got them wrong."

Did I die and go to heaven not realizing it? Because Miles surprising both me and my best friend with smoothies at work is so freaking cute, making my heart work overtime inside my chest.

Ava takes hers greedily and takes a sip of the purple liquid. "Berry is my favorite. Rylee, you better keep him."

I blush and turn my gaze to the sand because the feelings bubbling inside make it hard to look at him right now.

"I'll go round up the kids and get them settled for skills. Take five, Ry." She turns her attention back to Miles. "Thanks, Miles," she exclaims, then walks past him and toward our students in the water.

I stay seated on the sand since I'm unable to move because my legs feel weak from his sweet surprise. "Hi," I murmur.

Miles crouches and tucks a stray strand of my hair behind my ear. "Hi sunshine, you okay?"

There goes my heart.

I shake my head. "No, I'm not. You showing up at work to surprise me with a smoothie because it's hot is the nicest thing I think anyone's done for me. It's making me want to jump your bones when I'm supposed to be working."

He gives me his signature cocky grin. "Baby, get used to it. I'll always want to spoil and cherish you."

He hands me the yellow smoothie, and I already know it's my favorite – pineapple mango.

This man keeps reminding me of the Miles from my childhood, the one who was so sweet to me, the best friend I could be myself with. That part of him is still there. In fact, I think it's entwined itself with my soul and built a bond over the years that withstood the test of distance, emotionally and physically.

Now that we're back on good terms, I can see it more clearly than ever and although it scares me, it also fills me with something warm and fuzzy.

"Thank you," I whisper, my voice trembling with the emotions pooling in my gut so I take a sip of my drink.

He smiles, and his eyes gaze through mine as if they're looking straight into my soul. That's always been our thing. If Ryan did something stupid, we'd look at each other with a knowing look. If I got scared during a movie, his eyes would find mine and I'd feel his reassurance, surrounding me like a comfortable blanket.

"What are those for?" I ask, breaking our trance as I peer down at the bouquet in his arms, but I can't see the flowers because the wrapping is pulled up to block my view intentionally.

Miles tugs the wrapping down and hands them to me. "Something beautiful for my pretty girl. They reminded me of you so I got them."

The bouquet is beautiful, filled with sunflowers, white lilies, pink tulips, and greenery. I can't help the tear dropping because all of this is overwhelming.

"No, no. Don't cry, Riles. I seriously can't stand watching you cry, it guts me," he admits, his voice full of worry as he wipes the lone tear away.

I smile up at him brightly. "I'm crying because this is so freaking kind and unexpected, my brain doesn't know what to do right now."

"You can kiss me as a thank you, then get back to work because I'm not going to take you away from your job, and I need to get going."

"I think I need you to help me up because my legs feel like jelly," I admit, slightly embarrassed. I place my flowers and smoothie in the sand, then hold up both hands to Miles who's standing above me now with a smirk on his gorgeous face.

He grabs them and helps me to my feet. I go to brush the sand off my legs, but he crouches and wipes them off for me.

Seriously? He needs to stop before I drag him somewhere private to thank him.

As soon as he's standing, I waste no time and lift up on my toes to kiss him. My lips land softly on his, and I kiss him sweetly to show him know how much I appreciate him and his gifts. He kisses me back just as tenderly, cherishing me as he said earlier, his hands staying on my waist.

I break the kiss, remembering I'm at work, and step away from him. "Where are you off to? Or does it make me clingy and annoying to ask that?" I stumble over my words, suddenly feeling awkward.

He plants a soft kiss on my lips. "It's not clingy or annoying, sunshine. I'm off to my sister's to help with the house. Can I see you later?" he asks, removing any sense of awkwardness I was feeling over how much I felt for him at that moment.

"We're making homemade pizzas tonight. You can come over around five if you'd like?"

He beams at me. "A night with you and pizza? Yeah, I'd like that."

I smile back at him just as brightly, but then it fades once I remember our biggest problem: Ryan.

"What's wrong?" Miles asks, immediately picking up on

my worry.

"Ryan and Ava will be there…" I trail off.

"And you don't want him to know?"

"No, I don't. Not yet, anyway, not until we figure out what this is together…without him getting involved. Is that okay?"

"Honestly, I thought about telling him about us because I don't want to sneak around and hide you as if you're not meant to be shown off. But, I also get where you're coming from," he says, his voice clogged with emotions at the end as we're both reminded of why he left all those years ago, to avoid ruining our relationships with Ryan - who's so important to both of us. "Just so we're clear, you are important to me, and I'm not picking him over you, but if that's what you want, then we'll do it."

I'm speechless for a moment at the sincerity in his words. "You're important to me too. That's why I want a chance to do this without the weight of everyone else. Just us for now, please?"

He nods. "And what about Ava? She knows everything, so do we trust her?" he asks playfully, making the mood lighter.

"She may be dating Ryan, but her heart belonged to me first. She won't say anything. She's rooting for us too much to ruin anything."

"Her and I have that in common then," he says so low, I barely hear it.

But I do, and my knees tremble as he says goodbye, and we part ways for the remainder of the afternoon.

As Ava and I run through the rest of the afternoon with our students, I can't help but worry about tonight any chance my mind gets a free second. How in the hell will I act like I'm not…whatever it is that I am with Miles? The last time my brother checked, Miles and I were just becoming friends again. Now we're *more than* just friends.

This is going to be fun.

CHAPTER FIFTEEN

Rylee

This is so not fun.

Don't get me wrong, we've been having a good time, laughing and carrying on as a typical group of friends would. Hell, it's going even better than I thought it would.

When Miles showed up with a pack of seltzers, I was nervous that, somehow, we'd be outed and Ryan would be onto us. But while I was drowning in overthinking, I forgot that Miles and I were best friends first, so it really hasn't been hard at all. It's actually been really nice to be ourselves with each other. There's nothing to fake or pretend because that's what we are. Minus the fact that I now want to kiss him when he looks at me while he laughs, or snuggle into his chest while we wait for the pizzas to finish cooking.

So it's still us but with some *minor* changes.

Now, back to the point where tonight isn't so fun—the stolen touches and glances whenever no one's looking.

For instance, while we were cutting vegetables together, Miles purposely brushed his chest against my back to get a knife. Or when he briefly held onto my pinky with one of his fingers while Ryan had his back turned to set up the Bluetooth speaker. Or when Ava dragged Ryan to the garage to "look for something" leaving Miles and I alone for a few minutes where he pressed me up against the counter and kissed me until my lips were tingling along with my clit.

So basically, it's been torture. The little touches have been edging me all night, and I feel like I'll detonate soon. I am so sexually frustrated that I may even come simply from a good make-out session with him if we get the chance.

We're watching an episode of our favorite sitcom while eating our homemade pizzas on the couch, and of course, mine has pineapple on it. Ryan and Ava are snuggled on the pull-out section of the couch like the love-sick people they are while Miles sits next to me at a distance that's normal for two friends, but not close enough for my liking.

I don't even know what we are, but I want him closer to me. I crave it.

Since we're sharing a blanket, I decide to sneak my right hand under the blanket. I glance over at my brother. He seems engrossed enough in the show and Ava that I don't think he noticed my hand going underneath the cover.

I reach for Miles's side of the cushion and try to find his hand, but I don't have to go too far because his hand quickly collides with mine. I feel a rush of relief once our hands are interlocked. His thumb gently strokes the top of my hand, and I shiver. I can sense him smiling to himself, and I press my lips together to try and hold mine in.

We spend the rest of the show doing this, secretly taking turns as we stroke each other's hands with our thumbs. I take this time to think about everything that's happened over the last two weeks and how it went from dreading Miles's return to not wanting him to leave.

Our friendship and physical attraction are off the charts, and it would be easy to fall in love with him. I can already feel myself slipping into that territory. I've always been a hopeless romantic, and being around Miles makes me forget how to think rationally.

Ryan pauses the show and quickly sits up. We both let go but refrain from making any movements so that Ryan doesn't question why we're moving under the blanket.

Ryan beams, his green eyes full of excitement. "Guys, I was thinking—"

"Congrats, I know that's hard for you sometimes," I tease, eliciting a chuckle from Miles and Ava.

Ryan glares at me. "We should go to the cottage with the team when Mom and Dad leave for New York."

"Oh my gosh, yes," Ava exclaims, sitting up.

"When would that be?" I ask because I don't know how I'm going to survive being around Miles all weekend without being all over him. I'm hoping it's not for another month. That way we can give our relationship time to grow before we have to tell him.

"In four weeks, they're leaving August 1st. We can go up a week after on a Thursday night and come home Sunday."

Miles answers instead. "Because there's no chance we are forfeiting a game on Monday."

"Exactly. So, what do you guys say? You in?" Ryan asks, his excitement rivaling that of a five-year-old on Christmas morning.

"Duh," Ava says.

"Sounds fun," I reply, although there is nothing fun in being tortured all weekend, not being able to touch Miles. Tonight was just a glimpse of what that will be like and I don't think I'd be able to resist not being near him.

"I'm in," Miles chimes in, but I can tell he's thinking the same thing I am.

We are going to be absolutely screwed that weekend.

"Great, I'll text the team and set it up," Ryan says, heading toward his room to grab his phone. He leaves it in his room whenever we have company because he likes to be fully present.

Ava collects our plates, and I know better than to argue because she's adamant that whoever cooks doesn't clean. Plus, she's just going to throw them in the dishwasher so there wouldn't be much I could help with there since Ryan cleaned the counters once Miles and I were done cooking everything.

"That's going to be fun," Miles remarks.

I roll my eyes at him. "Oh yeah, so much fun."

He scoots closer, invading my space. He brushes his nose against mine. "It's not for a while, be here with me now."

I realize how much Ryan, Miles, and I have in common. We grew up being outside all the time, and even though we use our phones like anyone else, we also value the importance of being present in the moment.

Until I see a text from Ava light up my phone on the ottoman. The only reason I break away from him to check is because I have a feeling she's about to give us some alone time.

I hear the creak of the top step as I open her message and confirm my theory.

Ava

> I'm going to do some things to your brother you probably don't want to know about.
> Stay downstairs and have some fun ;)

I scoot closer to Miles and let him read over my shoulder as I text her back.

> Isn't he going to avoid being a rude host and come back downstairs??

Ava

Nope, he'll be tied up if you must know. So, he has no way out. P.S. You guys are friends, so he'll assume you can chill without him, without touching each other, even though I know you can't, LOL. K bye. Have fun!

I groan and throw a hand over my face, attempting to erase that first sentence from my brain forever. Miles's body vibrates beside me, and I look over to see him laughing his ass off.

"Oh, I am so going to tease him about that. Who knew he was so kinky?"

"Sadly, I do now," I mumble in response which only makes him laugh harder. I let out a laugh too, because his laugh is infectious, and I can't help myself.

My laughter stills when Miles takes my phone out of my hand and tosses it on the cushion behind me before crushing his lips to mine. He kisses me like it might be our last time.

This man is hungry for me, and I'm equally as famished. He's been working me up all day and I need a release. Which is what gives me the confidence to swing my leg over his hip and straddle him. Once I nestle into his lap, I feel him harden beneath me, and I squirm in response.

I love that he's so attracted to me because, at times, I find it hard to believe that I turn Miles on.

His hands rest on my hips and squeeze. "These lips have been driving me insane all night. I need more," he rasps against my lips, claiming them once more as he devours me.

I match his energy, kissing him just as fiercely. I suck and nip at his bottom lip when his tongue enters my mouth, I whimper. His unique scent of mint and pine invades me, heightening my arousal. I grind against his hard length, reveling in the relief the friction brings.

"Rylee," he groans and stills my hips.

I frown at him. "I need you, please. I'll be quiet."

He mulls it over for a second and sighs in defeat. "Fuck, I need you too. Think you can be a good, and quiet girl?"

I nod fervently. "Yes, yes. Now kiss me."

He chuckles. "Needy tonight, are we?" he teases, his hand trailing under my dress.

I shiver under his touch. His lips trail down my neck, pressing gentle kisses. "Yes, you've been getting me worked up all night and if I don't get relief soon, I'm kicking you out and going upstairs to use my vibrator."

He stills his mouth and hand that is achingly close to my already wet panties. "Not going to fucking happen. Now shush and let me take care of that for you."

His mouth is on the swell of my breast, kissing and sucking, as his hand moves my panties to the side so I do as he says.

Suddenly, music booms from upstairs, and I internally thank Ava because I have no idea if I'll be able to be quiet. This urges Miles on, and he lifts me up, his hips following up to push down his shorts and boxers. His cock springs out between us, and I hover above him, feeling a bit unsure now as that monster stares back at me.

"I'm not going inside you just yet, don't worry," he says, his tone soft and caring.

God, I love that about him— I mean *like* because I am not in love with him. Nope.

"Okay, and I do want you inside me soon…just not with my brother upstairs."

He pulls me back down onto him, and the feel of him bare beneath me sends desire shooting down my spine and to my toes.

"I know, and I'm in no rush. But I am in a rush to get you off before we get caught."

"Please," I beg.

He responds by yanking the front of my strapless dress down, exposing my breasts, which are eager for his touch. Miles wastes no time, sucking a nipple into his mouth, eliciting a quiet moan from me. My hands grip his shoulders tightly.

He pulls away for a moment, his hand gently patting my ass. "Roll those hips for me, Riles."

I find myself liking it and wishing he slapped it harder, but I'll store that thought away for another time.

I do as he says, grinding against him as he sucks the other nipple into his mouth while his hand works the other. My need builds and I roll my hips harder into him, dragging my wetness across his hard length, so hard and fast that I feel like I might slide right off of him. It's almost embarrassing how wet I am right now.

I look down between us and the sight of my arousal coating his cock drives the orgasm building in me.

"That's it, baby. Take what you need from me. Rub yourself on my cock, and show me how needy you are to feel me inside you," he murmurs against my breast, his beard rough against my chest.

It'll probably leave marks, but I don't care right now. I slide back enough that I feel his tip near my entrance, and I whimper a little louder than I would like.

Miles's hand comes up to cover my mouth, his thumb slipping between my lips, and I suck on it, hard. He reaches between us, gripping his cock and taking over control. He rolls his hips, the motion causing the head of his cock to slide between my slit, hitting my clit just right.

I moan around his thumb, my eyes rolling into the back of my head at the insane pleasure coursing through my entire body. His groan vibrates against my chest, and my orgasm rips through me. I come, moaning into his hand when he suddenly removes it.

"Baby, I'm going to come right about now, I need-"

Somewhere to put it because we're on the couch.

Ryan is upstairs, and we can't have a mess. I quickly lower to my knees between his legs and wrap my lips around his cock. God, I love having him in my mouth, and I wish he wasn't about to come so I could be down here longer.

Miles has ruined me in every way. Who knew I would be like this?

He comes in my mouth within five seconds. It's salty and not the greatest, but it's him, and I love it for that reason. Once he's done, I lift my head and wipe my mouth to ensure there's no evidence left.

When I look up at him, his expression is bliss from his orgasm. I smile, and he returns it with a dazed one.

"You didn't have to do that Ry, I would've just come in my pants and left," he says quietly.

I pull up the top of my dress and lift myself back onto the couch as he puts himself back into his pants. "I told you, I like going down on you. I don't want you to leave yet, so I'm glad I did that."

"I'm not going anywhere," he whispers. "Come here."

I nestle myself closer to him and he wraps an arm around my waist, pulling me onto his lap. His arm rests on my back to keep me up while his other hand caresses my thigh. I place my hand on his chest and revel in this quiet moment we have together, just us two.

We stare at one another, seeking, searching, and talking to one another while remaining silent. It's perfect until I hear the music upstairs stop, signaling that they're finished too. I look up at Miles and pout my lips.

He smirks at me and kisses my forehead softly. "Soon, Riles."

I slide off his lap, my body recoiling at the distance between us. A few moments later, Ava and Ryan come down the stairs with big smiles adorning their faces.

Ew.

"Sorry about that, I stayed up there to text them, didn't want to be rude and be on my phone," Ryan lies poorly.

Miles and I both start laughing, unable to contain it. My brother couldn't lie even if his life depended on it.

"Did Ava learn how to tie a rope with Dad during a summer or...?" I ask.

Ryan turns pale. "Ava, what the fuck?"

"I couldn't be rude to our friends. I had to tell them we would be awhile and to just watch the show without us."

He shakes his head. "You're lucky I love you."

"Yeah, I really am."

They're so in love. It's both cute and sickening at the same time.

All four of us continue watching the show like we didn't all just have an orgasm break.

Later that night, I lie down on my bed, my mind reeling from tonight's events. I don't only mean what happened between Miles and I, but everything before that.

The four of us hanging out felt so natural and easy. From

Ryan and Miles making stupid jokes, to Ava and me giving them shit or Ava and Miles ganging up on me while Ryan sat back and smirked. Our group flows nicely, and if Ryan takes it well, hopefully, it'll all work out. I can see the four of us vacationing, buying a cottage together, and our babies growing up alongside one another.

Okay, babies? I might be getting ahead of myself, but I want it all, and with him, only him.

Thinking of Miles has me rolling over, grabbing my phone off my nightstand, and texting him.

> Thanks for another orgasm, much appreciated.

Miles
> You make me laugh like no one else.
> You're more than welcome.

> Good. Laughter and orgasms can be our thing.

Miles
> Damn straight it is.

> 😊

Miles
> You were soaked today...you have no idea how badly I wanted to fuck you.

> Sorry?

Miles

Sorry? That was fucking amazing. The wetter
you are the better, Riles. It's hot.

Miles

I'm serious, I didn't mean it in a bad way,
I only brought it up to see where your
head is at in regards to sex.
(No pressure of course, just curious).

I really wanted to too. But I'm glad
we didn't. I don't want my brother
anywhere nearby for that.

Miles

I also don't want him around either,
he might try to tie me up.

Okay and on that note I'm going to bed.

Miles

Good night sunshine

Night hot shot, wishing you kinky
dreams of being tied up by Ryan ;)

Miles

I'll be dreaming of fucking you, sweet dreams pretty girl.

CHAPTER SIXTEEN

Miles

It's Saturday, which means I've had four long fucking days without seeing Rylee. Sure, we've texted, but it's not the same. I don't want to scare her by blowing up her phone, but I also want to talk to her all day. I want to know every detail she perceives to be mundane about her day because I've missed out on so much of her life already that I don't want to miss another second.

Since I don't work during the summer, another perk of being a teacher, I have a lot of free time. But when all I can think about is Rylee, it's torturous. I spend most of my days working out in the morning, then head to my sister Sydney's house for the day.

She and her husband moved in a few months ago to prepare for the twins' arrival, and the house desperately needed renovations. Despite all the work it needed, Syd demanded to live here because she always rooted for the underdog. Her husband, Martin, is an engineer, so I think he also enjoyed the prospect of rebuilding their dream home from the ground up.

Martin completed all of the foundation work, from the flooring to drywalling and installing all new windows. Syd mentioned they still needed help painting, and completing the deck outside, so here I am. Sweating my ass off in the humid heat of a Michigan summer. I was finishing cutting a piece of wood for the deck when my sister comes out of the sliding door, waddling and carrying over two glasses of water.

"Syd, go sit down. If we want water, we have two feet," I scold her because she's seven months pregnant with twins. She shouldn't be moving more than she has to already.

"Don't waste your breath. She doesn't know how to relax," Martin adds.

Besides Ryan, Martin is the next closest thing I have to a best friend. Sure, there was a group of guys I hung out with in college, but the bonds didn't run that deep.

He looks at Syd, his face full of concern. "Cariño, por favor. Siéntate y relájate. Puedo cuidar de ustedes tres." *Honey, sit back and relax, please. I can take care of you three.*

"Would both of you quit it? I am pregnant, not dying," she scoffs, handing me a glass. She turns to Martin, her hand not letting go of the glass she's handing him. Her demeanor softens and she lets go of the glass. "Sé que puedes, y lo harás. Te amo por eso," she tells him. *I know you can and will, and I love you for that.*

Syd learned Spanish after their first date, claiming she already knew he was the one, and wanted to learn for him.

My sister is sweet, but she's also feisty. She doesn't take shit from anybody. Growing up, I always worried I would have to give her the "don't break his heart" talk instead of giving it to whoever she was dating because I worried she didn't have a heart for the longest time. When she fell in love after their first date, I found it quite funny because she was adamant that she wouldn't.

Martin and I took a long sip of our water, temporarily soothing the heat basking onto our skin.

"I can't wait to deliver these babies so I can get to interior designing the hell out of this place," she exclaims, her hands intertwining in front of her chin as her imagination runs wild.

Syd is an interior designer, which is how she met Martin when their companies were working on the same project. They never met face to face until their first date and only communicated via email until he finally asked her out.

"I can't wait to meet my niece and nephew, Miles and Miles," I boast, wiping a bead of sweat from my forehead.

"Good one," she says dryly. "When are you going to settle down and give me a niece or nephew, huh? You're only getting older."

Martin laughs. "Dale un carajo mi amor." *Give him hell, my love.*

He ventures to the shed to continue measuring pieces of wood, clearly wanting to avoid getting involved in this conversation. I don't blame him because I don't either.

Do I want kids? Yes. But I only want that with Rylee. I can't imagine it any other way.

But I also can't tell Syd that.

I lift my hat and run my fingers through my hair. "My students are my kids. That's more than enough."

Syd stares at me, her gaze penetrating my soul as she tries to see through my half-assed excuse. "Miles, who is she?"

I run another piece of wood under the saw machine, the loud sound giving me a few moments to come up with an answer, but I got nothing.

"I don't know, but when you figure it out, tell her to give me a call, would you?"

The corners of my lips curve into a smirk. I feel my phone vibrate in the back pocket of my shorts, cutting off what I was about to say. I itch to grab it, but I know Syd will be all over me if I do. As much as it pains me to ignore it for now, I do.

I stay for another twenty minutes to finish cutting all the wood, then say goodbye to my sister and Martin, hopping in my truck and cranking the air conditioning. I wait for the cool air to fill the space in my truck and pull out my phone to find a text from Rylee.

Riles

So...I'm going on a date tonight.

What. The. Fuck.

I shake my head and reread it again, and again.

Did she not understand she was mine? Mine as in only me, no one fucking else.

I pull out of the driveway a bit more aggressively than I should and speed over to where the source of the rage pumping through my blood is. It takes me twenty-five minutes to get there, and by the time I do, I am nearly losing it. The whole drive here, I kept wondering who, where, why, and what the fuck.

It takes me three strides to reach the front door, and as I knock on it, I realize Ryan's truck is missing. Perfect, because I don't think I could put on a front for him right now. I wait ten seconds, every single one setting my nerves on fire, until Rylee finally answers the door and my rage momentarily ceases when I take her in.

Her hair is in a low bun and she's wearing a white t-shirt that's tied in the front, and a red floral skirt that hits her knee, a slit showing most of her sun-kissed leg.

I'm suddenly annoyed all over again because who is she looking this dressed up for?

I step into the house, and she locks the door behind us.

"Hi," she says, sounding smaller than usual.

It hits me right in the gut as I realize my face isn't the

kindest right now. My jaw is tight, eyes blazing. I take a deep breath and try to relax my features.

"Didn't realize we were going out tonight. A heads up would've been nice," I say dryly.

She winces, and it's only then I realize how upset she looks. The pain I feel from her being upset is far worse than thinking she's going on a date with someone else. As long as she's happy, and not hurting, that's all I want.

She starts to ramble, her arms covering her chest as she tries to shield herself. "I'm sorry, I sent the text trying to make light of the situation and—"

I reach out, gripping her wrist and pulling her softly towards me. She willingly comes into my arms and rests her head on my chest. We both take a deep breath, calming ourselves, but seeing how nervous she is has me on edge.

I run my fingers lightly up and down her arm and gently ask, "What situation?"

She exhales into my shirt. "Ryan asked me to go on a double date at the movies tonight with him, Ava, and Nick, a guy at his work. I tried to say I wasn't interested, but Ryan went on this rant about how I'll never find someone if I don't try."

I see red for a moment, picturing some guy with his arm around Rylee. Rylee laughing with him, kissing...

No. I need to stop before I lose my shit.

"And you can't tell him you found someone already," I fill in for her, my voice low because while it's a statement, part of it was a question.

Rylee lifts her head off my chest and replaces the absence with her hand as she nods. "I have, but I can't tell anyone. He's protective, cocky, sweet, and so beautiful I question if he's even real. You know him?"

I see her smile for the first time since Tuesday, and it feels like my oxygen has been renewed. Add that to her compliment, and my heart is doing fucking gymnastics in my chest.

The previous tension chips away and I smirk. "Yeah, and he's really pissed at your brother for making you do this."

"I'm sorry. What did you want me to do? I can't tell him yet," she says pointedly, her brief playfulness gone again.

I gently hold her chin, tipping it to look at me. "Riles, I'm not mad at you. Just promise me something, okay?"

Her gaze softens. "Anything."

I release her chin and trail my hand down her neck. She visibly shivers and I grin knowing the power my touch has on her. I continue my descent lightly down the middle of her chest, and her stomach, slowly stopping right before her pussy.

I lean into her, and whisper in her ear, "He doesn't touch you anywhere, especially not here." I cup her pussy through the fabric of her skirt, eliciting a gasp from her. "Or here." I bring my hands up to cup her breasts, earning me a breathy moan. "Or here," I say icily.

My hands snake their way around her back and I grip her ass, tugging her body tightly to mine. "Most important of all, not fucking here," I whisper against her lips before claiming them in a passionate kiss.

Rylee flushes and I can feel her heart beating erratically against my own. "Anything else?"

"To be crystal clear, he doesn't get to kiss or touch you. Unless you want me to end up in jail for assault," I say, deadly serious.

"Don't be dramatic, Miles."

"I wouldn't test me, Rylee. Let Nick kiss you and find out just how protective I really am," I answer, my grip on her ass tightening.

She steadies me with her eyes, and I know she's about to

challenge me. "Hmm, how possessive are you, hot shot? Would you be okay if he kissed me like this?"

She leans up and kisses me softly at first, her hands cupping my face as she pours herself into the kiss. Then, her tongue quickly comes into play, demanding access. I willingly give it to her and savor the taste of her tongue against mine. Her mouth tastes like her, a sweet and sour mix of candy. She tastes like *mine*.

I break the kiss, needing to take back control of the situation. If she wants possessive, I'll show her possessive. "If he kisses you like that, I might end up in jail for more than assault."

I snap, taking her lips back with mine. I nip and suck on her bottom lip. Our breaths mingle as our lips lightly scrape one another's. Instead of kissing her, I bend and lift her into my arms. I need to leave her with more than a kiss so she doesn't forget who she belongs to during her date.

She gasps as I set her down on the dining room table and sink to my knees. "W-what are you doing?"

I skim my hands up and down her smooth legs. "Making sure you remember who you belong to. How much time do I have?" I ask, slowly pushing her skirt up over her stomach, revealing her white lace panties.

I faintly hear her mumble something, but my mind can't comprehend what she's saying as I take in the sight of the soaked lace, her hidden, sweet pussy waiting to be devoured.

Even though I hate the jealousy coursing through my veins, I'm glad seeing me this way turned her on. Knowing that she wants me just as much as I want her.

"What was that, baby?" I ask, my voice husky and raw as I pull her panties down and revel in her bare, glistening pussy.

All for me. *Mine*.

"About fifteen minutes. He just left before you got here to go get Ava."

I groan as I fist her panties into my pocket. "Dammit, that's not nearly enough time, but I'll take it."

Rylee leans up on her elbows. "What do you mean?"

I grip her hips and bring her body to the edge of the table so that her pussy is exactly where I want it. I lower my lips to her inner thigh and place a kiss there, "Ry, I want to spend hours devouring you. I get off on getting you off, understand?"

Her head falls back. I kiss my way up her inner thigh, to the top of her pussy, and finally her clit. I lightly flick it with my tongue, teasing and testing it before fully diving in and taking it between my teeth.

Rylee's fist comes down hard on the table, which only motivates me more. My tongue travels down her pussy, licking and sucking as I go.

She tastes so fucking good.

My tongue finds her hole, and I fuck her with my tongue as my fingers play with her clit.

"Miles," she moans, and hearing my name on her lips goes straight to my already hard cock.

I stop. "Baby, look at me," I demand gently.

Rylee lifts herself on her elbows, and I'm pleased to see the lust in her eyes, the slight part of her mouth, and the flush on her cheeks.

I lift my hand up to hers and intertwine them, resting them on her stomach. "Keep your eyes on me while I remind you whose tongue you come all over."

I bring my lips back to my second favorite pair of lips she has. I suck and lick her like a starved man, devouring every inch of her perfect pussy.

"Who does your pussy belong to?" I murmur against her as I insert two fingers inside of her.

"You," she cries out.

"This pussy only drips and comes for me, got it?"

"As if it could ever belong to anyone else," she whimpers and her legs shake.

That's the answer I was looking for.

I slide my fingers out of her slowly, before slamming them back inside as I suck on her clit. I pump into her erratically while my lips suck and worship her clit.

"Miles," Rylee screams, her back arching off the table as she comes all over my face.

"I want another one. Be a good girl and give me one more," I demand, bringing my fingers to my mouth and licking them clean. I bury my face back between her legs, so much so I can barely breathe.

She's the sweetest and best thing I'll ever taste.

Rylee eventually comes again, her orgasm bouncing off the walls as she screams my name. I begrudgingly take my mouth away and take her panties out of my pocket. I use them to wipe between her thighs, then tuck them into my pocket.

I'll be keeping those.

Then I pull her skirt back down and smile when I notice she has an arm slung over her eyes.

"You okay?" I ask, leaning over her body and nudging her arm with my nose.

She lifts her arm, and her lips form a peaceful smile when our eyes meet. "I don't think I'll ever be the same after that," she admits, her voice barely audible.

I can't help but chuckle. "Good, so when douchebag tries to touch you tonight, remember this. Remember whose name you screamed so loud the neighbors probably heard."

Rylee raises her hand up to cup my cheek, and I lean into her touch. "You have nothing to worry about, Miles. I promise I won't let him touch or kiss me."

Her words fill my body with warmth, but they still don't erase the jealousy that it should've been me there with her tonight.

"I trust you," I say, my voice low but steady.

Rylee tries to sit up and I step back. Once upright, she grabs my face between her hands and kisses me, her lips licking her own arousal off mine. It's sweet, loving, and with a touch of fierceness. Just like the Rylee I know.

We pull back for air, and her eyes fall on my erection. "I wish I could put you in my mouth or—"

I whimper, cutting her off. "Baby, please don't finish that thought. I am hanging on by a thread here."

The lights from Ryan's truck flood the living room window, and we break apart. Rylee quickly runs to the bathroom to fix herself up and I sit at the dining room table, adjusting myself while I think of something to say to Ryan.

I come up with nothing because I can only think about how I devoured his sister on the dining room table only minutes ago.

Ava and Ryan come in, and two very different looks come my way. Ava, who knows about Rylee and me, gives me a pointed stare with an arched eyebrow while Ryan looks momentarily confused.

"What brings you here?" he asks.

"I just came by to see if you wanted to hang out tonight, but Rylee told me you guys are going out already," I say calmly, the lie flowing effortlessly from my mouth.

"Do you want to come with us?"

Part of me wants to say yes, so I can make sure nothing happens, but I just told Rylee I trust her. And I do. I want her to believe it. Besides, if I see this guy, I'll probably lose it.

"No thanks. The game is on tonight anyways. I don't want to miss the Lynx and Panthers playing each other."

Finally a true statement.

Rylee emerges from the hallway, and my breath hitches in my throat. She looks stunning, the same as always, but the post-orgasm glow suits her well.

"Wow, Ry. You're glowing," Ava observes as if she just read my mind.

I narrow my eyes at her and she just smiles in response.

"Thanks. I just need to get my chucks, one second." She mumbles as she rounds the staircase.

"Rylee, you can't wear your yellow chucks on a date," Ava says, her tone admonishing.

"Why not?" I say out loud, internally cursing myself for slipping.

Everyone turns to look at me, but I quickly recover. "I just mean that guys don't really care what type of shoes you have on. He won't notice."

"Add in the fact that I don't care. If he doesn't like me in my chucks, then he isn't the one," Rylee says before running up the stairs.

She's always been herself, and I love that she doesn't try to change for anyone else.

I stand and wish Ryan and Ava a good night because the longer I stay, the more my resolve slips.

Once I get in my truck, I immediately text Rylee.

> I hope you enjoy the movie, but not the date.

She texts back while I'm driving, so I wait until I'm parked to answer her.

Riles

> I'll try! (the movie I mean, don't worry)

156

> If he tries anything, text me and I'll come to get you.

> Also, I'm taking you on a real date this week.

I'm in bed with a plate full of food and the baseball game on as I wait for her reply. The setting is semi-perfect. Rylee being here, next to me would be the icing on the cake.

Riles

> Maybe I'll wear something other than my chucks for you.

> I like you as you.

Riles

> I wish I was cuddled in bed with you, watching the game and wearing comfy clothes.

> You just described the wet dream I had the other night.

Riles

> Funny.

> You can't pull a 'me' move on me, Riles. Get your own moves.

Riles

Stop making me smile. It's going
to get them suspicious.

Never, it's my life goal to keep that beauty up there 24/7.

Riles

When are you free this week?

Riles

Ava, Claire, and I have Sunday funday
tomorrow. It's a girl thing we try to do
twice a month. Our camp isn't running
Monday during the day. Or Tuesday
evening is good if you are looking for
something soon. The rest of the week
is free. Whatever works for you
honestly, I don't want to be difficult.

Oh gosh I'm rambling, just ignore it and
give me a day and time

I love seeing her get nervous because while she comes off
so confident and competitive most of the time, I know the vulnerable parts she keeps hidden.

Tuesday I'm supposed to go golfing with Ryan and some of the guys from the team. Monday during the day is okay to start? We can figure out the rest of the week as it comes.

Riles

Sounds good! The movie's about to start, talk to you later 😊

CHAPTER SEVENTEEN

Rylee

alfway through the movie, images of what happened two hours ago on my dining room table invade my brain. There was something erotic about watching Miles go down on me and giving me the best orgasm I've had thus far. Now that I'm reliving it in my head, my clit is throbbing against my soaked thong.

I'm the worst date ever.

Honestly, Nick is great. He's taller than me which is already a hard feature to come by for me, has long, black hair tied in a bun, and an outgoing personality. The man's not hard on the eyes, but, he clearly knows that all too well.

Miles doesn't have to worry about him pulling a move on me because the guy can't stop talking about himself long enough to even give me a once-over.

I learned about his failed hockey career, about being on the farm team for the state's professional team before he got injured, his dog's bladder issues, and how his mom and sister need to make up after all these years. I think all he knows about me is my name if he even remembers it.

I had a bad feeling about this from the moment Ryan made me come along, and now all I want is to be in my bed, preferably snuggling Miles. I don't know what that is even like, but I imagine I would like it.

I often forget how many firsts I still haven't had yet, and it makes me feel like I'm behind, as if someone's keeping score on who reaches these milestones first. I know that's not true, but sometimes my inner critic is a real bitch.

I'm pulled out of my thoughts when I feel a cold arm fall around my shoulders.

Seriously, is he a teenager?

I flinch at his touch, and at that moment, I accept what my heart already knew. I don't want any man touching me besides Miles. Nick's arm around me feels wrong, and I know I'd want to rip a girl's arm off if I saw it on Miles. I grab his hand and lift it off my shoulder, returning it to his side.

Nick's eyes nearly fall out of his head, but he quickly recovers, a scowl forming on his lips as he crosses his arms and turns his attention back to the movie.

God this is awkward.

I can feel the heat coming off his body from the silent rage he's in from being rejected, which I assume is the first time. Is this how he pulls girls? He talks their ears off about himself, and they fall prey to his lame moves?

Couldn't be me, even if I was as single as a Pringle.

I debate about escaping this mess when my phone vibrates. I pull it out as a welcome distraction.

Miles

How's the movie?

Tell you later. Taking an Uber home.

Miles

The hell you are. I'll be there in ten minutes.

A small smile forms on my lips.

I have great friends who would do things for me, but there's something about the person you like going out of their way to care for you.

Relief settles into my system, knowing that I will be escaping this torture. I grab my purse and pretend I'm excusing myself to the washroom but on my way out I text Ava.

Nick tried to pull a move and things got awkward. Tell Ryan I started my period and needed to leave ASAP. I took an Uber home.

I pray Ava is smart enough to turn her brightness down so Ryan can't read the message. My phone vibrates as I walk out into the movie theater lobby, the smell of buttered popcorn filling my senses.

Ava

I got you babe. Text me when you're home safely.

I push the doors and wait outside for Miles. It's a warm summer night, and I look up to the sky, but there are no stars out tonight.

Fuck.

I take a deep breath and let the last five minutes go. Instead, I focus on the butterflies in my stomach as I anticipate seeing Miles's face soon, but my inner critic slowly creeps in.

He's so gorgeous, sometimes I can't comprehend how he finds me attractive. I'm sure he's slept with beautiful, flawless women I could not compete with even on my best day.

I take another deep breath, push the critic out, and make way for more positive thoughts. Clearly, he is attracted to me, so I need to get my head out of my ass.

The screech of tires around the corner pulls me from my thoughts, and a shiver runs down my spine.

He's pissed.

I replay the text in my head and realize it left room for interpretation as to why I was leaving the movie early.

His black truck comes to a halt, and Miles hops out. Within seconds he's in front of me, his eyes wildly scanning my body and my eyes to see if something isn't right.

"What the hell happened?" he asks, his voice tight in an attempt to control his anger.

I cup his face with my hand, my fingers rubbing against his beard in a soothing way. "Nick didn't look or talk to me directly all night, which was great, but then he tried to put his arm around me during the movie, and I removed it. It pissed him off, so I left. End of story."

Miles's eyes close for a moment, and when he reopens them, they're blazing. "I don't like that he touched you or how he reacted. But I'd rather not ruin the rest of our night by going in there and beating him to a pulp, so let's go before I do that," he says.

He removes my fingers from his cheek and kisses them before stepping back and opening the door for me. Once I'm settled into the passenger seat, he closes the door and within seconds, we're driving away from the movie theater.

The car ride is silent, Miles trying to calm himself down next to me. I don't even want to imagine how pissed off he would be if something else happened.

I shudder at the thought of Nick's hand snaking down to my chest.

I take the opportunity to stare at Miles while he's distracted. He's wearing a Lynx cap with a black shirt that clings to his biceps and gray shorts. Casual, yet so attractive.

Call me biased, but I'm a sucker for a guy in a baseball hat, especially if said guy is named Miles.

He breaks the silence first. "Did you think I'd let you take an Uber?"

I shrug my shoulders. "I don't like to ask for help. I can take care of myself."

Miles glances over at me, and although it's brief, I can tell he's upset by my comment.

"I know you can, but I want you to let me take care of you. I want to be that person for you," he says, his voice sweet and soft, melting my heart.

I'm not used to having someone else to rely on, someone to take care of me. But I'm beginning to like it.

"And what would that be?" I ask because, in all honesty, I have no idea what we are. We've gone from being childhood best friends to me hating him, reconciling, flirting, and so much more. I don't know what any of it means.

His grip on the wheel tightens, his throat bobbing. "What do you want me to be? Cause I know what I want you to be, Riles."

Those damn butterflies again, soaring around my stomach wildly at the mention of his nickname for me.

"And what's that?" I ask trepidation in my voice at his response.

He glances at me again, and this time I see nerves, a change from his usual confident demeanor.

"My girl. The one I slow-dance in the kitchen with. The one I grow old with, travel with and laugh with. The one I can be myself with and come with," he says sincerely, smiling over his last comment.

Screw butterflies. Every inch of my body lights up at his words. Did he have to be such a sweet talker too? How is he so perfect?

I smile. "The math teacher does know how to put words together. Nice job." He glares at me, and I put my hands up in mock defense. He just spilled his heart to me, and here I am teasing him.

I reach across the console for his hand and intertwine our fingers. "Sorry, it was too easy. I promise not to tease you as much, I swear."

His head jerks in my direction. "No, I like when you tease me, but, don't avoid my question from earlier. What do you want me to be? You know what I want now."

I take a steadying breath, and with all the confidence I can muster, I say, "For you to be mine. My boyfriend, exclusive, whatever you want to call it. I like you okay?" I finish, my free hand covering my face from embarrassment.

I hated being vulnerable.

The truck comes to a stop, and I realize I'm in my drive-way. Miles turns off the engine and leans over to pry my hand off my face. I peer at him shyly, and the look on his face is swoon-worthy.

He's looking at me like I hung the stars in the sky. It's too much for my heart to handle.

"Good, because I like you too, Riles," he says softly, his hand coming up to tuck a strand of hair behind my ear.

"God only knows why," I mutter quietly because my brain cannot fathom how this is possible.

His eyes darken at my comment. He shakes his head. "We're talking about this in bed. Let's go."

I don't ask why, I simply comply because I'm exhausted. It's only 9:30 pm, but waking up early during the week meant I could barely make it past nine, even on weekends.

Miles quietly follows me into the house, up the stairs, and into my room. It's the first time I've had a guy in my room since, well, since the last time we were friends.

It's changed a hell of a lot since then. Gone are the purple walls and SpongeBob comforter. I now have light gray walls with white accents. My bedspread is white with yellow pillowcases. Plants fill a corner in the room, and my desk takes up a portion of one wall.

It's pretty minimal, despite the photos that hang over my dresser opposite my bed. In university, Ava and I started taking photos on film and hanging them on my corkboard.

I search through my dresser and find my pajamas— an old baseball shirt and cotton shorts. I leave Miles, who's analyzing my photos with a smile, in my room and slip into the bathroom. I quickly change, brush my teeth, and do my skincare routine for the night.

Once I finish, I open the door and see Miles lying on my bed casually, as if we do this all the time. He pulls the comforter back for me.

He pats the open spot. "Come here."

I oblige and climb into bed, sitting next to him as we lean our backs against the headboard. "Hi," I say, my voice a mere whisper.

He's been so quiet, and I know he's about to give me shit for my comment earlier about not knowing why he likes me.

"Hi," he responds, looking at me intently.

I could drown in those blue eyes. Their green specks are

more prevalent, making it nearly impossible to look away. They were my warning sign that we were about to have a heart-to-heart.

He pulls me onto his lap. We're now sitting face to face, forcing me to take in everything he's about to say.

His eyes are steady on mine. "You want to know why I like you, sunshine?"

I nod, the lump in my throat making it hard for me to form words.

"I like you for so many reasons. I can't possibly list all of them, but I'll try. You being a teacher tells me you have a heart bigger than most people, but I already knew that. I like how whenever I'm near you, I feel lighter. More like myself. I like how those around you radiate in your glow. You're sunshine, you make everything around you better and brighter. Your smile takes my breath away. It's so goddamn pretty. Your soul, your heart, that smile, everything about you reminds me of what it feels like to come home after a long trip away."

Breathe in and out, I remind myself because I don't think I've moved a muscle since he started talking.

"And these legs," he says, his hands skating across my thighs and eliciting goosebumps in their wake. "They were made to be wrapped around my waist. This ass is perfect," he groans, squeezing my ass and causing me to gasp.

His hands slide up my waist, and I suck in a breath, "Your body is beautiful and I love every inch of it. These tits." He cups one in his hand and squeezes. "They were made for me. Your hair drives me wild, and those little freckles around my face remind me of the peace I get when looking up at the stars at night. And your eyes are fucking gorgeous, I could lose myself in them," he says sweetly.

I can't help the tear that escapes and his thumb brushes

it away lightly.

"You're so beautiful it makes my chest ache whenever I look at you. Everything about you is perfect for me."

My heart soars at his words, beating rapidly against my ribcage.

Did he seriously say all of that or am I dreaming?

Tears poke at my eyes again because this might be the most beautiful thing someone has ever said to me. God, I am such a hopeless romantic, and I'm hopelessly falling for this man.

A tear escapes, slowly strolling down my cheek and Miles gently swipes it away.

"Just so you know, these are the only tears I am ever okay seeing you with, got it?"

Why is he so perfect?

My heart can't handle it. It's never experienced this kind of lo— nope, not saying that four-letter word just yet.

I lean my head closer and softly press my lips to his as my hands cup his jaw, his stubble rough beneath my fingertips. He wraps both arms around my back and pulls me flush against him as he kisses me back longingly.

Our kisses are soft, gentle, and sweet just like his words. It's unlike any kiss we've ever had before. That fact alone causes shivers to erupt all over my skin. We continue kissing for what feels like forever, our lips savoring and caressing one another.

Miles pulls back and kisses my forehead, his lips lingering there for a moment. After all he's said tonight, and the way his lips moved with mine, I can honestly believe that he cares about me.

I break the silence. "So, we're dating then?"

Miles pulls back, bringing his striking gaze to mine. "Yes, and before you ask if I'm sure, the answer will always be yes."

I smile at that because he knows me too damn well.

"Oh god," I mutter, as my nerves start to creep in. "What if Ryan finds out sooner than we want? What if he doesn't approve? What if I'm a shit girlfriend? What if you get tired of me and leave—"

Shit. I wasn't supposed to say that last part out loud.

Miles tilts my chin up. "Breathe, baby."

He gives me a few minutes to do just that and after a few beats, he confidently answers all of my worries.

"If he does and doesn't approve, we will figure it out together. But I highly doubt he won't. We're adults, Ry. He can't control what we do." He takes a breath, then continues. "I know you've never dated, but neither have I, so I honestly have no idea what to do. But you're not a shit person, Ry. There is no way you would be a shit girlfriend, okay?"

I love how calm he makes me, his words etching themselves into my cells and calming me from the inside out. But part of me is waiting for the last shoe to drop. What would he say to my worry about him leaving?

I don't have to speculate for much longer because he looks at me intensely when he says, "I'll never get tired of you. I will never get tired of making you laugh and smile, protecting and cherishing you. And I'll never get tired of making you come."

I clutch at my chest, feeling my admiration for him growing like a bad weed, spreading into every crevice possible. "You know for a domineering ass, you've got a pretty sweet side." I smile, my eyes glassy with unshed tears. "I'll never get tired of you either."

His face changes into a small smile, a look of pride in his eyes. "Good, because I got a full-time position as a grade 8 teacher at Westchester, so I am not going anywhere. I'm moving back for good. And even if I didn't get the job, I wouldn't go back to Arizona. I can't tear myself from you again. I'm not strong enough."

He's moving back for good?

I don't even know where to begin processing it all. I hadn't even thought of him going back when we started moving towards building an 'us.'

"Congrats, hot shot. I'm so proud of you."

I give him a cheeky smile because I'm really happy for him. It's such a huge accomplishment at his age.

I clash my mouth to his in excitement and kiss him fiercely. Before the kiss can escalate, I hear my phone vibrate on the side table— it's Ava's special ringtone.

I groan and climb off Miles, opening her message to read they're on their way home.

Shit.

"You have to go. Ryan and Ava will be here soon," I say reluctantly.

Miles nods, and we walk to the front door together, hand in hand. I love how physical he is. His need to always be touching me fills me with some unexplainable emotion.

Before I can unlock the door, Miles tugs on our hands and pulls me into him. He lifts me, and I wrap my legs around his waist like they were meant to do.

"Good, I see your legs learned their place," he mutters before kissing me with such intensity.

As if he loves me.

I shake the thought away. I know he cares for me, but there's no way he could love me. Not yet anyway. I'm hopeful though because God knows I'm close.

"I wish I had time for these legs to be wrapped around my head," he tells me with a mischievous smile on his lips as he winks.

I laugh and roll my eyes, pushing him towards the door

where we kiss once more before parting ways. I watch his truck cruise down the opposite end of the street.

A few moments later, Ryan pulls in. Perfect timing.

I run upstairs into my room and hop into bed with the biggest smile my face has ever felt as my legs squirm involuntarily from joy.

CHAPTER EIGHTEEN

Miles

I wake up early, which is unusual for me on a Sunday, but I want to get this day started. I spend a good portion of the morning dealing with contract paperwork for the board while my mother makes my favorite blueberry muffins.

I love that woman and her muffins, but ever since I got the job, I've been looking online for a condo to rent. I recently found one for a decent price close to the school, a twenty-minute drive from where I live now, and contacted the landlord immediately.

I could afford a house with the salary I'll be making now and my investments, but I'm thinking of the future, especially Rylee's and mine. In the next year, I hope we move in together, and I know it's smarter to start smaller. We can save and build the house we want later on with the help of my sister and brother-in-law.

After finishing all the paperwork, I clean up around the house, go to the gym, and plan our date and it's only noon.

Fuck this day was dragging. All because I was eager as hell to see her tomorrow.

Not knowing what to do for the rest of the day, I drive up

to the local dog shelter to spend the rest of my Sunday there.

I did my volunteer hours here back in high school, and I loved it. It was time that was spent meaningfully, and I thoroughly enjoyed chatting with the two elderly twins who ran the place, Doris and Boris. They used to tell me stories, some of which I would've rather not known and made me feel like one of their own grandchildren.

Plus, I got to spend time with the dogs, which are arguably the best thing to bless this planet besides Rylee.

I park my truck on the side of the road and stare at the shelter. It looks better than I last saw it. The sign looks fresh, a new paint job must have been done. There's a new front window that lets passersby see the adorable dogs roaming in the play area and a new patio at the side of the building, a garden bed full of bright flowers decorating it.

It looks good and it makes me happy to know things have gotten better around here since my last visit.

"Oh my lord, Doris, is that who I think it is?" Boris exclaims, her glasses perched on her nose as she peers at me.

Doris's head sticks out from the back door. "It is. It's our sweet boy, Miles Anderson," she confirms, beaming.

"Hello, ladies. It's nice to see you both. How have things been?"

Boris yanks me to her in a hug, which I return, before letting me go and taking a step back. "Great, still kickin'. How have you been? You grew up so nicely," she boasts.

I can't help but chuckle. Boris was always the funnier of the two, and Doris the affectionate one. Other than that, they looked exactly the same. Small frames, and hair as gray as the sky currently.

"I'm good. I'm actually moving back here and was wondering if I could volunteer a few days a week before school starts?" I ask, hopeful.

"Boy, if you ask me another stupid question like that, I am going to throw you out," Boris spats, but her eyes are bright.

Doris comes out of the back room and strolls up to us. "Of course, sweetie."

Boris and Doris exchange a look, one I'm not sure how to gauge, but I don't have time to overthink it because Boris blurts out, "You tell Rylee how you feel yet?"

I blink a few times at her remark. What? Did I hear that correctly?

"Uh, I have no idea what you're talking about," I deflect, crossing my arms over my chest.

Doris chimes in. "Miles, we overheard you talking to the dogs when you spent here in high school. 'Rylee looked so pretty today, I miss Rylee. Should I tell her I like her?' Blah, blah, blah."

My gut drops embarrassed they overheard. I rarely feel this way, and it must show because Boris takes pity on me.

"It was the sweetest thing to hear. Most boys your age would've been talking about how to get up her skirt."

Her comment makes my nostrils flare.

"Boris, would you stop getting him riled up? Miles, sweetie, have you talked to her?" Doris asks, her eyes wide and expectant.

"Why don't we go in and you can show me what needs to be done? Then, we can catch up," I suggest because them staring at me like two moms demanding answers is making me nervous.

They comply and I spend the next two hours grooming and playing with dogs as I tell them everything that's happened since I left. Minus the intimate stuff, they don't need to know that.

Once I'm back in my truck, I see I have a text from Ryan, asking if I want to meet up at GOAT, a local sports bar. I text him back, saying I'll meet him there shortly.

A few minutes later, I walk into the bar and immediately spot his blonde hair at a high-top table near the large screen TV, the Lynx and Beavers game playing.

"Miles, how's it going? Sit," he says, gesturing to the stool in front of him.

My eyebrow shoots up in question because Ryan doesn't usually talk like this. Something must be up.

Fuck does he know? Should I just come clean?

I take a seat and decide to play it cool, letting things play out. "Good, busy but productive day, you?"

He taps the side of his beer with a finger, his nerves showing.

Hmm, that's odd too.

"Cool, cool. I'm good, just—"

Our waitress cuts him off, "Evening boys, what can I get y'all?" she asks, her southern accent cutting through.

I don't miss the way she looks at me, her brown eyes suggesting, but I decline her advances by averting my eyes down to the menu and rattling off an order of water, fried pickles, and soft pretzels. Ryan orders water as well, knowing he has to drive later and needs to sober up.

I pull out my phone and pretend to be busy to avoid the waitress. Her fingers lightly brush my forearm when she reaches across to grab our menus, and I instantly withdraw my arm, still avoiding her gaze.

Take a damn hint.

"I apologize for my friend. He doesn't know how to act when a pretty girl looks at him," Ryan says, his tone underlining a 'dude, what the fuck.'

"All good, honey," she calls out, her voice drifting as she walks away.

I lift my head up and glare at him.

Ryan gives me a quizzical look, then punches me lightly in the shoulder. "She was good-looking and clearly interested. What's wrong with you?"

I level him with a blank look. "Why don't you tell Ava how pretty that girl is, huh?"

He rolls his eyes at me. "Look, we're secure in our relationship. We can admit other people are attractive while still knowing we have more than that with each other. It's human nature, people are good-looking. But no one will compare to Ava for me, ever."

My expression slowly morphs into a sly grin. "God, I love whipped Ryan. I'll take this version over the heartbroken over Jade one."

"Don't," he warns cringing. "We don't talk about that. It was a phase, never to be mentioned again."

"Oh no, I will never forget grade 8 Ryan posting sad songs on his social media, commenting hearts on all of her pictures—"

"Don't forget when I went to her house and tried to sing my way back into her life, that was the best part," he teases, making fun of himself.

We both crack up at that. He was an emotional mess after that breakup.

Our waitress interrupts us by placing the water on the table, and this time I don't look away when she makes eye contact because I should try not to be an asshole. But I do end up giving her a non-welcoming look, so I guess I'm still one.

"You can look at me like that any day, sugar," she half whispers, winking at me before turning on her heels and heading back to her other tables.

I grimace and roll my eyes because clearly, I can't win.

"So, tell me why you're not taking her up on her clear-as-day offer to fuck her?" Ryan asks bluntly, leaning his body halfway over our circular table.

I lean back and answer him with a partial truth. "I'm not interested in hooking up anymore. I want to date."

Ryan leans back, his hand coming up to grip his chest. "What? The ladies' man of Arizona State finally wants to date? Since when?"

"You make me sound like a whore. So what if I hooked up a couple of times in college? Most of them were repeats, my number is still under ten, just saying."

He takes a sip of water, waving me away. "Yeah, yeah. I like to twist your arm. Now, tell me why the sudden change? You've never had a girlfriend. I always assumed you'd be a bachelor for life."

Now this is where I have to partially lie because he doesn't know that I'm dating his sister, and even if I wasn't, I wouldn't date anyone because they weren't her. That's why I've never dated anyone else.

"Me too, but seeing Syd and Martin, and you and Ava all the time now put things into perspective. I want that," I answer, truthfully this time.

Ryan pretends to wipe a tear from his eye. "Damn, my best friend is finally growing up. Welcome, join the table of love and heartache, my friend."

"What do you mean heartache?"

I always assumed it would be smooth sailing with Rylee. I didn't anticipate hurt into the equation when I thought of us getting together.

He laughs. "Love is great, don't get me wrong. But the

worry, thinking of what could go wrong with them or watching them in pain. Yeah, that shit hurts."

I nod in understanding. "Understandable, but the reward's worth it."

Ryan's eyes widen. "Jesus, who are you?"

I flip him the finger and roll my eyes just as our waitress arrives with our food.

Great, here comes round three.

"Incoming, hot food for some hot stuff," she drawls, her gaze pinned on me.

I look away and thank her.

"Let me know if y'all need anything, anything at all you hear me?"

I finally crack because she's bordering on desperate now. "Look, I appreciate the interest, but I'm not looking for anything right now."

There, I was firm but not a total asshole either.

Her lip curls in distaste at my rejection, and she storms away, leaving us in peace.

I reach over to grab a fried pickle when I catch Ryan scrutinizing me. "What is it?" I ask.

"How come you don't want to try dating her?"

"I'm not sure if you caught it, but the desperation was practically dripping off her. I'm all for a girl putting herself out there, but if someone's not biting after one or two tries, give it up."

He shrugs in agreement. "That's fair. Can't say I would be attracted to that either."

We spend the next few minutes eating our food and talking about the ball game that's on. The Beavers are up by one, and it's the bottom of the seventh inning, with the Lynx up to bat. They could tie it here and send it into extra innings.

The excitement is brewing in the bar. You can feel it

growing around us. They have two outs, and their last chance at winning is up to bat. The hitter swings and connects with the ball, sending it out to the outfield, and the entire bar is at the edge of their seats. Until the centre fielder jumps and catches the fucking ball. Game over. Everyone boos, and the atmosphere is a lot less exciting than it was a few minutes ago. That's baseball for you.

I look over at Ryan and notice he's been playing with his napkin, repeatedly folding and unfolding it. "You okay? You seem a bit off tonight."

He peers up at me, and, suddenly, he looks like a shy schoolboy.

What the fuck is going on?

"I… it's a big deal, and I don't want you to make fun of me."

"Nonsense, when have I ever made fun of you?" I comment, full of sarcasm.

"Uh, about twenty minutes ago to be exact. My soul is still feeling the pain of that interaction," he says, dramatically.

He's such an idiot sometimes.

We both laugh, but I quickly tone it down and get serious. "Seriously, what's up?"

He takes a deep breath, pulls a box out of his pocket, and I know exactly what he's about to do. "I'm proposing to Ava at the cottage, not in front of everyone, of course, but there's a spot the two of us always like to go to together, and I plan on asking her then."

He opens the box, and in it is a silver engagement ring, a square-shaped diamond in the middle with smaller diamonds bordering the larger one.

"Ryan, that's awesome. I'm happy for you both, honestly. You're perfect for each other," I say, smiling brightly.

His smile is just as bright. "Thanks, man, but I'm a bit

nervous."

"Why? Afraid she'll say no and ruin the rest of our trip?"

"No, I just don't want to mess it up."

I give his shoulder a squeeze. "It'll be perfect as long as you're honest, don't stress about it. And if you need help to pull it off, I got you."

"I appreciate that, Miles. You're my best friend, the best one I've ever had, you know that, right?"

My hand drops and I wrap it around my drink. "I know, the same goes for you."

"You know, I'm really glad you and Rylee could patch things up. It's nice to all hang out again, and I know she missed you," he says.

I instantly feel guilty that we're dating behind his back.

"Yeah, me too. It's been really great. I uh, missed her too. She's a good friend," I reply, stumbling over my words.

Fuck me.

Ryan doesn't seem to notice. "The whole thing with Jaxon made me realize she's growing up, and I hate it. Look out for her, will you? We can't let her end up with some jackass."

I take a sip of water, finishing it off to gather my words. "Yeah, she deserves the best."

The best of me, that is.

CHAPTER NINETEEN

Miles

I t's finally Monday which means it's date day with Rylee and we have a baseball game. I couldn't ask for a better day.

I go to Ryan's house around 10:00 am, not wanting to waste any more time. With a bouquet of white lilies because my Mom raised me right.

I park and walk over to their front door. I knock and Rylee answers within seconds.

She is a sight for sore eyes. She's wearing a white t-shirt and light jean shorts that show off her long legs, with, of course, her yellow chucks. Her hair is in this half-down, half-up style, with two ponytails on each side of her head.

It's cute, well she's cute.

"Hi beautiful," I say, handing her the flowers.

She blushes in response. "Thanks. You look good, really good."

I look down at my simple outfit— a navy shirt, black joggers, navy chucks, and my baseball cap. I kept it simple because I know Rylee. She'd rather do something adventurous and fun than go on a fancy lunch outing.

"Thank you, baby. You ready to go?" I ask, itching to get our date started.

Rylee's smile lits her face up. "Yeah, let me just put these in water. I'll be right back."

I smile, watching her literally run back into the house. She seems a little nervous, and it's adorable.

I step through the door as she darts around the corner and runs right into me. I catch her easily and steady her. "Easy, sunshine."

She chuckles into my shirt and rests her chin on my chest. "Sorry, I've missed you and I'm a bit nerv–"

I don't let her finish and lean down to press my lips against hers because they were begging to be kissed. I start off softly, letting her take the lead. She continues to kiss me but amps it up a bit by pressing her lips more firmly against mine, her hips rolling into mine.

I grip her ass and groan into her mouth, before reluctantly pulling away.

"You're safe with me, okay? We're best friends, so let's hang out like we normally would, but add some kissing in there."

She nods and takes another calming breath. "Okay, and maybe more than kissing?"

I blink at her in shock, then grin. "Of course, whatever you're comfortable with. Now let's go, I want all the time I can squeeze with you before baseball."

I take her hand in mine, let her lock the door, then walk her to the passenger side of my truck. I open it for her, and once she's settled, I close it and go around the hood to hop into my side.

Our car ride seems to remove any of Rylee's worries for good once we get onto the highway, the music on and our conversation flows easily.

I get off on an exit, and she realizes exactly where we're going once I'm pulling into our destination.

"Are you… are we going to the park we played T-ball at?" she asks, sounding a little emotional.

"Yeah, we're going to play some one on one. I'm dating a competitive girl, so I need to show her I can challenge her," I answer, feeling good about my choice after seeing her reaction.

Her knee starts to bounce, and she claps her hands together. My girl's excited.

"Oh, it's so on. What are the rules, hot shot?" She sits up a bit straighter, and cracks her knuckles, gearing up to kick my ass.

It's hot.

I park my truck and turn to face her. "I brought a soft bat and blow-up ball because it wouldn't work with the legit stuff. We play ten innings, and the person with the most runs wins. We pitch to each other, and the pitcher has to field the ball once it's hit. Once you get it, throw it at me, and if it hits me, I'm out. We still have three strikes, but only one out each inning."

"Game on. I hope you're okay with hurting your ego a bit on our first date," she teases, sticking her tongue at me before hopping out of my truck.

Little does she know, I'll lose to her any day just to see her smile.

I grab the equipment from my trunk, then meet her on the turf. I pull a coin from my pocket and nod toward her. "Your call, heads or tails?"

"Tails."

I flick the coin up into the air, catch it on my palm and flip it over, an old president staring at us.

Fuck yeah.

Rylee frowns for a moment, then straightens up. "You're going to need all the help you can get anyways."

I chuckle as she grabs the bat and sets up at home plate while I head to the pitching mound. The diamond is used for kids' baseball, so it's a lot smaller, which is perfect because I want this to be more fun than the torture it would be if we did this on a standard field. Since we're not using legit baseball equipment, the balls aren't going to go very far, just far enough for a bit of competitive fun.

I pitch her a nice, high lob because those are her favorite. She connects with the ball, smashing it over my head and into center field. I take off towards the ball, and by the time I turn around, she's rounding second, and heading to third.

I take a second to time it right, then throw the ball, aiming it right for third base, but Rylee hears the swoosh of the ball and misses it by picking up her pace.

She turns and smiles at me as she crosses home plate. "That's the best you got?" she huffs, a bead of sweat dripping down her forehead.

"It's the first inning, calm down Miggy," I say, taking her spot at home while she goes to the pitcher's mound.

The next eight innings were back and forth, making us tied during the top of our last inning.

I want to beat her because I know it'll rile her up. I've had fun regardless though, and I think she has too. We teased the shit out of each other and laughed the entire time. But now, it's time to play for the win.

Rylee's back at home plate. It's her last time to score a run because if I score the next one and she doesn't, it's game over. I give her an easy pitch, not because she can't hit a curve or fastball, but because I like when she challenges me too. I want her to hit the ball and make me work for the out.

She smashes the ball, sending it into right field, close to the foul line, which means I need to fucking sprint. I race my way over there, and when I turn around, she's already rounding second.

Fuck, she's fast.

I run forward and wind up my arm, preparing to throw her out at third, but I stop when she suddenly slows down. Confused, I watch her turn toward me, walking backward toward third base.

I wind up my arm again just as she quickly grips the bottom of her shirt and lifts it over her head. Fucking hell. She's wearing a pale blue lace bra, and it's making her boobs look delectable.

I'm frozen to the spot, even when she starts running home because all I can do is watch the way her breasts bounce as she runs.

It isn't until she starts cheering that I realize she played me.

I grunt, trying my best to remain playful while my cock is urging me to play with her. "I think that counts as grounds for cheating."

She pulls her shirt back down, and I frown. "I didn't hear that in the official rules earlier."

She winks at me, then takes up residence at the pitching mound.

"Are you going to cry when I beat you, sunshine?" I tease, setting up at home plate.

Rylee arches an eyebrow, all business, she's not messing around. "Not going to happen, so keep dreaming. Ready?"

I nod, and she throws the pitch. My bat connects with it, and, just by the sound, I know I fucked up. It pops up into the high sky, giving Rylee plenty of time to catch it, which she does.

A wide smile forms on her lips, and she throws her hands up in victory. I can't even be mad because seeing the look on her face is better than the satisfaction of winning.

I approach her at second base and she halts her celebratory dance party.

"How does it feel to be a loser?" she chuckles.

I abruptly pull her into my chest, wrapping my arms around the small of her back.

I nuzzle the side of her head with my cheek, and whisper in her ear, "Losing to you feels like a win when I get to see that smile on your face."

She melts into my arms. "Don't ruin my gloating moment by being soft, dammit."

A deep laugh emits from my belly, and I kiss the top of her head. "Cute."

She tilts her head back to look at me, and the softness in her eyes warms my chest. "Thank you for this date. It was perfect. My first and best date yet."

I frown at her. "It's not even close to being over. Let's go." I nod toward the equipment.

We collect and store it in my truck. Rylee puts her hand on the passenger door handle, and I gently swipe it away, opening it for her.

"You don't need to do that every time you know," she says sincerely with a shy smile.

"Riles, you need to get used to expecting more of me because I'll always give that to you." I lean in and press a kiss to her lips.

God, I do love this girl.

Her hands snake up my chest and rest around my neck, tugging on my hair.

I pull back before we get carried away, and walk around to hop into my side. I start my truck, hop on the highway, and head toward Target.

We pull into the parking lot and she looks over at me, confusion written all over her face. "Uh, Miles? Why are we at Target?"

I smirk. "Another challenge for my girl. You up for it?"

The right side of her mouth tilts up in response. "I'll always say yes to an opportunity to kick your ass. What is it?"

"The challenge is we have to buy for each other to see who knows the other best. There are three categories: something the other likes to eat, something they'll use, and something to make them smile."

"Oh, you are so going down. I know you too well," she says, pride etched in every word.

I like how confident she is in how well she knows me.

I can't help but grin as we head out and into the store. We split up and do our best to avoid each other in the store. Since it was my idea, I'd already picked out the items making it easy for me to find and check out before her.

I wait for her inside the truck and hide the things I got for her in the back seat where she won't see them.

A few minutes later, Rylee walks out of the store, her items hidden in a large party bag she must've bought.

Clever.

I get out to open her door before she gets to it, but she halts her steps and she yells at me, clutching the bag to her chest. "Nope, save your chivalry. No peeking."

I put my hands up in peace. "Fine, I'll let it slide this time," I mumble.

While I know she can easily open her doors and take care of herself, I want to do it for her. I want to care for her like no other man ever has or ever will.

She puts her bag in the back, but I don't glance at it because I know she won't be very happy with me. One year when we were kids, I knew my birthday gift was hidden in Rylee's room, so I took a peek.

Rylee loves giving gifts, and she was really pissed when

she caught me.

Once seated and buckled in the front, I head back to her house, the clouds darkening the sky above. Soft rain pelts against my windshield, the kind of rain that's welcome on a warm summer day.

I park in the driveway, knowing we have another three hours before Ryan gets home and another five before we have baseball. Time seems to fly when I'm with her, and it's a bittersweet feeling.

Her brow raises in questioning. "Why are we back at the house?"

I unbuckle myself. "Because there's still a fort to build. That's where we will exchange the gifts."

I don't miss the mixed look of shock and appreciation that fills her face as I hop out, grabbing my bag from the back. I cover my eyes to avoid looking into hers to be safe.

The fort idea came to me late last night when I was thinking about us and how that fort represented something pivotal in our relationship.

When I decided to disappear from her life like the idiot that I was.

Tonight, that changes. This fort will show her how much I've changed since then, and change our relationship in a way I hope is better than the last time we spent time in one.

"Give me your keys and wait in here until I have the door unlocked," I say, the light rain making my shirt uncomfortably wet.

Rylee unbuckles herself and glares at me. "I won't melt in the rain you know."

"Yeah, well you in a wet, white t-shirt is going to derail the rest of my plans, so sit your pretty ass still until I get it unlocked, got it?" I demand playfully.

She rolls her eyes again, and I can't wait to see her do that under different circumstances.

Rylee tosses me the keys, and I quickly run up the steps to her front door, unlocking the door and waving her on. She reaches behind her to grab the bag, then hops out and runs toward me, smiling.

I shut and lock the door behind her. We then head downstairs to the basement to set up our fort, eager to share our gifts.

I move toward the laundry room, and take off my shirt, flinging it over my head, the dampness making my skin uncomfortable. I throw it in the hamper and don't bother getting a new one.

I grab a few spare blankets and pillows, then head back to the living room space, where Rylee has already gathered some bar stools.

I place them down when Rylee turns around. Her mouth drops open. "You… Jesus, Miles."

I smirk. "Something wrong?"

She shakes her head, realizing she was staring. Not that I mind. "Nope, pass me a blanket and help me set it up."

I do as she says, and we build our fort together in comfortable silence. Once it's built and sturdy, with blankets, fairy lights, and pillows inside, we both crawl in with our bags behind our backs.

It's not a large fort, the space cramping us together. We're so close that my senses are swarmed with her signature vanilla and cherries scent. It's intoxicating.

We settle into the space, and it feels like déjà vu. The last time we were in here, I kissed her before I pushed her away seconds later.

But this time? There's nothing holding me back from taking her as mine.

CHAPTER TWENTY

Miles

"**A**lright, losers get to go first," Rylee quips, shooting me a cocky grin.

"Wait till you see what I got you. I think I'll be classified as a winner," I say, putting my bag in front of me. I pull out a bag of sour patch kids. "Something you love to eat."

She beams like a kid on Halloween and takes the bag from my hand. "Okay, good choice."

"Something to use." I grin, handing her a pineapple-flavored chapstick. "I liked the taste on you."

I tasted this on her lips the other night, and I wouldn't mind tasting it again. This one is partly for me. What can I say? I can be a selfish bastard.

It doesn't surprise me that she tastes like pineapples, considering she's loved them ever since our obsession with SpongeBob as kids started.

She blushes, realizing the meaning, and places it next to her candy. "Oh."

"Lastly, something to make you smile, well, other than me," I joke.

She scrunches her nose at me. I take out the pineapple-stuffed pillow and hand it to her. It's her favorite colour and a memento from our childhood.

The smile lighting up her face is so bright, it makes the sun look dull in comparison. Rylee reaches for it and hugs it to her chest.

I tug her closer, needing her to wrap me with the energy she emanates with her smile. "You like it?"

"I love it." She smiles, leaning forward to kiss me softly before she grabs her bag.

Honestly, I don't even care what she got because the simple fact that she was thinking of me while trying to get me something I would like, makes me feel like I've already won.

"Something you love to eat," she says, pulling out peanut butter m&m's, my absolute favorite.

I grab it and eagerly tear the package open while she gets ready to pull out the next item.

Her cheeks turn the darkest shade of red I've seen yet, and I can't help but wonder what she got.

"Come on, let's see it," I urge her.

"Something you can use," she says, taking out a single medium-sized condom.

Laughter rumbles deep within my chest, and I can't stop.

Her face twists in mock hurt. "What's so funny?"

"Come here," I say, inviting her to settle between my legs.

When she takes too long, I grip her hips and bring her closer.

My hands rest on her hips, holding her in place and I tease her. "You think that'll fit me?"

Her mouth gapes open, and she feigns shock, her eyes drifting to my crotch. "Oh right, you might need a smaller size. My bad."

I scoff. "You've sucked my dick, Riles. You sure as shit know it's not small."

"I guess we'll just have to wait to test that out," she teases, her scent consuming the small space between us.

I know she bought the wrong size just to fuck with me and I love seeing this playful side of her, where she teases me without restraint.

She surprises me by reaching behind her and pulling out the last item. "Here's something to make you smile," she whispers, holding a box of large-sized condoms instead.

"Rylee." I groan, frustrated with my need for her while trying to balance my respect for her wish to take it slow. "Filling you will make me smile, but there are so many things you do already that make me smile. We don't have to if you're not ready... that wasn't the point of the date. I'm not trying to get into your pants. I just wanted to make you smile and have fun today."

Rylee shocks me again by straddling me, her hands cupping my face. She eyes me seriously. "Miles, you are too sweet for my little heart. I want to give myself to you, fully." She pauses before going in for the kill, "Please fuck me, Miles. I need you, *now.*"

My self-restraint vanishes. I grip her ass, squeezing as I yank her even closer.

Our lips crash against each other, both of us lost in the frenzy of our emotions. My hands roam over her body while she tugs at my hair. She grinds into my erection, seeking friction, and moans into my mouth, almost making me come.

Fuck, I need to get it together.

I pull back, and she lets out a soft whimper. I run my knuckles across her cheek.

"Slow down baby. Let me cherish you."

Her eyes soften. "Yeah, I think I'd like that. These feelings are just… a lot. I've wanted you inside me since you brought me flowers this morning."

I chuckle at that. "You can have me anytime you want."

She smiles, and I shift my body, wrapping an arm around her waist as I lower her to the blanket. I hover over her and all the air leaves my body when I stare down at her. She's so fucking beautiful, and all mine, eager for my touch.

"Lift up," I whisper, my voice low and rough.

She follows my command and lifts her hips, allowing me to pull her jean shorts and panties off. Rylee sits up once they're off, and removes her shirt, throwing it over her head.

She moves to take off her bra, but I beat her to it, unclasping and dragging it slowly down her arms and off her body. Her nipples are hard and eager for my touch. I lean down to suck on one when Rylee places her palms on my bare chest.

"Now, I want *you*, naked," she orders.

What guy in their right mind would say no to that?

I lift off her as smoothly as I can in the low-ceiling fort and remove my shorts and boxers. My erection rests against her belly, and it twitches when her nails dig into my back. I need to know if she's ready for me because I'm more than fucking ready for her.

I rest my weight on my left arm and kiss her while my other hand trails down between us, stopping my descent when I reach her pussy.

Her fucking soaked pussy. I love how easily turned on and ready she is for me.

I part her lips and brush her clit lightly, teasing, and her body bucks up into mine. Her hard nipples brush against my chest, reminding me of their need for some attention.

I lower my body and suck one into my mouth, long and hard, before licking and kissing her entire breast. My hand lowers until I reach her center, and I start with one finger, feeling her out, before adding another.

Rylee moans and arches her back, bringing her breast closer as I continue fucking her, slow, then fast, driving her to the edge.

I lower myself until my head is right between her thighs when I feel her tighten around my fingers. I lick her pussy, enjoying how she tastes and soaks my face.

I was going to let her come on my fingers, but I couldn't resist tasting her. I remove my fingers, and she groans in frustration.

I smile against her before my lips wrap around her clit and I slam my fingers in her.

"Miles," she yells, her thighs wrapping around my head.

I slow my ministrations while she rides her orgasm out, and I revel in my reward. I lift my head and watch Rylee as her body relaxes, her expression in a daze from the high.

I love knowing *I* did that to her. Me, no one else.

I reach for the large condom pack, pull one out and tear it open, placing it over my cock.

I hover back over her, and Rylee's eyes meet mine, pure joy and lust in them. Her arms come up to rest around my neck, her finger drawing lazy circles. I lean forward and kiss her forehead, my lips lingering as I take in the moment.

I am so fucking grateful she's mine.

"You ready, Riles?" I ask softly, my nose brushing her cheek, my breath scattering over her cheek.

"Yes," she breathes, her voice filled with need.

I grip my erection, place the tip at her entrance, and look at her with a softness I've never given anyone in bed. "Let me know if it hurts too much, okay?"

She nods as my tip nudges inside her. Fuck. Fuck. She's so goddamn tight already, and this is just the tip. I take a deep breath and inch myself in more, my eyes focused on her, watching for any sign of discomfort.

She looks okay to me, so I push in a bit more until she bites her lip and her brows narrow.

I stop instantly, my gaze frantically searching over her body. "What's wrong?"

"N-nothing, it…you feel so good, Miles. Don't stop. Keep going, please," she pleads.

I give her what she wants and push until I'm halfway in and almost combust from the sensation.

I bring my hand between us to stroke her clit, and her body loosens up more for me, allowing me to slide fully to the hilt, loud sighs leaving both of us at the feeling. I hold myself still and stare into Rylee's eyes which are locked on mine already.

The fort. Our past. Our now.

Her gray-blue eyes staring intensely at mine. Mine full of love. Her warmth choking my cock. I've never had someone consume me this way, so fully and completely.

Emotions build inside my chest, the warmth spreading throughout my body. I rest my forehead on hers.

Rylee frowns. "What's wrong?"

I shake my head. I don't want to tell her I love her during our first time because she may think I only love her because she let me fuck her, and that's not it.

I've loved her for as long as I can remember.

"I'm just overwhelmed, baby. By your beauty, your heart, this moment. By us, right here, right now."

Before she can respond, I kiss her gently and thrust my hips. Savoring every feel of her around me, the way her walls clench when I reach that spot. My hips rock in, and out of her slowly, each thrust deep and hard.

"I need more," she pants against my lips, her voice strained and her body tensing.

She's close, and thank God, because so am I. I've been close since I slid inside her. But she needs more, needs *me*.

"You don't know what you're asking for." I lean in and kiss her neck, sucking before nipping at the soft skin.

A whimper leaves her lips, and it only adds to the fire building in my body.

"Miles," she groans as I roll my hips. "Give it to me. Fuck me like I know you need to. Like I need you to."

I still, my body in shock at her words, but once they register, I let my instincts take over.

"You want to be fucked, baby?" I ask, pulling my cock nearly all the way out and sitting back on my heels, leaving the tip just inside her.

She nods, and her confirmation seals the deal. My girl will always get what she wants.

"When you can't walk later, remember you wanted this. *You* wanted my cock driving into you so deep that you'll be feeling me for hours, leaving no confusion about who owns this pussy."

"I think I need the reminder," she muses, provoking me.

She knows how to get under my skin, and right now it's working. I grip her thighs and yank them up in front of me, resting her calves on my shoulders. My hands leave her smooth legs and tug on her hips, shifting them so she'll feel me deeper.

"Let me remind you then," I rasp, then rock my hips up aggressively, right to the hilt.

Her eyes widen at the new position, feeling how much deeper she can take me this way. My vision blacks for a moment at the sensation. She feels so fucking good.

"Miles," she moans, and that breathy little cry sets me off.

I slam in and out of her roughly, my thrusts hard and fast as her walls suck me in with each one. I wrap my hands around each thigh, gripping her smooth inner skin to use them as leverage.

"Hold on to my shoulders," I warn her because I'm about to deliver on her request.

Her hands come up to grip my shoulders, her nails digging into the skin. Gripping her thighs, I piston in and out of her more rapidly than before.

Harder. So much fucking harder.

My cock slams into her without abandon, my balls slapping against her slick skin. Rylee's moans fill the fort, loud and without care, my name spilling out of her lips.

I feel her tighten around me, and her orgasm barrels through her body. She shakes under me, body writhing as her walls suck me in so fucking tightly like they never want me to leave. I somehow find the strength to hold off, not wanting this to end. I release her legs, letting them settle around me, then flip us so she's on top.

And what a fucking sight it is.

"Turn around and ride my cock," I command.

Her bottom lip parts as she sucks in a breath at my words. A dark glaze takes over her eyes, her desire evident, and it makes me want to puff my chest in pride.

Mine.

She does as told, and lifts herself off my cock with a slight wince, maneuvering her body so her ass is now in my line of sight.

I give it a light tap, not knowing if she's ready for anything rougher yet. "Make me come."

Rylee moans, throwing her head back, her waves draping down her back as her hands land on my thighs to steady herself. She slowly lowers herself down every inch of my length, and we both moan at the movement. She rocks on top of me, grinding forward, then sliding back with more pressure, rubbing herself down to give her clit friction.

"Lift up and down too," I remind her.

Rylee leans forward, shifting her hands from my thighs to my knees. She lifts up, and I marvel at the sight. The way she's coated the rubber with her arousal.

Fucking hell, I'm not going to last much longer.

The breath leaves my lungs as she slams down, a ragged whimper leaving her. She finds a rhythm, riding my cock, and I bite my lip at the sight.

My pretty girl. A fucking masterpiece.

I grunt with each bounce she does on my cock, unable to control the sounds leaving my lips. I grab her hips, stilling them. I let her experience some control, but it's going to be me that fucks her into our orgasms. I lift my hips and begin fucking her with rapid thrusts.

"Are you going to come for me again, baby?" I rasp, my hand reaching around to play with her clit. "Be a good girl and cover my cock with your cum."

My words set her off, her orgasm shooting off her lips as she moans my name out over and over again. Her pussy clamps around my dick, so hard I almost black out as I come too, my body jerking upwards and I lose all sense of being.

Holy fuck, I've never come so hard in my life.

I hear the mingle of our ragged breaths when I come back down from the high. Rylee lifts up and falls back onto my chest, our sweaty bodies pressed together.

We stay silent for a few beats, sated and overcome with our new connection. At least I am.

With a deep breath, she rolls over to lie beside me. "Consider me reminded," she says with a satisfied grin.

I smirk at her, knowing damn well I did what she asked. "You okay?" I ask, needing to know what she's feeling.

She mentioned only having sex once, and her body isn't

used to taking me.

"I'm more than okay. That was... wow. I might be addicted, just so you know," she says, her cheeks tinting with a pink shade.

"I'll be your dealer anytime you need me," I say, brushing a piece of sweaty hair from her forehead.

Her hand caresses my back gently. "This has been the perfect day Miles, I–"

She's not able to finish her thought because we hear the front door close.

Fuck. Fuck. Fuck.

Ryan's voice booms from the floor above us. "Rylee, Miles, you guys here?"

Our eyes widen in fear of being caught.

I quickly throw my shorts on and whisper, "I'll go out first, and tell him I came to swim. I'm not leaving you like last time, okay?"

This is different, I need her to know this.

She sits up and kisses my cheek. "I know. Now go before he comes down here."

I usher out of the fort, and fix myself in my shorts, condom still on. I walk up the stairs, uncomfortable as hell.

I get up the stairs and see Ryan in the kitchen unloading his lunch bag. "Hey, I came by to hop in the pool before baseball. You get off work early?" I ask.

"No worries man. My house is your house, you know that. But, yeah, I did." He responds, mindlessly throwing dirty dishes in the sink. "Where's Ry at?"

"She was watching a show downstairs. I was just about to head in the pool when you came in." I answer, guilt bubbling up because that is not at all what happened.

"Cool, I'll join you in a few. Let me get changed," he replies, not an ounce of suspicion in his tone, somehow making me feel worse.

I nod and head back downstairs, seeing the TV on, her favorite sitcom playing. Rylee must've heard me, and she's lounging on the couch, fully clothed as if nothing happened. But I can see her cheeks are still flushed, her lips swollen.

We make eye contact and smile knowingly before I head into the bathroom and dispose of the condom.

That was fucking close, and as much as she wants to keep this a secret, I don't know how much longer we have before it all comes clean.

CHAPTER TWENTY-ONE

Miles

Today has been a great fucking day, despite the interruption. Ryan and I chilled in the pool, and Rylee even joined us for a while. It reminded me of the old days, the three of us together enjoying summer.

Minus the guilt weighing heavily on my shoulders for what I did to his sister before he showed up.

I leave Rylee's house before they do, wanting to give myself some extra time to stretch. I pull into the diamond's parking lot, grab my ball bag, and head to field number 3.

Playing baseball professionally in university taught me the importance of stretching before a game and practicing yoga every morning to keep my muscles loose.

While I stretch, I think of Rylee because when doesn't she consume my thoughts?

I don't need to be with her 24/7, but that doesn't mean I don't think about her 24/7. She consumes me, even when I'm not with her, and that hasn't changed since I was sixteen.

After twenty minutes of stretching, I see Rylee's Jeep pull into the lot, and my full attention focuses on her.

Rylee and Ava make their way to the diamond, and I admire her the entire way because Ryan is nowhere in sight, which is odd. It takes everything in me not to run up to her and wrap her body against mine, to kiss and claim her in front of everyone here. But, even if he's not here, his team is, and they're his friends, not mine. Which means I can't do what I really want to.

Rylee throws her bag on the bench in the dugout. "Ryan got called in at the last minute. I guess there was a bad accident on 94. He'll most likely be there till tomorrow afternoon."

"Hopefully everyone makes it out okay," I respond, my chest aching when I imagine her being the one in an accident.

Fuck this, I need to hug her. Friends can hug each other, right?

I cut the distance between us and pull her into my arms, my hands resting around the small of her back.

She gasps. "Miles, what are you doing?"

"Hugging you, you weirdo," I say into her hair.

I can feel her chuckle against my neck, and I have to temper the effect her laugh has on my dick.

"I know, but no one can know yet. Remember?" she says, her arms coming around my back, squeezing.

"Friends can hug each other, right?" I point out, taking a step back because I know I don't want any of her guy friends hugging her any longer than that.

She pins me with a glare, her eyes rolling a second later and she chuckles again.

I lean into her, my mouth close to her ear. "You sore, baby?"

I wasn't gentle with her, but, in my defense, she asked for it.

She sighs softly, her breath skimming over my cheek. "A little, but I feel great. I've never felt this good, pinky swear."

I pull away from her to see if she's lying, but her eyes tell me she's not. I see her pinky out in the air, waiting for mine, and I wrap it around hers. We get lost in the moment, my mind replaying the feeling of being inside of her.

I feel myself about to grow hard when a hand claps down on my shoulder.

"You want to warm up?" Sean asks, and if he suspects anything is happening between Rylee and me, he doesn't show it.

I nod and we jog to the outfield to warm up. We start with light tosses and eventually move up to longer throws.

The game starts, but so does the rain. It's not hailing, or lightning, which, in baseball, it means we'll play anyways.

While most of the team is annoyed about the rain, I look over to first base from my spot at shortstop, where I'm filling in for Ryan, and my girl is all smiles. Her attention is directed at the home plate, her hair now darker, as she waits for the batter, her head bopping to whatever song she's singing in her head.

God, I love her. I really fucking love her.

With rain comes the increased potential for injuries, making the usual red dirt softer and harder to run into. It also makes the ball wet, and some idiots tend to forget this and throw the ball without a proper grip, sending it anywhere but where they intended.

I'm not worried about myself or Rylee since we've both played long enough to know how to prepare ourselves and adjust. But who I don't trust are the idiots we're playing.

During the warm-up, half of them downed some beers, and I'll be fucking livid if anyone hurts Rylee because they're not fully focused.

The first hit comes off the bat, stopping in the dirt a few feet away from me. I run to scoop it, and quickly make sure I have a good grip before sending it over to Rylee, knowing she'll catch it.

With her back foot on the bag, and her left leg out front, she barely even has to move to catch it. The inning continues without a hitch, and we easily get three outs without letting them score.

Our lead-off, Sean, is up to bat while Rylee, who can't sit still, is pacing in the dugout waiting for her turn. I gently grip her elbow with my fingers, causing her to stop.

"What's wrong?" I murmur, my voice low.

She sighs and takes a seat beside me. "I always get nervous for the first at bat."

She starts fidgeting her knee, so I place my hand on it and trace circles on the inner part with my thumb. Her lips part slightly, and her leg ceases its movement. I reluctantly remove my hand, not wanting to draw the team's attention.

"I got you, always," I whisper, low enough, only for her to hear.

She smiles, her eyes intently watching Sean hit a double and round first base to second.

Ava is up next. Then, it'll be me and Rylee will go right after.

Before I get up, I think of a way I can motivate her competitive personality.

"If I get on base, and you don't, I won't eat that sweet pussy of yours for a week."

I hear her sharp intake of breath before she chuckles. "That's fine. I can get the job done. I don't need you."

My insides twist at her words because I *want* her to need me. Not in the way that she can't live without me, but more in a way where she craves me.

I'll show her how helpful her toy can be, but remind her that I'm the one who owns her pussy.

I think my plan is backfiring on me because I already know I can't go a week without tasting her. Not after knowing what she tastes like.

I stand, needing to focus before I go up to bat. Rylee stands too, and I quickly whisper in her ear, "Pretty sure the neighbors heard you screaming *my* name earlier."

Before she can react, I get my bat and swing a few practice swings. I look over my shoulder, and Rylee is waiting for her turn, her middle finger slyly rubbing her jaw.

I wink at her and take my position at the plate. The first pitch is a ball, an outside pitch, but the second one is perfect. I make contact and send the ball flying over right field, allowing me to round first. The outfielder still hasn't retrieved the ball, so I keep going to second when Eric yells at me to get to third, and I do.

We clap hands, and I catch my breath while Rylee steps up to the plate.

She gets into her stance, readying to lift and put power into her swing. She quickly glances at me, and takes the first pitch, cracking the ball right over my head and out to left field.

I quickly run home, scoring our third run. I watch Rylee round first and head to second, but it'll be a close call because the outfielder whips the ball to second base. The player there catches it and sticks his arm out to tag Rylee, but his turn is so rough, he knocks her on her back.

The ump calls it an out, but I barely register it.

I see red, and before I know it, I'm running over there. Rylee gets up off the ground and intercepts me before I can get to him, her hands on my chest. "Miles, don't. I'm fine, it was just an accident."

The player shrugs his shoulders and says, "Sorry."

Sorry, my fucking ass. I sidestep Rylee, my hands tied into tight fists at my side.

"You're going to be sorry when I break your goddamn arm," I snarl, nostrils flared, and chest heaving rapidly. I want to tear him to shreds.

Rylee puts her hand on my shoulder, attempting to tug me back, but I don't budge.

"Relax, Rylee's not made of glass," the guy says calmly like he didn't understand that I was two seconds away from tearing him apart.

Rylee is so precious to me. I don't want to so much as see someone give her a dirty look, let alone this.

"Austin, I suggest you shut up," Rylee says, flicking her gaze to him, and it's clear that they know each other from years of playing co-ed softball.

It still doesn't make me any less angry.

"I didn't realize how close you were to me," he says nonchalantly.

I take a deep breath.

Don't lose your shit, I tell myself, but the image of Rylee getting knocked back is making my blood boil. Rylee's death grip on my shoulder keeps me from breaking his arm.

"This happens again and I won't walk away like I am now, got it?" I threaten him, my voice cold.

Austin chooses to remain silent, his gaze unwavering as I turn to wrap my arm around Rylee's shoulder and walk with her back to the dugout.

"Before you ask, I'm fine. I didn't land on my head or anything," Rylee says quietly, and I can feel her gaze on me.

I glance down at her and take a deep breath. She's okay, I need to relax. I nod tightly, my jaw ticking as I do it.

Rylee glances over to Claire and Ava heading toward us. "I appreciate you sticking up for me, you didn't have to."

Before I can respond, the girls pull her into a hug. I keep walking into the dugout and mull over her words. I didn't have to? I know she's never had a boyfriend, so maybe she doesn't know what to expect. But Christ, is the bar really that low? She needs to expect more than just the bare minimum from me.

With time, I tell myself.

The rest of the game goes off without a hitch, and I put myself in the outfield to avoid coming into contact with Austin. I can't make any promises that I won't trip him or worse.

We're now tied in the last inning. The opposing team is up to bat, which means if they score, the game's over. But if they don't, we play another inning and would win if we score first. We just need to hold them off.

I ask Sean to switch me because, although he's good at shortstop, I don't trust his nerves to not throw a shitty throw at Rylee.

The first hit is a pop fly near first base, and Rylee easily catches it.

That's my girl. One down, two to go.

We need this win to secure our first-place spot in the playoffs starting in two weeks.

Their last batter is none other than Austin. That bastard eyes me as he sets up on the plate, then flicks his gaze to the pitcher. He swings, but misses. He looks pissed, his lips tight as he gets in position again.

This time, the ball rebounds on the ground right next to me.

Fuck yeah, I'll get to throw his ass out and extend the game.

I pick up the ball and throw it to Rylee. She lunges, trying to stretch and make the catch before Austin reaches the bag but then it happens.

Austin loses control of his footing, slips on the dirt, and barrels right into Rylee. If that wasn't bad enough, it happens right as she tries to catch the ball. Instead of it landing in her glove, her body gets shoved forwards and the ball collides with her collarbone on her way down. I can hear the pop as it hits her.

Everything seems to happen in slow motion, but in reality, it all occurred within mere seconds.

I am going to kill him.

I can't think of anything besides wrapping my hands around his neck and beating him until I see red all over his face. I start charging toward him, but when I stop in my tracks when I hear Rylee's shouts of pain.

Fuck. Fuck. *Fuck.*

I sprint over to Rylee, who's curled up on her side, her left hand holding her right arm in pain, her eyes shut tightly.

"Shit, are you okay Rylee?" Austin asks out of breath as he stands.

Fuck it. I lunge toward him, my fist rearing before connecting with his nose. I must've taken him by surprise because his entire body topples over as he groans in pain and holds his nose.

Good. He's lucky that's all the time I can spare over him.

His teammates rush over to help and our team slowly starts to circle around us. No one bothers mentioning the hit because both teams know it was deserved.

I get on my knees beside Rylee, my hands shaking as I reach for her. "Riles," I croak, my voice raw.

Rylee must've heard the anguish in my voice because she stupidly sits up. "I'm fine, I can take care of it." She takes a strained breath and attempts to stand.

My hand gently pushes on the shoulder opposite to the collarbone she is holding, forcing her to remain seated.

Something inside of me wants to snap. She just took an 80-mile-per-hour ball to the chest and she thinks she can just take care of it on her own? Leave it to Rylee to fucking think that.

"Sit the hell down, now," I order, sounding a bit harsher than I intended, but seeing her in pain ignites something feral in me.

She glares at me and shakes my hand off with her shoulder, the motion causing her pain as she lets out a small whimper that tears at my heart.

Fuck this.

I lean in closer and wrap an arm under her knees, and the other around her back, carefully hoisting her up in my arms as I stand. I expect her to protest, but instead, Rylee clutches her collarbone and nestles her head in my neck, inhaling deeply.

As much as she hates being cared for, and would deny liking it, I can feel the way her body relaxes in my arms. A warmth spreads in my body only for a moment before I remember why she is in my arms in the first place.

Ava runs past us, yelling for ice, as she heads toward the pavilion.

I kiss the top of Rylee's head, not caring who's watching, as I carry her to the picnic bench beside the dugout.

I carefully sit down with her still in my arms. "Talk to me, baby. Do I need to bring you to the hospital?"

Fear claws its way through my spine as I imagine rushing Rylee to the hospital, and waiting hours through surgery, seeing her in pain for weeks...

Rylee's gaze meets mine. She shakes her head and tears pool in her eyes. My chest swells with pain as I gently tuck a piece of her hair behind her ear, my fingers lingering to trace lightly over her jaw.

Something suddenly dawns on me. While this was mainly Austin's fault, I can't help but feel partly to blame. None of this would've happened if I hadn't whipped the ball so hard or even thrown it a bit lower.

"Riles, I'm so fucking sorry." I choke on the lump in my throat.

"For what?"

"Had I not thrown the ball so hard, you wouldn't be in this pain," I admit shamefully. I let the game get to my head instead of taking it easy.

Rylee's hands cup my cheek, and I lean into her hand, letting it soothe me for the time being. "Miles, stop. You and I both know I easily had that catch. If Austin didn't slip none of this would've happened. You didn't run into me, he did. Stop looking at me like you hurt me," she demands, her gaze intense on mine.

She's comforting me when I'm supposed to be the one comforting her. I grab her hand and kiss her knuckles before resting our hands against my heart.

As if suddenly remembering where we were, Rylee tries to wiggle off my lap. "Miles, we can't–"

I tighten my hold on her. "I don't give a shit who's around. You're in pain, I'm not leaving your side."

A small smile forms on her lips and she looks at me intently, an unreadable expression on her face. Ava and Claire interrupt us by bringing Rylee an ice pack. Claire hands it to her, and Rylee places it over her collarbone, grimacing when it makes contact.

"I already told the team to give you space Ry. They know how you are when you get hurt. Mrs.I-don't-need-anybody's-help," she admonishes.

I scoff at that lightheartedly because it was true.

"And don't worry, I'll make sure everyone knows not to mention any of this to Ryan," Ava says, flailing her hands in our vicinity. "If he finds out about you two from them, you'll really lose any chance of him taking it well."

"Thanks, girls, I appreciate everything," Rylee says softly, sniffing back the tears threatening to spill. "Now, go kick some ass and finish the game."

The girls nod and tell her to text them with updates and if she needed anything. Then, they're off to finish the game. I flick my gaze over to the opposing team's dugout, and Austin is lay-ing back on the bench with bloody paper towels and an ice pack.

Good. He deserved it.

I press my lips to her forehead. "Do you want to go or stay?"

"Can we go?" she asks softly.

Her answer makes my heart beat faster because I honestly expected her to say 'I'll drive myself, you stay and play.'

"Are you sure you don't need to go to the hospital? If it's broken Riles, the sooner we get there the better," I remind her.

She shakes her head. "It hurts like hell, but it's not broken. I broke the other side once years ago, and the pain isn't the same."

A part of me feels guilty for not knowing that, but that's what I get for leaving. I want to ask how she broke it, but I decide on stashing the question away for later.

I stand. "Whatever you want Riles, I got you. Where are your keys?"

She points to her bag and I walk over to grab it, slipping it over my shoulder. I know we need to take her Jeep because I don't have a key to her house yet.

I pull out my phone and quickly text Ava, asking her to grab my bag because I am not putting Rylee down until I get to her Jeep. And I sure as hell am not leaving her in there unattended. Call me overprotective, I don't even care.

I open the door with one hand, still holding her up with the other, then place her gently in the passenger seat, buckling her in. After confirming she's safe, I throw her bag in the trunk, then round to the driver's side and hop in.

Rylee smiles at me. "You're cute when you're flustered. I'll be okay, it just really hurt at first."

I give her a reluctant smile. "Hmm, let's not make it a habit. I already worry about you enough as it is."

She rolls her eyes. "You don't need to, but I do appreciate you taking care of me, so thank you."

"Don't thank me yet. Wait and see how good of a job I do tonight," I say, pulling out of the parking lot.

"Tonight?" she repeats, her tone unsure.

I gaze at her, my jaw tight. "I'm not leaving you alone tonight, Ry. I told you that. Your brother is working all night, hell, probably will all day tomorrow too after that crash. Let me take care of you tonight, please."

She nods and grabs my hand, resting our joined hands over the middle console.

I drive us home.

CHAPTER TWENTY-TWO

Rylee

"Let me help you," Miles offers as I struggle to get the rest of my clothes off to shower. He helped me take off my jersey already, leaving me in my sports bra and shorts to analyze the yellow and green bruising already forming.

It hurts when I move, but it's a hell of a lot better than having it broken. It'll be manageable with ice and painkillers.

The last time this happened, the player ran right through me, the impact of his elbow falling on my left collarbone breaking it. The pain was indescribable, but I refused to cry in front of anyone, and the only person I let help me was my brother because he was studying to be a nurse.

Letting Miles take care of me is a lot for me because I grew up always taking care of myself. I always feel guilty having someone worry about me, it makes me feel like a burden.

When he took off my shirt, the look in his eyes was murderous. His greenish blues turned dark, his jaw tight, and his breath shaky. I told him about my previous collarbone injury to ease some of his worries so that he'd realize today's incident wasn't as bad. It slightly helped him relax.

"Okay," I say, feeling a bit insecure.

Having him see me bare during a non-intimate moment makes me anxious, but I do my best to put the worry away.

"Don't move your right arm. I'm going to lift your left one to get your bra over your head, then I'll slide it over your head, and down your right arm, okay?" he states calmly.

I nod, and he does just as he said, gently lifting and removing my sports bra. He is so gentle and careful, I don't feel an ounce of pain and my heart swell at his care.

It's funny how a couple of weeks ago, I wanted to hit him with a bat, and now here he is, helping me out of my clothes.

I go to cover my chest when he catches my wrists and puts them at my sides. "You're beautiful, Ry. Don't hide from me please."

I take a deep breath and try to relax as he bends down to take off my shorts and underwear.

"Fuck," he mutters, lifting my left, then right foot, and discarding my clothes into the laundry bin.

"What?" I tease, knowing exactly why he cursed. I'm wet, but how could I not be when he's touching me and being the sweetest? It was a siren call that went directly between my thighs.

"I'm not touching you like that tonight. Let's get you washed up," he insists, leaning over my bathtub, and letting the water run.

My momentary disappointment fades when the tenderness of his words hit me, wrapping me up in their comfort. I watch as he puts a sugar cookie-scented bath bomb in the water, the sweet aroma filling the air.

He sets up two towels on the counter and lights a candle he must've found in my room. My heart expands in my chest as I watch him lean over the tub, testing the water to make sure it isn't too hot.

I love you is on the tip of my tongue, but I don't say it. Instead, I take the hand he's holding out to me and step into the warm water.

"How's the water?" he asks, dipping a cloth into the bath, and lathering my body wash into it.

"Perfect," I mumble, feeling dazed as the bubble bath soothes my body.

Miles grins at me. He clears his throat, his expression turning serious. "Relax, and don't even think about moving. Got it?"

"Since I can't move, can you kiss me?" I plead, my eyes locked onto his lips. I might be rethinking my whole 'I don't need anyone to take care of me charade' because I'm currently loving it.

His lips meet my eager ones and he kisses me reverently, his lips moving slowly against mine, conveying how much he cherishes me without having to say it.

I attempt to delve my tongue into his mouth, but he pulls back before I get the chance. "We're supposed to get you clean, baby, not dirty."

I pout, my eyelashes fluttering. He shakes his head and lightly splashes the water at me. Then, ever so gently, he pushes my good shoulder back until it hits the wall of the tub.

Cloth in hand, Miles begins washing me. He starts at my neck, then goes down to my good shoulder and arm. When he brings his hand back up, he hovers it over my bad shoulder, where the bruises lay on my collarbone. His hand shakes slightly as his eyes roam my bruises, so I still it with my own.

"I'm okay," I tell him, hoping to ease his worries.

Pained blue-green eyes meet mine. "Watching you go down...the way you screamed in pain. Those two things are going to haunt me, baby."

My chest tightens at his confession. I don't even know what to say because I get it. My stomach sinks at the simple thought of the situation being reversed.

I bring his hand to my lips and kiss each of his knuckles. The same rough hands due to years of playing baseball, and fights, being so gentle with me.

He leans forward, half of his body hanging in the tub, and presses his lips lightly against my bruises, leaving feather-like kisses on each one. My heart thrashes against my ribcage. He smiles against my skin and pulls back, his eyes lighter than a moment ago.

I release his hand, and he lightly presses the cloth to my bad shoulder, looking at me the entire time to gauge my reaction. I nod at him so he knows it's not painful, and he continues over my bruises with the utmost concentration, his brows narrowed. He lathers the rest of my body, leaning me forward to get my back, down my legs, and between my toes.

Miles takes a deep breath, knowing there are two places he has left to clean. Between my thighs and my chest. Part of me hopes he'll lose control and make me come. But the other part of me is enjoying this intimate moment sans orgasms.

Grabbing a different cloth with my non-scented body wash, he does as I expect and washes those areas with the same care, except this time, a moan slips past my lips when his hand brushes between my thighs.

Drawing in a deep breath, Miles sighs audibly. "Riles, don't."

A breathy laugh flows past my lips. "Sorry, my body likes your touch too much to get the message this isn't that type of touching. Even if it wants it."

"Ry–" he grunts.

"Sorry, I'll stop talking." I pretend to zip my lips, throwing the imaginary key over my head.

He shakes his head, then moves his body to sit on the edge of the tub, my shampoo and conditioner beside him.

"But, I will tell you that usually, girls wash their hair first," I tease him as he pours cups of water over my hair, wetting it.

Miles scrunches his nose at me. "Are you judging my bedside manner?"

I laugh at that, my cheeks pulling up high, and he joins in, laughing along with me. All laughter ceases once his hands start massaging the shampoo into my hair. Holy hell. This man's fingers deserve a gold medal. He can fuck me into oblivion, and give one heck of a scalp massage. I'm never letting him go.

His fingers move delicately over my head, and he takes his time to focus on lathering every strand. My eyes shut close to enjoy the moment as I try to avoid letting a moan slip again. A hand comes over my eyes, shielding them as warm water cascades down my hair, washing the suds away.

"Don't use conditioner on my roots, okay? And make sure you use a decent amount, it's good for my curls," I tell him when I hear him pumping the conditioner into his hand.

"Noted," he hums, his hands lathering up my ends. He takes his time, and I nearly fall asleep, feeling so at peace under his touch.

He lifts the drain from the tub and it brings me back from my near slumber. But what wakes me up is Miles's corded muscles wrapping around my back and legs, lifting me out of the tub.

He sets me down and quickly wraps me in a towel, patting me down and ensuring I'm tightly wrapped up.

"I don't know how to do the head wrap thing with the towel, but you can tell me," he says, sounding almost shy.

This might be my favorite version of Miles, the one so insistent on taking care of me and doing a damn good job at it.

I instruct him on how to fold it, bending over so he can do it, and when I lift, he's sporting a wide smile.

"What?" I ask him, his eyes making me feel warm despite

the cool air blasting through the vent.

"I want to do that for you every day," he admits.

He's so precious. My golden boy, and he's all mine.

He leaves and returns with an oversized t-shirt of mine, then helps me get into it. And apparently, that is all I am wearing to bed.

"I think you forgot my shorts," I quip, my eyebrows raised.

His eyebrow mimics my own. "Last time I checked, quite literally, you don't wear anything underneath."

"Not like it'll matter tonight," I mumble, strolling past him to do my skincare routine.

Suddenly, I feel him behind me, his hard length pressed against my ass and he whispers in my ear, "I've been itching to get back inside you and paint you with my cum, but rest is what you need right now, baby."

I never thought it could be possible to come from words alone, but it might be time to revisit that belief because, wow.

Before I can respond, he moves my hair and kisses my neck sweetly, then disappears once more into my room. With an unfilled desire, I finish up my routine, apply my hair products, and brush my teeth.

I walk into my room and catch a whiff of my diffuser, the lavender blend filling the room with a calming aura. Miles is relaxing on my bed, his hands behind his head and an ice pack beside him. My side table has a full glass of water and two painkillers.

I climb onto my bed beside him and down half of the water with the pills. I put the glass back on the stand and turn to meet his gaze. His eyes are gesturing me to lie down, and so I do. He gently places the ice pack wrapped in a towel on my collarbone and turns his body to face me so I can see him more comfortably from my angle.

"How does it feel?" he asks tenderly, his fingers drawing lazy circles on my shoulder.

"Sore, but I'll be okay. Thank you for everything Miles," I say softly, my eyes unable to tear away from him.

"I take care of what's mine," he states, his fingers resting gently over my heart.

He said it so simply, like it was a mere fact, such as the sun rising each morning.

I don't know how to reply, my mind and heart are in a frenzy. So, I lie there and stare at the man I know without a doubt I'm falling in love with. Feeling vulnerable scares me, but I can either live and love, despite the potential heartbreak, or I close myself off and break my own heart.

I'm going with the first option.

Miles's hands trail down my arm, over my hip, and down to my thigh. My breath hitches in anticipation, but my hopes are crushed when he stops in his trail. "Your quads must be sore from the wet dirt. Want a massage?"

"Yes," I reply instantly, suddenly feeling the soreness at his reminder.

Miles gets off my bed, grabs my lotion, and settles back on the bed, nestling between my legs as I spread them to make room. My shirt still covers the area I want him to touch, but part of me is disappointed that it didn't hitch up higher in the process to tempt him.

Miles squeezes some lotion into his hands, then begins rubbing my right quad, his deft fingers knowing exactly what they are doing. He switches from applying pressure to rubbing softly over my sore muscles.

I sigh wistfully. "How are you so good at everything?"

I regret it as soon as I admit it because, knowing his cocky ass, he will use those words against me one day.

He chuckles. "Did you really just say that? Did the pain-killers get to you?"

I wish I could lift and playfully slap his shoulder.

"Don't forget it because I'll never admit that again."

He begins massaging my foot and switches the conversation. "Let's play twenty questions."

"What are you fifteen?"

"I want to know every detail about you," he replies so honestly, it makes me feel bad for teasing him.

He releases a knot in the arch of my foot I didn't know existed, and with a choppy breath, I say, "I love that. Ava and I used to answer the questions for each other to see who knew the other best."

He moves to massage my left quad. "Hmm, I like your version more. Explain."

"Okay, so we go back and forth picking questions. Then, we answer the question, but for the other person," I explain.

"Think you can prove you know me better?" He challenges, digging into a tense spot on the inside of my thigh.

"Oh, I know I can, I'd be worried if I were you," I shoot back, trying to suppress the moans and sighs of relief I want to let out.

This man's hands are magic.

"I only worry about you, not me," he replies, working his way down to my calf. "Let's start easy. First question, what's my favorite food?"

I don't even have to think twice about it. "Blueberry muffins, specifically your mom's."

He always had one for his lunch. They were heavenly, and my mouth salivates at the memory. It has been so long since I've had one, eight years exactly.

He squeezes my foot. "Correct. Yours is sour patch kids.

Although that's not really food, the second choice would be pineapple. I remember one summer you ate it all day long. You categorically refused to eat anything else."

I laugh at the memory. "While you and Ryan teased me that I would lose my tastebuds if I didn't stop. Jerks."

He shifts his body to lie on his side. "You were cute when you got mad. I couldn't help it."

I shake my head and continue with the next question. "What is something I do that no one else knows about?"

Miles doesn't even take time to think and says, "You used to write letters to the kids at the hospital, and I'm pretty sure you still do."

How the hell does he know that?

As if I voiced the question out loud, he continues, "It was before I stopped talking to you. Ryan and I were looking for your baseball glove because I forgot mine and it happened to be on top of a letter you were in the middle of writing. I couldn't help myself but read it. You have a big heart, Ry."

My heart skips a beat. "We had to do it once for an assignment, and for me, it stuck. I wanted to do anything I could to make their time in the hospital a little more enjoyable. Even if it was just for a few minutes as they read my letter," I explain, my fingers reaching out to grip his forearm.

His hand comes to rest on top of mine. "You radiate sunshine, Riles. I'm sure each kid was touched by your letters."

"Thanks," I smile. "Now for you, I know you used to volunteer at the dog shelter. My dad went there one day to drop off a dog he found on the side of the road, and mentioned seeing you working in the back. I was the only one home when he told me, and I was so excited to tell Ryan about it. But, when he got home, I never ended up telling him because a big part of me loved knowing that I knew something he didn't know about *his* best friend."

"I actually went there yesterday. I'll start volunteering in my spare time."

Could he get any more attractive? My best friend, a college baseball player, teacher, sex god, and dog lover? Jesus.

"Next question," he starts. "Where would I like to have sex?"

I burst out laughing. "And there it is, I knew this wouldn't stay PG 13." I take a breath and then say, "Hmm, I would say on your parents' boat. I doubt you've taken anyone on it, or at least I hope not. It would be special for you because of how much you love it."

Miles blinks, his mouth falling open. It takes a second before he finally replies. "You've been paying attention all these years. And no I haven't."

"I was, for the ones I could," I whisper, not wanting to make a big deal out of this.

He leans in closer and kisses my forehead. "Sorry isn't good enough to describe how I feel–"

I cut him off. "It's water under the bridge Miles, let it go. We're focusing on the present, okay? Now, tell me where I'd want to get down and dirty."

His face goes from regretful to sinful within seconds, a knowing smirk forming on his lips. "Bath or shower."

My mouth gapes open. "How did you–"

His thumb brushes my bottom lip. "I saw how wet you were for me before you got in. I just connected the dots. Do you know how hard it was for me to sit there and not give you everything you wanted?"

"You're gorgeous beyond belief, and have a dirty mouth that turns me into mush. I can't help but be turned on every time you're near me," I admit, my voice smaller than I'd like.

He closes his eyes for a moment and inhales deeply. "Jesus Ry." He takes another breath as if it's a struggle for him to control himself. "Okay, next question. What is my biggest regret?"

My heart sinks in my chest. *Why would he ask me this?*

I take a shaky breath, then exhale. "Shutting me out of your life for 8 years."

I don't want to assume I was his biggest regret, but I know him well enough to know he regrets it.

I get my confirmation when I see the pained look in his eyes.

His face is hard, but his tone is soft. "Yes. Ask me why I went to Arizona."

My eyebrows narrow. "I already have. You told me it was because you got the scholarship and loved the sunny weather. Right?"

He shakes his head and his hand reaches for mine to place it over his heart.

"That's partly right." He pauses. "I had to leave because I loved you. I knew if I stayed, I wouldn't be able to stay away from you. I've loved you since I was 16, and that will never go away. There's no place far enough to erase you from my mind, and my heart. I thought I was doing the right thing by putting distance between us, but I was wrong. Now that I have you, I wish we had done this sooner."

Holy hell.

With a shaky breath, he continues. "I love you more than I ever have before, and I don't think it's ever going to stop growing. If you ask me tomorrow if I loved you more than today, the answer will always be yes."

My heart is going to combust. On one hand, I feel like my blood is suddenly honey coursing through my veins, making me feel all warm and fuzzy. But on the other, I want to yell at him in disbelief because how could you leave someone you claim to love?

I stop myself from reeling and remind myself that we were young, and we agreed to move past it. As much as I want to dissect and pick at the past, it'll only ruin what we have now.

Love. Unconditional, and undeniable. So, I'm choosing to focus on that instead.

My throat feels too raw with emotions, so, instead of talking, I unlace my hand from his, and bring it up to cup his chin, dragging his face towards mine.

Our lips touch tentatively, as if for the first time. His lips feel like they were made for me, the way they mold perfectly to match mine with each touch.

We explore each other's like an R&B love song, slowly, passionately, lovingly. I add a hint of dirty by prodding my tongue at the seam of his lips, demanding entrance.

His lips part, and I take advantage, my tongue stroking his, tasting the mint he had earlier. I moan into his mouth and it causes Miles to pull back, breathless.

"Baby, we have to stop," he says, sounding ragged.

I whimper and pout. This man just admitted his love for me after caring for me when I got hurt and he expects me to not want him?

Sometimes I forget how irritatingly rational he is.

He smirks. "I'll take extra care of you when you're better, deal?"

I huff. "Fine." I roll over to lie on my uninjured shoulder, my back to him.

He chuckles quietly and moves his body to cradle me. His arm wraps tightly around my hips, pulling me to his chest, and I instantly feel how hard he is against my ass.

"You okay over there?" I tease, a yawn escaping my throat.

"Just because I am saying no, doesn't mean my dick got the same message."

I hum, liking the idea that he's torturing himself as much as he's torturing me. The last thing I remember before drifting off to sleep was that I have never shared a bed with a man before, and how I've never felt more at peace in my entire life.

I love Miles Anderson.

CHAPTER TWENTY-THREE

Rylee

I stir in bed, the chirping of the birds and sunlight peeking in through my blinds telling me it's early in the morning. Too early for my liking, especially on my day off.

Ava texted me while we were driving home yesterday to let us know they'd won, and that she canceled our camp day today. I felt awful about having to cancel on our kids because I knew they looked forward to it each day, but I knew she secretly loved it.

My collarbone isn't throbbing like it was last night, and I am pleased with the bearable soreness of it. But, what I am not pleased with, is the ache between my legs from waking up in Miles's arms.

It started last night and only seemed to amplify throughout the night. I press my thighs together, hoping to relieve some pressure, but of course, it doesn't help. I squiggle out of his embrace and sigh quietly.

The ache is becoming unbearable. I reach over to my nightstand, slowly pulling the drawer open, and grab my vibrator. I know it'll probably wake him up, but part of me is counting on that.

If this doesn't get him to touch me, I don't know what will.

I spread my legs under the comforter and press my vibrator on my clit. I take a breath and turn it on. The sound is somewhat muffled, the fan in my room blocking out a decent amount of the noise.

The relief is instant, and my other hand travels further south to insert two of my fingers inside of me. I stifle a moan as I begin riding my fingers while pressing the vibrator harder against my clit.

"Ry, what is that noise–" Miles rasps, his voice raw from sleep.

He pauses once he opens his eyes and sees me—my parted lips, the flush on my cheeks, and the way my knees are spread under the blanket.

He rips the comforter off the bed within the next second to get a better picture of exactly what that noise is.

I hear his sharp intake of breath, and he curses under his breath and mumbles something about Jesus. I look at him and see the tight set of his jaw, the way it ticks when our eyes meet.

"What the hell are you doing?"

"Taking care of what you wouldn't."

I moan, the pressure building within me. I am so close to coming.

He snaps, and suddenly, he's lying between my legs. "I'll be the one earning all of your moans and orgasms, Riles. Turn it off and let me take care of it," he demands.

I want to make him beg and push him to the edge, just like he did to me. So, I ignore him and keep going.

His features turn murderous as he watches me, his hands clutching the sheets.

Good. I shove a third finger inside me and moan, thrusting them in and out.

"Baby, you're killing me. I need to touch you," he growls.

"Now you know how I felt last night," I breathe out, on the edge of coming.

Miles must sense it because, within a second, he rips the vibrator out of my hand, turning it up a notch and pressing it firmly against my clit. I buck under the pressure. He removes my fingers and brings them up to his mouth, licking them clean. The vision shoots sparks up my spine.

"You're only allowed to come on my tongue, fingers, or cock, got it?" he orders.

"Make me," I challenge because I love this feistiness between us.

This constant back and forth, two competitive people trying to one-up the other. My words are his undoing and suddenly he's face first into my pussy, the vibrator still pressed on my clit.

Miles gets right into it, with no build-up or slow teasing strokes. His tongue is vicious as it sucks and licks. My nerves are on fire, and when he removes the vibrator, and replaces it with his mouth, sucking hard, I nearly explode.

My fingers pull on his hair, tugging the brown mess as he brings me to the edge of insanity with his tongue.

Miles inserts two of his fingers inside me, fucking me with them relentlessly. His pinky finger prods the hole below, seeking permission. I moan my response, and he gently eases it inside.

It feels different and new, but so fucking good. I love being filled with him. The sounds of my wetness slapping against his fingers, his pinky breaching the tight hole below, and his tongue devouring my clit, cause me to release an ear-piercing orgasm.

I come violently, my legs shaking. He removes his fingers

but continues licking my release as I orbit into a new planet from my orgasm.

Before I have time to come back to earth, he wraps his arms around my waist and pulls me into his lap, my legs wrapping around his hips. I can feel his dick poking beneath me, begging to escape its confines.

"What are you doing?" I ask as he lifts us off the bed.

"Fulfilling my girlfriend's fantasy," he says casually. "How's your collarbone?"

Shower sex. I don't care if my arm is broken, there is no way I was passing this up.

"Good, I'll let you know if it hurts too much," I reassure him, giving him a quick kiss as he shuts and locks the door behind us.

Miles puts me down gently, then removes his sweats in one swift motion. God, he is perfect– long, hard, thick, and all man. He removes my shirt just as quickly while being careful enough not to raise the arm that is attached to my sore bone.

I drop to my knees, and before he can protest, I put him in my mouth, tears pricking at my eyes once he hits the back of my throat. I release him and kiss the tip before spitting on it, and swirling my tongue around his slit.

His thighs tense beneath my touch, and a moan escapes his lips. I love knowing I'm turning him on. I lick his length up and down, before giving his balls an appreciative suck.

"That fucking perfect mouth of yours was made to suck my cock, wasn't it?" he groans as his hands fist into my hair.

I suck him more deeply into my mouth. He takes over control, fucking himself into my mouth, and I love every second of it. I love seeing him lose control and give himself to me.

"Up," he orders hoarsely.

I obey and stand. He takes my hand and drags me into

the shower, turning it on. We both jump from the initial chill, but the heat of our bodies allows us to ignore it as we ravage each other's mouths.

Miles pulls back from me. "Are you on the pill? Because I'm clean and want to take you raw. I want nothing between us, baby."

I never understood why girls were into this until now because I wanted nothing more than for Miles to fill me up with his cum, and claim a part of me.

"I just started getting the shot six months ago, and I'm clean too," I pant, our lips grazing the other's as we speak.

"I'm going to take you quick and hard."

"Okay," I rasp, my mouth taking his in a hard kiss.

Miles hitches my leg around his hips, grinding his erection against my pussy as we make out like we can't get enough of each other.

He suddenly drops my leg and swings my body around so that my back is to him.

"Hands on the wall, and spread your legs for me," he demands.

I obey, and I feel my arousal drip down my thigh. His knee nudges my legs further apart and he slides his dick through my arousal, teasing.

"Miles, *now,*" I demand.

His hard cock slaps against my pussy, making me jolt from the sparks of pleasure. "So mouthy. Let's see what I can do about that."

I feel his tip nudge against my entrance briefly before he slams into me in one quick thrust with nothing between us.

"Fuck," we both moan at once.

I understand what the hype is about now because feeling him bare is a sensation I won't forget anytime soon. I can feel every inch of him, the way it pulses inside of me. Every single thing he has to offer, I can feel it.

"Don't move, unless you want this to be over in ten seconds. Just give me a minute here."

We both take the time to adjust and hold onto our control in the quiet sound of the water running filling the space.

Ryan's voice shouting my name while running up the stairs cuts through the silence. Fucking hell.

I rapidly turn my head to look at him, my eyes wide.

The asshole grins. "That's one way to get me to gather my control."

I shush him, and seconds later Ryan is pounding on the door, while I can feel Miles pulsing inside of me.

"Ry! Are you okay? Ava told me what happened," he shouts over the shower noise.

"Yup, all good," I shout back, my voice strained.

God, I hope he didn't see the vibrator on my bed.

Miles chooses this moment to rock himself out of me slowly, then thrust himself back to the hilt. Fuck me, I mean he is, but holy fucking hell. I have to bite down on my arm to avoid screaming.

"Ava said Miles took you home. Did he take good enough care of you? Are you okay?"

Miles drives into me again, and whispers in my ear, "Hmm, how about that Riles? Am I taking *good* care of you?"

Fuck. I am *not* going to come while my brother is on the other end of the door, I can't. My mind is a mess, the pool of heat in my core building with every rock of his hips. I don't think I can even form words.

"Rylee?" Ryan shouts.

"Are you going to be a good girl and say yes?" Miles whispers again, thrusting into me again, and causing my eyes to flutter shut.

"It's still up for debate," I shout back.

Miles' fingers dig into my hips and my answer is met with a playful slap on my ass.

"Rylee, what was that?" Ryan questions.

I turn around to meet Miles's gaze, and nearly come from the look on his face. He's hungry, and knowing it's for me puts my mind in a tailspin.

"Do that again but harder."

He slaps my ass again, but this time it's harder, the sound echoing.

The doorknob jangles. "Rylee," Ryan shouts, his tone agitated.

"Sorry, I keep dropping my shampoo. It's slippery," I tell Ryan, hoping he can't tell how ragged my voice is.

"Be careful, I'll check on you later. I'll run to the store to get ingredients for your favorite soup."

Once we hear the front door slam, Miles's restraint snaps. He pounds into me relentlessly, his cock thick and hard as it reaches a place he's never reached within me. He gets so deep in this position, I almost can't handle it.

Miles's hand wraps around my neck, dragging my head back to his chest. His lips trace a slow, languid path from my shoulder, and up my neck, the opposite of how furiously he's pounding into me. The contrast nearly sends me over the edge, and I whimper into his mouth when his lips finally cover mine in a searing kiss.

"You're being such a good girl. Your tight pussy is taking my cock so well," he murmurs against my ear, nipping my ear lobe.

His words are my undoing, and I come fast and hard, squeezing the heck out of him in the process.

"Fuck, baby," he growls, filling me to the hilt and releasing himself inside of me.

The feeling of him coming inside of me is something I've never felt before and causes me to come again. I love feeling him inside of me like that, knowing it connected us in another way than we already were.

We both lose ourselves in our release, panting and shuddering as we come down.

Moments later, when our breathing is under control, he pulls out of me, and I wince.

He strokes my back gently, kissing my shoulder before he asks, "Did I hurt you?"

I turn around to face him. "I love it, but you are big. It's going to make me sore from time to time."

"Sorry, baby. I try to be gentle, but it's hard with you. I can't get enough," he admits, his forehead coming to rest on mine.

"Don't be sorry, I liked it. A lot," I say, slightly embarrassed as I remembered the light spanking he gave me.

He smiles, and it makes my heart pitter-patter. I smile at him and give him an order instead. "Turn around."

He doesn't ask why, he just does it.

I lather up some of my body wash, hoping he doesn't care to smell like vanilla and cherries. I run my hands across his back, spreading the soap around. I knead his muscles and end up massaging his back as I clean him off.

I take my time, admiring every inch of skin as I work my way around his entire body. He gets hard again, but I want to finish my task at hand and he lets me, his gaze never leaving me as I maneuver around him. He touches me faintly here and there, gentle whispers of his fingers on different parts of my skin, but never more. It's so soft and gentle, making me feel loved.

I remember suddenly that I never said it back to him. I smile to myself at the idea forming in my mind.

"Want to play a game?" I ask softly against his back, my

arms curving around his waist, my lips kissing his arm.

He hums.

"I'm going to draw something on your back with my finger, and you have to guess what it is. You only get one guess, so if you lose, I get to wash my own body."

"I'm listening," he says, sounding more alert.

I smile against his skin, then take a step back. I bring my finger up and lightly begin tracing the shape of a baseball, including the stitching inside.

"A baseball," he says confidently.

"One more?" I ask, my voice on the brink of betraying my nerves as he nods in response.

This time, my finger shakes as I lightly begin to trace 'I love you' on his back. Once I finish, I feel him shiver beneath my touch, and then he turns to face me.

His face is pure elation. His eyes are bright, and his smile widens as he looks at me with so much adoration. I nearly choke on the emotions clawing up my throat.

"I love you," he answers softly.

I nod, "Correct."

"Say it," he smiles, his eyes overflowing with happiness.

"I love you, Miles. It's always been you," I admit, my heart pounding fervently in my chest.

He cups my face with one hand, the other coming to rest on the back of my neck as he kisses me lovingly.

"I love you so fucking much, Riles" he rasps before plunging his tongue into my mouth, and soon enough we're both dirtier than clean, *again.*

CHAPTER TWENTY-FOUR

Rylee

A rumble of thunder awakens me, causing me to sit up in my bed, my heart pounding. I hate thunderstorms for two reasons. One is that they're just scary and loud, but the other reason is the memory that comes along with it. That night in the fort eight years ago. When Miles told me kissing me was a mistake and broke my heart.

Things are different now. I knew that and felt it to my core, but the memory still stung at times.

A ping on my phone steers my attention away from my thoughts and I pick it up, seeing Miles's name on the screen.

Miles

I'm at the front door. Let me in.

Wait, *what?*

I check my phone again for the time— 11:05 pm. Why the hell was he here this late at night? Plus, Ryan's not working tonight which means this could go downhill very quickly.

I hastily untangle myself from my sheets, and quietly make

my way out of my room, down the stairs, and to the front door. I unlock it and open it gently, hoping not to wake Ryan. He works at 5:00 am, so I'm hoping he's sound asleep in his room.

My heart twists and aches at the sight of Miles, his clothes are soaked from the rain, and his face is full of concern as he takes me in. I usher him inside, despite feeling overwhelmed with nerves at the prospect of us getting caught right now.

"What are you doing here?" I whisper-shout, locking the door behind us.

Miles's hand reaches out, tipping my chin up to look at him. "You're afraid of storms."

Four words, and they have the ability to nearly bring me to my knees.

"Miles, that's so sweet, but you didn't need to do that."

His brow raises. "You're telling me you wouldn't be up the rest of the night because of it?"

"Well…"

"Exactly," he looks at me pointedly. "Come on, let's go to bed, sunshine."

He laces our hands together and walks us to the staircase when I pause.

"Wait," I whisper, looking around the room to make sure Ryan didn't sneak down the stairs at some point. "I don't want us to get caught."

"We'll be quiet. Just lock your door once we're inside it. I'm not leaving you alone tonight," he says, finality in his tone.

He won't let me win this debate.

I nod, letting him hold my hand as we make our way up the stairs as quietly as possible. We're about halfway to my room when I hear the turn of a knob. I shove Miles behind the curtains that cover the hallway closet.

Ryan emerges from his room, looking dazed and confused.

"Rylee? What's going on? Did I hear the front door open?"

I freeze for a moment, then quickly regain control and rattle off a lie. "Nothing. I thought I heard someone knocking, but it must have been the wind from the storm."

Ryan glares at me, and my heart beats faster for a moment. Fuck, he knows, doesn't he?

"Ry, what the fuck? If you hear someone knocking at night, you come and get me. Not open the goddamn door."

Oh, that's why he's mad. Thank god.

"Right, sorry. I was sleepy and not thinking," I say, sounding breathless with relief from the breath I must have been holding.

Ryan studies me for a moment, turning more worried than pissed. "You okay?"

"Yeah, yes, great," I ramble, wanting him to get back in his room sooner than later.

"Oh-kay," he drags out. "Go back to bed, Rylee."

We both say good night and he finally turns and heads back to his room, shutting the door behind him.

I release a deep breath and hear a low chuckle coming from the closet. I pull back the curtain and press my finger to his lips, warning him to be quiet. He straightens his shoulders, and nods, a silent promise that he'll listen.

Once we're in my room with the door locked, Miles strips.

My mouth drops at the sight before me. He looks so good, and I'm already cursing him in my head because I'll want him to fuck me tonight, but it'll be hard with my brother across the hall.

"Did you run over here?" I ask, hoping the answer is no.

It's a thirty-minute run at least from his house so he better not have run that far in the rain for me, or I'll feel bad.

"No," he says, putting on dry clothes he had in a backpack I missed on his shoulders. "I parked around the block so he wouldn't see my truck in the morning. Then I ran here."

"Miles," I groan, "If you get sick, I'll feel awful."

He strides toward me, pressing my back into the door, his mint and pine scent washing over me, making me feel safe. "Riles, if you think for a second that I was just going to stay home knowing you'd be all alone and scared, then you don't know me like I thought you did. I love you, sunshine. Let me do that, okay?"

I swallow the emotions in my throat because he makes me feel everything tenfold. Every emotion, every experience always feels like more with him. I never knew love did that. It's scary yet fascinating.

"I love you, Miles, so freaking much," I whisper, right before taking his lips with mine and kissing him sweetly, to show him how much I appreciate him. "Thank you for being here."

He smiles against my lips, bending slightly to wrap his hands around my waist. He lifts me and my legs wrap around his waist. Which I'm beginning to learn is his favorite way to hold me.

Miles walks us towards my bed, when I say, "You like carrying me, don't you?"

He sits on the bed, my legs still wrapped around his waist, and he tightens his hold on my hips. "I prefer you close to me, baby."

"And why's that?"

"Because we spent way too much time apart already," he murmurs, his blue-green eyes full of regret.

I push back a lock of his hair away from his forehead, softly running my finger against it until the creases between his brows fade. "You know, every time something happened to me, you were always the first person I wanted to tell."

He looks pained by the admission, but also relieved. "Me too. You have no idea how hard it was to not reach out to you."

"It was hard for me too, you know," I admit.

He says nothing, but his gaze tells me more than his words could. I can see how sorry, regretful, and guilty he feels for his past actions. I don't like that I brought down the mood, in the midst of his sweet gesture, so with a shaky breath, I make myself vulnerable, which is something I hate doing.

"As a kid, you always made me feel safe. You were the one who made me laugh until my stomach hurt. I could always count on you, to be there for me no matter what it was. You kept me calm whenever I was upset, always knew exactly what to say to get me to smile again," I pause, watching his expression grow softer at my words.

"And now, it's more than that. I've never gotten goosebumps just from looking at someone. My heart has never pounded the way it does when you smile at me. You make me feel cherished, like I'm the most precious thing in your world. I just want you to know that I feel the same way. You're everything to me, Miles."

Miles brings his hand up between us to gently wipe away the stray tear falling down my cheek, his touch so soft like he's afraid he'll break me. "Riles," he whispers, my name like a prayer rolling off of his tongue, right before he brings his lips to mine, claiming me over and over again with every brush of his lips against mine, with every stroke of his tongue in my mouth.

He shows me how I belong to him as he makes love to me, quietly, slowly in the dark of the night. Our muffled moans and sighs are overshadowed by the booming thunder outside.

I've never enjoyed a thunderstorm as much as I did that night, Miles whispering dirty things in my ear while his body cherished every inch of mine.

My brother's best friend owned me in every way possible, and there was no way I could ever undo it.

CHAPTER TWENTY-FIVE
Miles

I have never played a more tortuous game of baseball in my life. Not only are we losing, but I have to pretend like I'm not dating the girl on first base who has my entire heart.

Ryan's here tonight, and so is Rylee, despite my incessant worries about her getting hurt. It's only been two weeks since the injury, and I still worry even though it was only bruised.

When I arrived, I said hello to Rylee like any other teammate, and it nearly killed me not to tug her into my arms and press my lips to hers. And when it was time to stretch, I had to do everything in my power not to openly eye fuck her as her long legs extended, displaying her muscles and curves for everyone to see.

I tend to be possessive when it comes to her, but I've gotten better. I don't like seeing anyone check her out, but knowing she's mine soothes the jealous beast inside that wants to rear its ugly head. They can look all they want, and honestly, I don't blame them because she's fucking beautiful but touching is where I draw the line.

That's when my possessive side of me will come back to play, and it won't be pretty.

It's the top of the seventh inning now, and we're down by five, which means if we don't score a run right now, the game is over.

Ryan goes up to bat first, earning us a double. Next up is Katie, who gets a single. There are two people on the bases when it's my turn, and there's pressure on me to score a run. I take a couple of practice swings, then dig my feet in, nodding at the pitcher to let him know I'm ready.

He throws me a low, but fastball, and I'll make him wish he didn't. I swing just at the right time and send the ball to the opposite field.

They're not expecting it, because a right-handed hitter usually hits to left field.

We take advantage of it, and both Ryan and Katie make it home, bringing us to 10 - 7. I stop at third base, bumping knuckles with Brandon who's coaching our runners.

Rylee is next, and if she's nervous, she doesn't show it. She simply smiles during her practice swing, then steps into the batter's box, a slight shimmy to her hips as she waits for the pitch.

I don't even think she knows she does it, but it's sexy as hell.

She hits the ball just right, smacking it down center field, at least a double if she can make it fast enough, which I know she can. I run home, then turn around and watch Rylee run to second base just as the outfielder cranks it to the second baseman.

Shit, she's not going to make it.

Rylee realizes this and decides to slide since it will increase her chances of making it before he catches the ball. She goes down swiftly, her slide clean and perfectly timed as the ump calls her safe.

The second baseman throws his hands up, yelling, "Bullshit! She wasn't safe."

My fists ball at my sides, but a hand lands on my chest. I look down to see Ava shaking her head at me, a silent warning that I need to relax. If I lose my shit right now, it won't be good for our *secret*.

Ryan's already storming over. "You got a problem with the call?"

"Yeah, I do. Just because she has *long* legs doesn't mean they made it there on time. She was out," the second baseman shouts.

The way his voice drawls over the mention of her legs makes me see red. I try to step forward, but Ava pulls on my hand.

"Don't even think about it. Ryan will not take this well right now, and Rylee will be pissed at you," she hisses.

"Fuck," I grunt in frustration, whipping my helmet against the chain link fence.

Not being able to defend my girl is sending me over the edge. All because our relationship is supposedly forbidden. I love her, and she loves me. It should be as simple as that, but I know that in reality, the best things aren't always simple.

My outburst rattles the ump and he throws his hands up. "One more word from either team and you will both be kicked out. Understood?"

Ryan gives the asshole one last glare, then makes his way back to the dugout where the rest of the team is while Sean goes up to bat.

"Tell me you gave that guy a piece of your mind," I seethe, my muscles straining with tension.

Ryan stops beside me, running a hand through his blonde waves. "Trust me, I did. I'm her brother, I know how to take care of her."

His words only piss me off more, reminding me exactly why I couldn't jump in and protect her. Ruining her relationship with him by exposing us too soon would blow up in our faces, and I don't think she's ready for that yet.

But I am. I'd walk through fire for her, but I need her to let me.

We end up losing the game, but it doesn't even matter because we secured first place in our division regardless. The team decides to stay for drinks, but I can't seem to get rid of the tension that's been there since the beginning of today's game.

Rylee must notice because she nudges her foot against my leg under the picnic bench. I glance up at her over my beer, and she motions her head to the right, asking me to follow her. She stands and rounds the table to head toward the back of the pavilion.

I wait a few minutes to not seem obvious, then make my way to her. I find her leaning against the wall where we kissed for the first time a few weeks ago.

As soon as she sees me, she kicks off the wall and marches toward me. Her hands come up to my beard, stroking it in a soothing motion. "What's wrong?"

I give her a stern gaze. "I'm pissed off because that asshole got to talk about you disrespectfully and I couldn't do a damn thing about it. Do you know how hard that is for me? To watch the girl I love get talked about like that, and have to stand and *watch?*"

She frowns at me, her usual bubbly demeanor fading. "I'm sorry Miles, but imagine what would've happened if you did. We both know it wouldn't have been ideal. You would've lost your shit and probably slipped up about us. That can't happen."

Her words hit me like a slap to the face. "Sorry that we're something to be ashamed of."

"Miles, no. That's not what I'm saying, you know I love you."

"But not enough to tell your brother, right?" I throw back at her.

Rylee's bottom lip wobbles, her eyes glassy. "That's not fair, we both agreed to wait until we gave this a chance first, and got our footing."

I wrap my arms around her lower back, needing to feel her despite the heated conversation. "Yeah, and guess what, Riles? I'm pretty sure we have steady feet, wouldn't you say? Or are we just saying *I love you* for fun?"

Her eyes search mine, and I know she knows I'm right. She's terrified but knows the truth needs to come out sooner rather than later.

She concedes, nodding her head in agreement. "Our relationship means everything to me, you know that," she says quietly, her eyes pleading for me to understand that, and I do. "How about after the trip? I don't want to ruin that for the group by fighting with Ryan and the trip getting canceled. Especially since you told me he wants to propose that weekend."

"Okay, that's fair," I say, lifting her hand off of my cheek and kissing each of her fingers.

I don't like fighting with her, but fuck if I wasn't pissed with everything that happened.

"Are we okay?" she asks, sounding slightly nervous. She bites down on her lip.

I answer her with a kiss, letting her know that I'll always love her, even when we're in disagreement.

I pull back before I get lost in her. "We're always okay, baby. I love you."

The smile that lights up my world appears wide and genuine. "I love you too, maybe more than sour patch kids."

I narrow my brows at her. "Maybe?"

She hums to herself for a moment, a sly grin on her face. "I don't know. It depends on if you can still do that thing with your tongue–"

She doesn't get to finish because I cut her off. "We're leaving, let's go."

I stalk back toward the pavilion to grab my stuff because I want to dive between her thighs as soon as possible. She laughs behind me as she follows, the sound relieving the tension in my body temporarily, knowing being inside her is the only thing that will cure it completely.

On my hasty walk back to the benches, I bump into someone and realize it's him. The asshole from second base. His beer knocks into his chest and spills all over his white jersey.

"Not sorry," I mutter because I meant it. I'm not sorry, not one fucking bit.

He doesn't say anything, which is wise, and I make my way back to the table, slinging my bag over my shoulder as I say goodbye to the team.

"I'm going to drive Miles home since he drank a few beers," I hear Rylee tell Ryan, coveting our lie for the night.

I've only had two, and I'm not close to being drunk, but it's what we have to do for now.

I just hope it's not for much longer because I'm tired of sneaking around. Especially when I want to shower my girl in love and claim her for everyone to see.

CHAPTER TWENTY-SIX

Miles

These past few weeks have been some of the best weeks of my life, despite having to sneak around. I divided my time between playing baseball, volunteering at the dog shelter, helping my sister, and hanging out with Rylee.

We spent as much time as we could together. We went on walks, golfed, had beach days, or simply relaxed together, her reading while I watched baseball games.

Oh, and lots of sex. I didn't take Rylee for one to be insatiable, but she just might be. The shower, the kitchen counter, my parent's boat, and a golf cart when no one was around.

Needless to say, it's been amazing. Minus, the part where we have to sneak around, planning our dates when Ryan's working to avoid any questions.

Occasionally, Ryan and Ava are there and we have to pretend, but even then, I don't hate it because she's still my best friend.

There are only five more days before our cottage trip. I should be excited to go, but I'm dreading having to pretend I'm not madly in love with my girlfriend.

Ry and I had agreed to keep our relationship a secret from

Ryan, so we could figure it out on our own terms before he goes big brother on us. At first, it made sense to me, but since that night at baseball, I've been wondering if that was the right decision.

Ryan might be more pissed when he learns we've been sneaking around this entire time. I have no idea how he'll react when she tells him after the trip, but most importantly, I don't know how she'll react to his reaction.

Would she leave me if that meant preserving her relationship with her brother?

I'm pulled from my thoughts when Rylee waves her hand before me. I snap out of it and remember where we're at.

My classroom for the next year at Westchester Elementary.

It's a decent-sized room, with all the basic necessities, but any teacher knows that to create an effective classroom experience, you need to dip into your own wallet.

We came early this morning to scout the place, then ventured to Walmart, Michaels, and Staples to get everything I needed.

I never knew how much I needed Rylee for this, but I do now. I'm a good teacher, but I don't have an eye for classroom décor like her. I love watching her come alive, a passion lighting her eyes when she gets ideas in her head and gets to put them together in real life.

"Sorry, what was that?" I ask her.

"I wanted to know if you agreed that these punctuation and grammar posters should go above the whiteboard or if you think they should go on the side wall?" she repeats, her hands pointing at the two different spots.

"Above the whiteboard, so the students can be reminded of it easily when they look up," I explain.

"Are you regretting bringing me here?" she blurts out.

I'm not shocked by her sudden statement because Rylee always says what's on her mind, but I am shocked by *what* she said.

My brows narrow in confusion. "What? Why would you even ask that?"

"You're letting me do whatever I want. I thought maybe you were just saying yes to everything to shut me up and please me, then change it when school starts," she rambles, her fingers toying with the others

"Riles, breathe," I say, taking a deep breath with her. "I'm agreeing because I agree, it's that simple. If I don't like something you don't think I'd tell you? You know me better than that," I remind her.

Her shoulders sag. "Ugh, you're right. I'm becoming more irritable as the trip looms closer."

I twine my fingers with hers, squeezing them in reassurance. "Ryan isn't going to find out. Stop stressing, sunshine."

Her words about regret spring our previous conversation from a few weeks ago to the forefront of my memory, when I asked her what I most regretted. I never figured out hers.

"What do you regret the most?" I ask.

She pauses for a moment, her hands gripping the chair she was about to use to stand on to hang the posters up. "You and that damn memory. I almost forgot you forget nothing," she teases.

"I know I'm supposed to answer for you, but I honestly don't know. I wasn't around," I grit out.

I know it's something we can't avoid bringing up because it was part of our story, but I still flinch every time.

Sadness crosses her features for a moment before she straightens. "I guess I would say not going to prom. Ava had a date, and I didn't want to go without one. It's so stupid. I know I didn't need a date to go, but when you're young, you don't always realize the stupid things you do until later. I always fantasized about it growing up, the dress I would wear, what my hair would look like, slow dancing with," she pauses, blushing. "With you."

My chest feels heavy because I wish I could've taken her to prom. Fulfilled her every wish and dream that night. Fuck.

"I didn't go either. It seemed stupid to me. Why spend hundreds of dollars on one night?" I joke lightly, trying to ignore the guilt in my stomach.

"That too. I didn't want to waste the money, but I made a bargain with myself. Since I didn't go to prom, I'll allow myself to splurge on my wedding dress. No limit, just whatever I want," she says, her cheeks flushing once more.

I've pictured Rylee in a white dress more than I'd like to admit, but hearing the words 'my wedding dress' out of her mouth puts a new spin on it.

God, I can't wait to marry her. Have her walk down the aisle, in a white dress looking so fucking breathtaking, swearing to be mine forever.

I want to comment about her dress, how I would pay for anything she wanted for our wedding, but I'm scared it'll freak her out. "You deserve whatever you want Rylee. Not just the dress," I say tenderly.

She smiles widely but hides her face as she turns to stand on the chair and hang up the posters. I stare at her ass, feeling myself grow beneath my shorts. The effect this girl has on me is insane.

"I can feel you burning a hole into my ass," she remarks.

"One day, it'll be my dick in your–"

I was about to say ass, and she knows it because she whips around so fast that she loses her balance. Time slows as she falls, but I quickly move and catch her in my arms.

"Good catch," she huffs, sending a loose wave out of her sight.

My dick throbs in my jeans, but I have to tell him no. She's on her period, and even though I wouldn't care, I know she does. She tends to get excruciating cramps and doesn't feel well all around, so sex is off the table.

I keep her in my arms, liking her here more than she will ever know. "You are a pretty good catch, I'll admit," I flirt with her.

We do this often, teasing and flirting like we're fifteen. Part of me wonders if we do it to fill the gaps we missed.

Her brows raise. "Is that so?" A smile takes over her face, and it lights me up from the inside out.

"The best and most important one I've ever made."

She kisses me, her lips ravenous as they meld with mine. I've never had this kind of connection when kissing someone before.

It's desperate, passionate, and leaves my nerves on fire.

Her hands wrap around the back of my neck, gripping my hair as she moans into the kiss.

Fuck me.

I switch my hold on her so she's now straddling my waist. I squeeze her ass and suck on her bottom lip. She whimpers and grinds on me, right against my already hard cock.

She is killing me and there is no other way I'd rather go out.

She suddenly untangles her legs from around my waist, setting her feet back on the floor. "Lock the door and sit in your chair," she orders.

I follow her command and walk to the door to lock it. I sit on my chair. "Look Ry, just because I'm aroused doesn't mean you need to do anything. I know you're not comfortable right now. Don't do this for me." I quickly say before she can move or say another word.

Rylee holds my gaze, annoyance clear on her features as she walks over to me. I think she's about to straddle me, but she surprises me and drops to her knees.

I'm about to stop her when she holds up her hand. "This is for me too, got it?"

I struggle, but I'm a goner once I glance at her determined, turned-on. I nod, and her lips turn up into the biggest fucking smile.

We quickly slid my jeans and my boxers down just enough so that my cock can spring free but not enough to leave me halfway naked in a school. There are no kids around, but the setting is still precarious.

She spits in her hand, a tip I taught her, and she firmly grips the base, blood pooling in my cock. She hasn't even started and my body is already on edge. She slides her hand up, squeezes around the tip, then slowly back down.

Chills shoot down my spine and before I can even process it, her hot mouth encases my cock. Fuuuuck. Her palms rest on my thighs as she swirls her tongue around the tip, then she quickly takes me as far as she can go.

It's nearly impossible to fully fit my entire length in her mouth, but she puts out a damn good effort.

I fist my hands into her hair. "Such a pretty girl with your lips wrapped around my cock."

Rylee was good her first time back in her laundry room, but I'd be lying if I said she didn't make progress since then. Her storm-blue eyes latch onto mine, and a moan erupts from her throat, sending vibrations against my cock.

She looks away, seeming overcome by the intensity, and my eyes roll back as she sucks me like she's savoring me.

A grunt rises in my throat, making my voice sound rough as hell as I try to warn her, "Ry, I'm going to—"

She takes me out, her lips hovering over my tip as she strokes my length. "I want you to come in my mouth."

She puts me back into her mouth and continues to give me the best blow job I've ever received. This. Fucking. Girl. I would never have thought her sex drive would be as high as mine.

And it's only with me.

That knowledge sends chills down my spine, and my balls tense up as I come into her mouth. Rylee continues sucking and licking my dick as I bask in the high of my orgasm.

As I come down from it, I realize I am never going to look at this desk the same way.

CHAPTER TWENTY-SEVEN

Rylee

I slowly rise and stir in my bed, but it doesn't feel like my bed. I open my eyes, blinking away sleep as I become aware of my surroundings.

I'm on the top of a bunk bed in the kids' room at my parent's cottage. The pale green walls and dark hardwood floors add to the rustic vibe of the house, everything is designed to make you feel surrounded by nature.

I love it here, being away from everything, deep in the forest in Whispering Pine's cottage country.

We came in late last night, and had all gone to bed after unpacking all the food and alcohol we brought. Which was a lot, considering there are ten of us here for the weekend.

Miles and I rode with Ryan and Ava. I want to say it was fine, and it partly was, but our secret is starting to gnaw at my insides as our relationship continues to grow.

Now that we've had time to explore it for ourselves, I know without a doubt what we have is real and hopefully, a forever kind of love. I think after this weekend, I'll sit Ryan down with Miles and tell him because I don't want to hide one of the best things in my life anymore.

I think I'm finally ready for that conversation. Just not immediately. I don't want to risk it and ruin everyone's weekend.

Miles is sleeping on the bottom bunk below me, while Sean and Eric are on the other bunk bed. Katie and Brandon are on blow-up mattresses in the living room, a decision made by a hundred-meter dash in a Meijer's parking lot on the way up here between everyone who was single, which is everyone besides Ava and Ryan.

(Miles and I too, but since nobody knows, we had to participate too).

Ava and Ryan took the main bedroom, while Claire and Lindsay shared the other small guest room. I would have liked to have that room for Miles and me, but that is obviously not on the agenda for this weekend.

A waft of eggs and bacon fills the room, making my stomach growl. I throw my blanket off and quietly climb down the ladder. A hand wraps around my ankle on the last step, and I nearly squeal until my body recognizes the familiar warm, large hand.

I crane my neck to look at Miles and I'm greeted with a sad smile.

"What's wrong?" I whisper, careful not to wake the two boys or alert whoever is cooking.

He lets go of my ankle, lays back down, and motions for me to come closer with his hand. I hesitate between not wanting to get caught, and not wanting to leave him in his bed when he's looking at me like that.

No one on the team knows we're together beside Ava and Claire. I was worried that they'd found out the night I hurt my collarbone, but Ava said they all knew we were good friends, and didn't suspect anything more.

I crawl into his bed, careful not to hit my head or get too cozy. I place my hand on his chest. He lifts a finger to my jaw, gently tracing the line back and forth.

"What's wrong?" I prod again.

He shakes his head slightly. "Nothing, I just miss you. That's all."

That can be remedied.

My lips meet his ever so gently to avoid making noticeable kissing noises. I try to pull back, knowing if we linger it'll be harder to stop, but he grips the back of my neck and holds me in place, deepening the kiss.

His chest thuds more rapidly under my palm, and that knowledge sends a chill down my spine. We both pull back at the same time, needing a breath of air.

"Better?" I ask, slowly crawling my way out of his bunk.

He moves with me, coming to stand beside me now.

"It'll have to do for now," he murmurs, quickly kissing me on the cheek before heading to the bathroom in our room.

My body aches for more too, but I know we can't. I take a deep breath and leave our room, noting the air mattresses deflated.

I spot Brandon and Katie perched on bar stools in front of the kitchen island, while Ava and Ryan are cooking breakfast.

"Morning gorgeous," Katie calls out.

While we're not super close like Ava, Claire, and I, we still get along really well.

"Look Katie, I know I'm irresistible, but I'm not open for business," Brandon interjects, and we all laugh.

If there was a picture in the dictionary next to the word cocky, it would be Brandon.

I smile. "Morning everyone. Do you need any help cooking?"

Ava turns to the griddle, pouring a dollop of pancake batter. "Nope. Brandon already set the table, and we're almost done cooking."

"Do you want me to go wake the rest up?" Katie asks.

"I got this," Brandon chimes in, cupping two hands around his mouth to yell, "BACON YEAH! WAKE UP YEAH!"

His love for Jersey Shore knows no bounds.

"Jesus, I think you blew my eardrum," Ryan mutters.

Within minutes, the rest of the team fills the kitchen, filling spots around the kitchen table or the island. Miles sits at the table, while I take a seat next to Brandon at the island, not wanting to be too close to him all weekend and draw suspicions.

I peer over my shoulder and notice he has a slight scowl on his face. Is he mad that I didn't sit with him? He wasn't clingy, but maybe he still wanted to sit next to me?

Ugh, I freaking hate this stupid charade, and I have no one to blame but myself.

"Alright, today's game plan is to head to Big Beaver Lake and rent a pontoon. We brought the jet ski up too, so Rylee will ride it. We'll spend the day on the lake, come back around dinner, BBQ, and fire for the night," Ryan explains, his need for organization never failing even on vacation.

Everyone agrees and talks about what we should pack for snacks and drinks, while Lindsay and Claire clean up the breakfast spread. I pack the snack bag, Sean packs the cooler, while the rest of the team gets ready for the day.

We pack into two vehicles and head towards the lake, the energy vibrant in the car. The music's cranked, and we're all jamming along to old pop songs we know by heart. Michelle Branch's song, Everywhere, comes on, inspiring Miles and Ryan to belt it out word for word. Ava, Claire, and I can't stop laughing.

Once we arrive, the boys go into Dad mode, unloading

everything and refusing to let us carry anything. Ryan goes inside to get the keys to the boat. Once he's back, the boys drop the snack and cooler bags onto the boat while Ryan and I unload the jet ski into the water.

Growing up by the lake every summer, our parents made sure we got our boating licenses and knew how to operate them.

I toss my oversized shirt into the truck, leaving me in my bikini. The yellow bottoms are cheeky, more than I'm usually comfortable with, but this set was so cute I couldn't not get it. The colourful striped top has a shoulder strap. It screams summer and joy, which is right up my alley.

"Alright, Ry. You know the area. You can either wait for us, or go now and ride around," Ryan tells me.

I roll my eyes. "Yes, boss." I wonder how the hell Ava deals with him.

"I'm just looking out for you Rylee. Who do you want to ride with you?" he asks.

Before I can even suggest anyone, Miles appears on the dock, strapping a life jacket around his bare chest. The life jacket looks tiny on him in contrast to the way his muscles accentuate his shoulders and arms.

"I'll go with her, just in case she wants to switch off at some point."

Miles is the only other person here with a boating license, and with Ryan driving the boat, it's the most logical option in case anything were to happen.

Ryan clamps a hand down on his shoulder, squeezing. "Thanks, man."

Miles nods and hops down onto the jet ski gently, careful not to tip us over.

"Drive safely. See you guys in a bit," Ryan says before turning on his heel to head to the other dock where our rental pontoon is.

I turn on the engine, loving the thrumming sound of the jet ski coming to life. Excitement builds in my body, goosebumps spreading in its wake.

I drive us out of the docking area, while Miles remains silent, his body barely touching mine. I find it odd, and it makes me anxious, but I choose not to overthink it and enjoy the moment.

Once we reach the buoys signaling that we're out of the docking zone, Miles suddenly scoots forward, the warmth from his body enveloping mine as his chest presses firmly against my back. Well, as close as we can be with our life jackets on.

I'm assuming his change in demeanor has to do with the fact that we're now far out and away from the boat, away from prying eyes.

His hands grip my bare hips, his fingers digging into my skin with enough pressure to make my clit throb.

A sigh of relief leaves his lips at the contact.

I roll my hips back involuntarily. My body clearly has a mission of its own.

"Having to watch you look so sinful in this fucking bikini all morning and not being able to touch you has been driving me insane," he groans against my neck, sending shivers down my spine.

I smile shyly. "You'll be fine, hot shot."

While I try to convince him he's fine, I'm not sure I am. I don't get to hear his response because I grip the throttle on the handlebar and send us flying forward.

The sun is high and the water is mostly calm, perfect conditions for me to press on the throttle a little harder since there aren't many waves to adjust to.

I can't help but smile. It's a beautiful day, the sun is beaming and I love the freedom that comes with being on the water.

Miles's hands slide from my hip to wrap his arms around

my waist, holding me as we enjoy the ride. His cheek nestles into my neck, and I can feel his smile against my sun-kissed skin.

The wake of a nearby boat creates perfect ripples of waves, and I steer us right into them. We jump the first one, and I would've nearly left the seat if it weren't for Miles's strong arms keeping me in place.

Miles shouts in joy, and it eggs me on to take the next one a little rougher. We jump the wave even higher this time, sending both of our asses off the seats briefly, before we smack back down.

Adrenaline erupts inside my body, swirling like smoke as the high builds. It also increases my arousal and I'm suddenly very needy for Miles's touch. It's been six days since he's last touched me intimately, and it feels like too damn long.

The lapping of the waves below us doesn't help the ache between my thighs as our hips clash with one another from the force.

"Miles…" my voice shakes, my need for him overpowering.

He picks up on it instantly, and it's then that I notice his erection bumping into me. "Do you trust me?"

"Yes," I answer because, after everything we've been through, how much love he's shown me, and despite my anxiety kicking in, I do.

"Drive to the bay stream on the right," he orders softly into my ear.

I follow suit and pull on the throttle. We reach the secluded area within minutes. It's a circle of water enclosed by trees, and not many people go here because you need a small engine like a jet ski to get to it.

As soon as we're through the stream, Miles starts peppering kisses along my neck, up to my jaw, and back. My eyes flutter shut at the sensation, and I feel one of his large hands fall on top of mine on the throttle.

"Let go and let me take over."

I let go of the throttle, keeping one hand on the other for balance. He brings his free hand to the top of my bottoms, his finger tracing the material back and forth.

"M-miles, what are you doing?" I rasp, sounding out of breath.

"No one's around and you trust me so, relax baby. I got you."

His fingers dive underneath my bottoms and I buck forward when his fingers lightly brush my clit. I gasp when his fingers trail further south until they reach my core.

"That's a good girl, always so ready for me," he growls against my jaw, his fingers driving inside me.

I turn my head to take his lips with mine, burning for that blissful feeling when they connect. We moan into each other's mouths as we kiss, pouring our longing and love into every ounce.

He fucks me in time with the waves. When we go up, he pulls out, and when we come down, I come down hard onto his fingers. My fingers trail his arm until I reach his hair, pulling tightly on the wet strands.

The pleasure building within me almost feels like too much. Feeling his warmth and build surrounding me, the exoticness of doing this on the water, and the way the waves play into the rhythm of his fingers.

The sounds as he finger fucks me don't embarrass me. It turns me on. His thumb strokes my clit lightly, once, twice, then he presses hard as his fingers curl inside me, and I go off. I come on his fingers, breaking our kiss to moan his name against his jaw as the high takes over.

Miles shudders behind me, and I feel his cock jut against my ass. I break out of the trance from my orgasm and open my eyes to look at him.

Did he just…?

"Did you…" I pant. "Come too?"

He seems shy, but he nods and smiles boyishly. "Yeah sunshine, I fucking did. That was hot as hell."

My lips part in astonishment. "I didn't even… how?"

He chuckles. "That's what happens when you're insanely attracted to and in love with someone I guess."

We both burst out in laughter and eventually make our way to the sandbar, meeting them just a tad later than we'd planned.

Hours later, the boys are throwing a football around in the water, while we snack and tan on the boat.

"Do I look red to you?" Lindsay asks, worry lines creasing her forehead.

Claire winces as she takes her in. "Just a tad."

She sighs dramatically. "This is why I stay inside. The outside isn't supposed to hurt us."

Lindsay is the least adventurous of the group, but we still love her anyway.

"But, I could get used to the view," she says, her eyes averting to the water where the guys are.

I follow her gaze until I land on Miles, instantly wanting to stake my claim on him.

"Why don't you just talk to him?" Katie perks up, clearly oblivious to how Ava, Claire, and I have tensed at the subject.

Lindsay hums. "Because I don't want to risk our group dynamic and make it weird."

Katie sits up tall, a light going off in her head. "Rylee, you guys are good friends. Why don't you talk to him for her?"

My insides boil, and I feel as red as Lindsay looks. Not going to happen. Sorry Lindsay, but hell no.

I try my best to keep my face blank and stay emotionless behind my sunglasses, as I take a deep breath. "Uh…"

I catch Ava and Claire looking at me with curiosity because they have no idea what I'll say. So, I go with the truth, well a truth from before. "Miles doesn't date, literally never has. He just wants to hook up."

Lindsay's eyes gleam. "That's fine with me. I've always wanted a fuck buddy."

I dig my nails into my palm, but before I can say anything, Ava thankfully speaks up. "He doesn't hook up with girls from his social circle, to avoid making things awkward. So, I'd drop the fantasy quickly."

I mouth a silent thank you to Ava, and she squeezes my knee in response.

"Ugh, what a shame. I'd give him the ride of his life." She grins, and I want to smack it off her face.

I physically can't sit here anymore because I'm worried I'll ruin everything and let it slip that he's mine, my jealousy threatening to bubble to the surface and topple over.

I stand and swing a leg over the side of the boat, hopping into the water. The coolness is refreshing, and I let it wash away the feelings Lindsay brought up in me.

Jealousy and anger.

Angry because I'm starting to hate this stupid secret, and jealous because I don't like to share.

I brush it off for now and make my way over to the guys.

"Go long, Ry," Eric shouts.

I halt my steps, as he rears his arm back and chucks me the ball. I make the catch, and he splashes the water in victory, cheering. I feel my smile make its way back to my face and I throw the ball to Sean, who misses and gets splashed by water instead.

We do this for a while until it's time to return the boat.

Miles offers to drive the jet ski back, and I oblige without fighting him because a full day in the sun usually makes me sleepy. Once we're out of eyesight from the group, I wrap my arms around him and rest my head against his back.

I revel in the way his scent wraps around me, the sound of the water, and the fact that right now, he's mine.

And hopefully, for every day that follows.

CHAPTER TWENTY-EIGHT

Miles

I t's our second to last night of the cottage trip, and I'm sad to see it nearly end. I've gotten to know the rest of the team really well, and it's nice to feel a part of a group that feels like family.

We've spent our days at the lake, playing volleyball, drinking games, and sitting by the fire. Yesterday, Ryan and I took off on our own for a while to set up the engagement spot.

He brought everything he needed, being the overly detailed guy he is, and it looked pretty fucking good if you ask me. He and Ava went after dinner around sunset and let's just say they didn't return until this morning.

Rylee was so happy she cried tears of joy, and it only made me more eager to get down on one knee for her.

Soon.

The fire burns away, the ember chips floating up to the clear sky, the stars visible this high north.

It's beautiful, but not as beautiful as watching Rylee watch them.

Her head is tilted, her neck craning to take in the various

bright spots in the dark sky. Those blue-gray eyes are wide, a mix of joy and peace swarming in them.

I love seeing that look on her, happy and content, it's how I want her to always feel.

"Alright, it's time to make things interesting. Who's up for a game of Kings Cup?" Ava suggests, a mischievous glint on her face.

Kings Cup is played using a standard deck, where each card represents a game of some sort. For example, ten is a category, so we go around the circle with a certain topic, and the first person not to have an answer or say a repeat answer has to drink.

Basically, it's a quick and fun way to get drunk because, with each card, someone has to drink.

Brandon claps his hands together. "I love when a jack gets pulled. 'Never Have I Ever' is my favorite."

"What don't we know about each other already?" Katie pipes up.

Brandon shoots her a bemused look. "Oh, you'd be surprised what we can learn about each other."

"Yeah, like that one time, we learned that Brandon once had a threesome in–" Ryan starts, but Brandon quickly cuts him off.

"Don't even say it–"

"A bathroom at a gas station."

The girls break out into a fit of groans and 'ew's,' while we guys break out into laughter.

"Listen, I was like eighteen and super horny. It's not every day you find one, let alone two willing girls at a rest stop. I saw an opportunity and seized it," he defends himself.

"You could've caught a disease from the grime in there," Ryan retorts.

"Who's talking right now? Wait, is it the guy who waited

till he was twenty-three to have sex? Because he wanted to be in love?" Brandon mocks, his hand placed on his chest dramatically.

"I thought it was sweet. Don't talk about my honey bun Bran, or I will cut you," Ava throws back at him, her words playful but there's a hint of seriousness as she defends Ryan.

I knew Ryan wanted to wait to have sex until he met "the one," but I didn't realize that was only two years ago. Not that waiting is a big deal, but I am shocked. He's a good-looking guy, and he had girls trailing after him in high school like a bee to sugar.

Brandon throws his hands up in surrender. "All good Ava. You know your love story makes my heart sing."

Ava's cheeks twinge red, but she continues setting up the cards on the wooden stump we use as a side table. A couple of rounds go by, and we're all getting a bit tipsy now.

"Brandon, don't get too excited, but look here, the first jack," Katie smiles as she turns the card to show everyone the jack.

This game is about to get real. Never Have I Ever always revealed things about people you never thought you'd know.

Brandon yelps, literally. "Alright, you guys know the drill. Five fingers up, and you drink for each finger you put down. The first person to lose all five fingers has to finish their drink."

We all raise a hand and I make eye contact with Rylee. She looks a bit nervous, probably not wanting to be forced to reveal something about us. But it's a game, and we can lie if needed.

Although, I am tired of hiding us. Not that I would make that choice for us and come out about us. I'd never do that without her being on board.

Katie hums. "Hmmm, never have I ever…jacked off using two hands."

All the boys put a finger down and drink, and I nearly spit out my drink when I see that Rylee is doing the same.

Eric beats me to asking her about it. "Rylee, please explain."

"Jesus Christ," Ryan mutters to himself, putting his hands over his ears.

Rylee shrugs her shoulders. "If you don't know why I drank Eric, then clearly you're doing it wrong."

My mouth drops. I think I just fell more in love with her.

Eric gapes. "W-what do you mean?"

Rylee chuckles, before biting her bottom lip, "One hand inside and the other…on my clit."

"That's kind of hot," Sean comments.

I shoot him a lethal glare.

"That's kind of my sister, so watch it," Ryan says, joining back in the conversation.

His words fail to bring a pang of guilt because I refuse to feel guilty for loving and treating his sister with the utmost respect. I'm not sixteen and stupid. I'm a grown fucking man who knows exactly what he wants.

Brandon loses the game first, and we move on to the next card.

Lindsay pulls a queen, the truth or dare card. "Ouuu, I want a dare," she brightens, sitting up straight in her chair.

"I dare you to kiss Miles," Katie says.

I instantly sober up. Everything goes silent. The only thing I can hear is the crackle of the fire and my own heart furiously pounding against my rib cage.

What. The. Fuck.

I know Lindsay is attracted to me, but I haven't once cared for it. If she knew about me and Ry, I know she'd back off instantly, which is another reason why I want to out us to everyone. I don't want to make the choice for us, but like hell am I kissing Lindsay, it would be cheating, and I'm not fucking doing that.

Ava and Claire look like a deer caught in headlights, but when I gaze at Rylee, I see something I've yet to witness.

Pure jealousy.

Her eyes are narrowed at Lindsay, her chest heaving up and down rapidly, and her hand is balled into a fist against her thigh.

"So, I'll take that as a no…awkward," Lindsay mutters, taking in the stark silence.

I don't know why everyone went silent, but maybe they sensed something was off, or Rylee and I have been more transparent than we thought.

"Don't be an ass, Miles. Kiss her, it's just a game," Ryan says, throwing me an exasperated look.

After our chat at the bar, he's probably confused as to why I'm not giving her a shot because Lindsey is an attractive girl who also happens to be a good person too.

But she's not my person. Not my Riles.

I swallow once, my eyes landing back on Rylee to get a read on what she wants me to do. But I get nothing because her head is tilted down, which means she's in her head.

Fuck me.

"Look, Lindsay, I–" I start, but Rylee cuts me off, shocking me with her next words.

"Take one step towards my boyfriend and I will lose my shit," Rylee says, her words crisp and protective.

Claire spits out her drink and Sean pauses his mid-air. Brandon yelps and Ava squeals, the rest of the group gasping in unison.

A part of me is so fucking happy that she was the one to say it, claiming me in front of everyone like I've been wanting to. I'm so proud of her.

But, the other part of me is anxious as for what is to come.

It's dead fucking silent again, and a look of shock adorns

everyone's face, even on Claire and Ava's faces who already knew about us.

They must be just as shocked as I am. Before I get to look over at Ryan, voices erupt.

Katie is the first to break the silence. "Oh my god, Ry. If I knew I would've never suggested that. I'm so sorry."

"I'm so sorry, Rylee. Miles is good-looking, but if I knew, I never would've made those comments on the boat yesterday," Lindsay apologizes, looking sincere.

Rylee only nods at her words, probably still in shock at what she just said herself.

"It's about time. You two were only eye-fucking each other all summer long," Eric comments.

"This is going down as the best game of Kings Cup ever," Brandon sighs happily, loving every minute of this.

Amid all the chatter, I look over at Ryan and he's fucking pissed. I can tell by the way his hand is clenching his beer, his eyes boiling with anger as they stare back at me.

"Rylee, please tell me you're fucking joking," Ryan says, every word dripping with controlled rage.

Rylee speaks up before I have the chance to defend her. "I'm not fucking joking Ryan. We've been dating for a few weeks, but we didn't want to tell you yet and have you ruin it before it even started."

He stands up and turns his attention to me. "How could you? I fucking told you to stay away from her, all those years ago, and again at the first party you came to this summer."

I stand up as well, ready to defend us. "Yeah, and I listened pretty fucking well the first time, didn't I? I left the goddamn state, for Christ's sake. I'm sorry I hurt you by lying to you, and breaking bro code or whatever, but I'm not sorry for loving her."

He steps closer to me, his body seething with rage. "Jesus, you love her? Was it easy, is that what you love? Or do you just love fucking your best friend's sister?"

I growl, my chest bumping against his. "Ryan, I love you like a brother. But talk about her like that again and we're going to have a big fucking problem."

"We already do have a big fucking problem. You got into her pants, now what? I know how this works for you."

Fury builds within me, shaking me to my core, so much so I'm vibrating with anger. I ball my fists at my side. "I already told you to mind your fucking words when her name comes out of your mouth. You know me Ryan, and I don't give third chances."

Hard green eyes stare back at me, and I know he's not backing down. Ryan steps into my space even more, shoving at my chest. "My sister isn't like the girls you hook up with. She's not just a place to stick your dick in and take off when you're done."

That's it, I'm about to punch my best friend. Rylee must sense it because she's suddenly wedging her way between us, her palms flat on my chest.

"Stop, please," she begs, her voice cracking.

The anger thrumming in my veins slows at her tone, realizing how much this is hurting her.

I start to worry. Would she choose him over me?

Ava joins in right after, standing and tugging Ryan backward. "Honey bun, you need to calm down. If you would give them time to explain, and see how much Miles loves her without judgment—"

"You've known this whole time, haven't you," he states, not asking.

"Of course, we're best friends. This also brings me to my next point, you're dating your sister's best friend and that's not an issue, but Miles doing it is?"

"You've been keeping this from me. Christ Ava, what else have you been hiding? She's my little sister, it's fucking different."

Sean interrupts. "Ryan, that's bullshit dude."

I almost forgot that we had an audience, but they're being respectful and letting us handle this on our own, except for Sean.

"Yeah, it is," Rylee says, head whipping in his direction. "Miles treats me with so much love, and respect. We're not just fucking as you so grossly put it, asshole. I don't see how you could find anything wrong with me being with someone who treats me like I'm his entire world."

I wrap a protective arm around Rylee's waist, needing to touch her, to let her know that I love her without saying it. Her body slightly relaxes under my embrace, and it eases the anxiety that was churning in my stomach. She's with me, and she's not letting Ryan push her away from me.

"I spent years hooking up with girls that meant nothing because of you Ryan. Because the only girl I ever wanted to be mine, I pushed thousands of miles away. I was so fucking torn up over it. Not being able to talk to her, or see her. It ate me the fuck up, so yeah I hooked up here and there, trying to push her out of my mind, and guess what? It never fucking worked."

Rylee turns to face me again, a tear falling down her cheek. I gently wipe it away, wanting to ease her pain as much as possible. I know the two of us fighting is hurting her because Ryan is one of the most important people in her life.

He runs a hand through his blonde hair, gripping his locks tightly. "Fuck, just give me a minute to process this. I'm too goddamn angry to think straight," he admits.

I get it. If roles were reversed and it was Syd, I'm sure I'd put up a good fight too.

"I didn't want to hurt you Ryan, you're the brother I've never had. But I couldn't change my feelings even if I wanted to. Rylee's been the one for me since I was sixteen, and that's not ever going to change."

I'm pouring my heart out to him and the entire softball team, but I could care less. I'll fight for her, for us, as much as I have to.

"Come on, Ryan, it's adorable." Brandon swoons.

His support gives me a rush of relief, not that we need others' approval, but it helps.

"My bad for the comment earlier about Rylee being hot," Sean admits, a tad shy, which is shocking.

I grin, tugging her into my chest. "All good man, you didn't know. And she is hot, but she's mine."

God that feels so good to say out loud for the first time. The rest of the team hypes us up, approving of our relationship. Rylee's head lifts from my chest, her face brighter than before, her need for praise and approval being fed. I smile at the sight of her.

I peer up at Ava, who's still trying to calm Ryan down. I take the reprieve from our fight, walking Rylee and me over to my chair, where I sit and tug her onto my lap. Ryan be damned, he may as well get used to it.

She doesn't hesitate, curling up into my chest as her legs draped over my chair. The team picks the conversation back up, moving on as if nothing happened.

I inhale her sweet scent of vanilla and cherries, smelling like home.

"I'm so fucking proud of you," I whisper into her ear.

She doesn't respond verbally, but her body does by nestling closer to mine. I tighten my hold and let my body relax as I have her in my arms freely for the first time.

Until I hear Ryan grumbling. "I'm going to get over them being together eventually, but I don't know if I can get over the fact that you've been lying to me."

Ava looks like she was verbally slapped. "Ryan, don't. Rylee is my best friend, and you're my fiancé. I knew once you realized how much he loves her, you'd be okay with it. If it was some sleazy asshole, yes, I would've broken Rylee's trust and told you. But that's not what happened here. So, either get your shit together right now or talk to me when you're over your tantrum."

It goes eerily silent for the third time tonight and my stomach churns.

Fuck, I don't want them to fight over this. I know it'll tear Rylee up if they broke up over this. I'd like to hope Ryan isn't that much of an idiot to do something like that.

Crushing his beer can in his hand, Ryan stands and walks into the cottage. Ava doesn't follow him and returns to her seat instead. Her eyes are glued to the fire, watching the flames dance.

The group continues their previous conversation, knowing it's best to not ask and just let them figure it out. But Rylee won't let this go.

"Ava, what's wrong?" Rylee asks her quietly, twisting her head to look in Ava's direction.

Ava shrugs her shoulders. "Honestly, nothing. He's a grown man, and I'm giving him the space he needs to process this. If he wants to be mad at me, so be it."

"But what if he doesn't? What if he doesn't forgive you and I'm the reason you guys break up?" Rylee rambles, her anxiety coming into play.

I run my hand up and down her leg reassuringly, trying to soothe her, but deep down, I'm wondering the same thing. They just got engaged, and if we caused their downfall, I'll feel like shit.

Ava props her arms on her knees and leans forward, determination set on her face as she looks at Rylee. "Rylee, stop. If we break up over something as trivial as this, then our relationship has issues that have nothing to do with you. That'll be on us. Besides, that's not going to happen. He's whipped. He might be pissed off right now, but he'll be apologizing by 8:00 am tomorrow."

"You want to bet on that?" Rylee asks, and I can tell Ava's words helped soothe her worries.

"Loser has to drive home tomorrow?"

Both girls laugh, and shake on it. "Deal!"

I wasn't sure what would happen when we finally told him, but this is more than I could ask. Rylee is content in my arms, and Ryan said he would try to get over it. I'll take it for now.

Everything will work out, I'll accept nothing less.

CHAPTER TWENTY-NINE

Rylee

ast night was… interesting.

That wasn't how I planned on telling my brother I was dating his best friend, but shit happens. There was no way in hell I was letting Lindsay get anywhere close to him. I know he wouldn't have kissed her, but I also knew he was struggling with not being rude because, to anyone else, it wouldn't make sense why he wouldn't just kiss her.

"I can practically hear your gears running, what's wrong?" Miles rasps, drowsiness evident in his voice as his body slowly awakens, as he tightens his arms around me.

I voice my worst fear. "I just…What if Ryan doesn't come around? Do you want to try and take a break until things cool off?"

I don't want a break at all, but I'm not sure how he's feeling.

Miles shifts us so quickly I barely have time to process anything. My back hits the mattress and he hovers over me, shielding us into our bubble.

"Riles, stop," he groans, sounding pained. "He loves you, he will come around to the idea. Give him some time, and baby?"

"Yes?" I ask, my body on edge as I wait for his response.

"The only thing I want to try is seeing how good your name would sound next to my last name."

My breath gets lodged in my throat as my emotions swell. Tears prick my eyes and a smile forms on my lips. It may sound crazy, but I feel like I've loved Miles my whole life, and I can't imagine not loving him for the rest of it, so the idea of talking about marriage doesn't scare me with him. It excites me.

"I love you," I whisper softly, my fingers tracing the outline of his lips. "I'm ready for Riles nights every night."

Before he can respond, Ryan enters our room, whisper-shouting. "Ry, Miles, come out here."

My body stills, our little bubble popping. Miles brushes his lips against my forehead, then crawls out of the bed, and I grumpily follow suit. I want to patch things up with my brother, but I also wanted to cuddle with my boyfriend.

We follow him out into the kitchen, tiptoeing as we go since everyone else is still asleep. Ryan sits at the dining room table, and we sit beside one another, opposite him. I peer over at the clock on the wall. 7:27 am.

Looks like I'll be driving home today. Unless he hasn't apologized yet, but judging by the state he's in right now, he seems remorseful.

He looks tired, like he didn't sleep well last night. There's dark spots under his eyes, and his hair is more disheveled than I've seen it in a long time.

"I want to apologize to both of you. I'm sorry Ry. The things I said last night were out of line. I know it wasn't fair for me to react how I did when I'm dating your best friend, but just know it's because you're precious to me. You're my little sister, I'll always look out for you. But seeing how he was willing to defend you last night, I know I don't need to. He's got you, just like he always has."

Ryan's not usually overly emotional with me, so hearing him say such loving things causes tears to return again.

"I'm sorry we kept it a secret. It hurt me to sneak around you, but we needed to try this for us, and our future. We're not in high school anymore, so, thank you. And Ryan?"

"Yeah?"

"I still need you too, you're always going to be my annoying big brother."

Ryan smiles at that, and I can feel the tension rolling off of him as his shoulders drop. He turns his gaze to Miles. "Miles, I'm sorry. You deserved more from me. It wasn't fair of me to think you weren't good enough to be anything real for Rylee. I thought last night about that night at the bar, and how you dismissed the waitress every time. You did that because of her, didn't you?"

My eyebrow quirks up at that because what the hell happened? What did this waitress do? I know Miles wouldn't do anything, but I can't control my jealousy when it wants to come out and play.

"Like I said. She's it for me," Miles says with such ease like it's written in the stars, unable to be undone.

"Good. Last thing, just keep it in your pants around me. Ava and I owe you that decency, and I would like the same," he cringes while smiling, seeming to feel lighter with each apology.

I cover my hands over my face in embarrassment because the last thing I want this early in the morning, or ever, is to talk about sex with my brother.

"Noted," I grumble behind my hands.

A piercing ring erupts from Miles's phone, interrupting the moment. *Thank God.*

We usually have poor reception up here, so whoever is calling got lucky.

Miles pulls the phone out of his pocket. "Hello?"

I can't hear whoever is on the other line, but from the look on Miles's face, it seems urgent.

I wrap my hand around his on the table, squeezing gently to let him know I'm there for him. Ryan registers our hands together but makes no comment as he too, waits to hear what's happened.

Miles hangs up and lifts his head. "Syd is going into premature labor. I need to go. Martin is away on a work trip and our parents are in New York with yours."

He stands abruptly, pulling his hand out of mine, and heads toward the kid's room to likely pack his stuff. I hurry after him to help him collect all of our belongings.

We're leaving the trip a day early, but that's okay. There's nowhere else I'd rather be than by his side, supporting him.

Ryan calls out after us. "I'll drive, you just worry about packing your shit up quickly. I trust Claire to lock up the cottage for us."

It's a three-hour drive from here to Grand Rapids, where Syd is most likely giving birth. She isn't due until September, and it's only August. It might be common for twins to come early, but it's still scary to think of all the 'what ifs' with premature births.

We pack all of our stuff in silence and are in the car, ready to go within ten minutes. Miles and I are waiting in the back of the truck for Ryan and Ava. I know he's stressing over the fact that she's alone right now, about to give birth earlier than expected to twins at that.

"Hey," I say softly, intertwining my hand with his.

His leg ceases its relentless bouncing and he brings our hands up to his lips, kissing each of my knuckles.

"I'm sorry if I'm not being... I don't even know what. I'm just worried sick right now."

"I know you are, and that's okay. What can I do to help you?" I ask, my heart breaking at seeing him so worked up over his sister.

The love he has for his family is sweet, and it makes me love him even more.

Miles takes a deep inhale and releases an even deeper exhale. "Just hold me, sunshine."

I nod, and he adjusts his body so that his head is in my lap, his body sprawled on the seat. I wrap my arm around his shoulder, tracing circles over his chest while my other hand gently plays with his hair.

Ryan and Ava hop in, and we're off. It takes a while for his body to relax, as I gently soothe him with light touches. I release a breath as his tension eases.

I didn't realize how much loving someone causes your feelings to amplify theirs. If Miles is worried, I'm freaking the fuck out. If he's hurting, my heart is aching. If he's smiling, I'm beaming.

As the trees pass by in a blur, I think to myself how grateful I am. Ryan may not be thrilled about Miles and I being together, but he's here. And that's a start.

CHAPTER THIRTY

Rylee

We got to the hospital within two and a half hours, courtesy of Ryan's maniac driving. Miles went in to see Syd immediately, but now that she was in full-blown labor, she asked him to wait outside. There are some things you just can't have your sibling be a part of, and childbirth is one of them.

Ryan and Ava went home and asked us to text them updates. I've been sitting in the waiting room for about seven hours now. Miles joined me at the five-hour mark, shock all over his face when he realized I was still there.

We've been inseparable since, our bodies making contact at all times, me in his lap, our hands intertwined, or a thigh pressed against a thigh. I've realized that Miles's love language is physical touch, especially when he's stressed out.

While alone for the first hours, I spent a lot of time with my thoughts. I thought about Miles, and how much he's shown and told me he loves me. And I feel like I'm not sure if I've done my part to that capacity.

So I went to the gift shop hoping to find something I could buy him because I love showering the people I love in perfectly curated gifts. I already bought Syd one for the babies, which I gave her a week ago when Miles and I visited.

I almost gave up when a certain item caught my attention, and an idea struck me. I bought the gift and worked on it while I waited out in the waiting area.

It's currently sitting in my bag, and now I'm regretting the whole thing. I'm worried he'll think it's stupid, or if he'll even care considering there are bigger things happening right now.

So, it'll stay there until I grow a pair.

"You think we'll win tomorrow?" I ask, my arm wrapped around his back and my fingers resting on the nape of his neck as I toy with the hair there.

"I know so. That championship title is ours," he says, but the words come out flat, his usual excitement gone.

Seeing him like this is taking a toll on me, which is what urges me to just give him the damn gift.

I bend over to my bag on the floor, pull the baseball out of my bag, and hold it up to him. "For you," I murmur, my cheeks flaming hot.

The side of his lips perk up as he takes in the black Sharpie scrawls all over the ball.

"What's this?" he asks, taking the ball into his hands and inspecting it further.

"It's all the reasons you're a good catch," I say softly, my eyes tuning glassy as I watch him read and take in each thing I wrote.

His face morphs into something else entirely. It takes me a second to understand it, but it's realization and relief, knowing I love him as much as he loves me

Our silent eye conversations.
Your ability to make me feel safe and protected.

The way you love your family so fiercely.

The fact that you volunteer to help dogs.

The way you've put everyone else's needs before yours, until recently.

How your lips fit so perfectly against mine.

The way you know me in and out – I think our souls are connected, or whatever deep shit people say.

You never let me win, you push me, and I love to push back.

How your smile grows with mine.

Your heart, for giving it to me entirely.

He's quiet for a few moments, turning the ball over and over again, taking in the words written from my heart.

I start to worry it's too cheesy for him. "It's silly, you don't have to keep it."

Miles's head snaps up, his eyes are soft as they lock with mine. "This is the best thing I've ever been given. I love it, and I love you, so much."

His mouth crashes onto mine, swallowing up any words that were going to leave my mouth. His lips are relentless, giving me all of his love while taking everything from inside me.

Love. Desire. Need. Affection. I'll give him whatever he wants.

"Ahem," a nurse coughs, interrupting our moment, which is probably a good thing because I was two seconds away from wrapping my body around him like a cozy blanket on a cold night.

We break apart, and Miles's attention is solely focused on the nurse, awaiting her news.

"Your sister is doing very well, and the babies are healthy. Would you like to go see them?" she asks, her red curls bouncing around as she nods her head to the hall to the right.

We both stand and follow the nurse until we reach Sydney's room, who's on the phone as we walk in.

"They're perfect," she coos to Martin, her eyes glossing over as she takes in her babies lying in front of her on the bed. One wrapped in pink, the other in blue.

"Tell Mila and Matthew that Papa will be there soon," he says.

I peer over at Miles, and oh fuck, there go my ovaries. He's crying as he looks at his little niece and nephew, pure adoration radiating off his body. I wrap my fingers around his and squeeze.

"God, I love them. Isn't that crazy? How, within seconds of seeing them, I already love them so much."

I beam at him. "No, it's not. That's what babies do. It's their magic power."

"I can't believe she actually named her babies after me. Mila is pretty close to Miles, and Matthew also begins with an M," he teases, his eyes crinkling.

"Sorry to break it to you, love, but her husband's name also starts with an M," I say with a pat on his back.

"That's okay, I just learned I prefer being called love over Miles anyways," he winks.

My body thrums with happiness and my mind imagines Miles looking at our babies like this.

This time, I don't stop myself from imagining it, because I want it. I want everything this life has to offer with this man.

CHAPTER THIRTY-ONE

Miles

My life has been a whirlwind this past weekend. Between the brief drama at the cottage, my sister going into premature labor, and now a tied game for the championship at softball.

Also, today is my birthday.

One day at a time, I tell myself, trying to focus on the game in front of me. It's the top of the last inning, and we're the away team, which means we get to hit first to try and score some runs. Then, we'll have to hold them off in the bottom of the inning to win.

Rylee is up to bat. If she crushes this ball like I know she can, we can easily secure a few runs to hold them off when they go up to bat next.

On the outside, she looks confident as she reaches the plate, her cleats swishing the dirt around until it's just right for her to get into her stance. But I know on the inside she's stressing out a little since there are already two outs, meaning if she gets an out, it's game over.

The pressure is all on Ry but I know my girl, she's got this.

The first pitch is thrown heavily inside, and Rylee doesn't take it.

The ump yells for a strike, the first out of three.

The second pitch is a ball that nearly hits her leg but she moves just in time. I scowl at the pitcher's back, but shift my gaze to Rylee, hoping she'll look my way before she sets herself up again.

To my luck, she does, and I try conveying to her to relax, and crush the fucking ball. She smiles and leans her chin down, telling me she got the message.

The third pitch comes in, and Rylee waits before swinging the bat at the right second. The contact of metal to ball pings in the air as she sends the ball flying into right field.

It catches their outfield by surprise since she's been hitting into left field all night. It soars over his head and Ryan yells at Ava and me to run home.

We do.

I round home plate and turn to see Ryan telling Rylee to run home, and she does. The ball is whipped in from outfield, so Rylee slides in order to make it on time.

"SAFE!" the ump yells.

We all cheer and I run over to Ry, picking her up in my arms and walking us off the field, swinging her around in a circle as she smiles so freely.

"You have no idea how badly I want to fuck you right now," I rasp into her ear, sliding her down my body.

She pulls her bottom lip beneath her teeth. "I've had a dream or two about you taking me in the dugout."

"It's my life's mission to make all your dreams come true, you know," I coo, turning my dirty words into truthful, heartfelt ones.

She leans up on her toes and kisses me sweetly, a yelp

escaping her lips as I palm her ass, pulling her into my body.

"Gross," Ryan mutters, crinkling his nose.

He comes to stand beside us, watching Brandon go up to bat. His ball is a pop fly, our final out. We all grab our gloves and head to the field, ready to defend our runs and hold them off.

I easily make the first throw to Rylee, who catches it by extending her long ass legs to beat the runner. The second hitter crushes a home run, so now we're only up by two. Their third player gets a double, while the fourth hits a pop fly that Ava catches in the outfield.

A new player is up to bat, and this is our shot at securing the last out to hold onto our championship title.

Eric's first two pitches aren't great, but his third pitch is a beauty. The hitter sends the ball right at me. It bounces off the dirt and takes me by surprise, connecting with my kneecap before I can catch it.

Holy fuck. I nearly black out from the pain.

I quickly throw the ball to third base, getting the runner from second out, then fall back on the dirt as the pain overtakes all of my fucking senses.

"Miles," Rylee shouts, her panicked voice getting closer and closer until she's kneeling over me.

Her hands cup my face, willing me to open my eyes.

"Are you okay?" Rylee's worry is palpable: the etch between her brows, the wobble of her bottom lip, and her widened eyes.

I sit up and hold my knee, trying to ease the sting. "Yeah baby, I'm fine. It just fucking took me out for a second, but I'll be okay. It's nothing some ice and a blow job can't fix."

She releases a breath, her worry replaced with a smirk. "I know the perfect lips for the job."

Instead of continuing to spar with me, she stands and holds out her hand. I take it and she tugs me up. My knee hurts like a bitch as I stand, and I know there will be a nasty bruise later, but it's all worth the rush of the game and seeing my team light up with our win.

"We won," Ry exclaims, jumping up and down with excitement.

God my girl is fucking adorable.

"I already felt like I won the moment you came into my life. This is nothing compared to that."

Rylee rolls her eyes. "You are such a softie. I love it, but we just won. Let's celebrate with our friends, get drunk, and have fun. And then tonight you're mine. I have a special gift for you, birthday boy."

"Hmm, does it involve you being a good girl for me all night long? Taking my cock however I please? Cause that would be the best gift," I tease her, leaning closer into her space, our foreheads touching.

"Was I a good girl when I let you paint my ass with your cum last night?" she says, her minty breath against my lips sending a shiver down my spine.

"Very."

My lips brush against hers, and I feel her smile against mine before I take her lips in a searing kiss. Kissing Rylee feels like the sunset on a summer night— soft, safe, warm, joyful and so fucking delicious.

This summer my family expanded by two. I reconnected with my best friend, became a part of the team, and returned home.

With Riles.

EPILOGUE
5 years later

"**M**ommy," my two-year-old, Lila, yells.

I look up from the laptop on the patio table where I'm working on report cards and toward the pool. My husband is holding our baby up in the air, a wild smile on his face as he brings her closer to smother her chubby cheeks in kisses.

My heart swells a the scene.

"Yes?" I ask softly.

"Bring my brover in the pool or wake up Mila and Mattew pwease!" she demands as Miles sets her in a floaty.

By brother, she means the baby in my tummy. Her cousins, Mila and Matthew, are taking a nap inside, which I'm currently envious of. Miles, Martin, Syd, and I took the kids to the park this morning, so they're exhausted.

Not Lila though. She's always ready to go do the next activity. Martin and Syd are having a date night, so we offered to watch their kids, knowing they'd enjoy our weekly get-together with our friends.

"I have one more comment to go, then I'll join you."

I got a permanent teaching position as the grade 2 teacher at Westchester public school three years ago, where Miles is still the grade 8 teacher.

Which is how I ended up pregnant with Lila because once I got busy having my own classroom to run, I forgot to get my birth control shot. And with lockable, private staff bathrooms, we were fucking any chance we got.

Despite the surprise, we were both ecstatic about the idea of having a baby. We had just gotten married and were planning on starting a family sooner than later.

The sun's rays catch my ring, sparkling, as I type on my laptop. My mind slowly drifts away to the night we got engaged, and I smile at the memory.

It was four years ago, only a year after we got together. He surprised me one night by recreating prom night for me. He decorated his parent's boat with fairy lights and had an Italian meal catered. Ava made sure I was dressed for the occasion, and it drove me crazy not knowing why I had to be so dressed up.

Miles and I aren't the fancy type, so I was stressed.

We danced until he got down on one knee with a rose gold band, a large diamond nestled in the middle, surrounded by smaller diamonds outlining the larger one. We then made love all night long under the chill of the starry sky.

It was perfect, just like he is for me.

A knock on our gate pulls me from the memory and the shrill cry of a two-month-old baby.

"Uncle Miles, Auntie Rylee, I'm hereeee," Nora screams as she bounces into the backyard, followed by Ava and Ryan.

Ava and Ryan follow behind, Natalie, their youngest, strapped to Ryan's chest.

About a month after the birth of Miles's niece and nephew, Ava found out she was pregnant. It wasn't planned, considering they had just gotten engaged, but it didn't bother them.

They had Nora and got married once she turned one, so

she could walk down the aisle as the flower girl.

Ryan joins me at the table with Natalie, while Ava and Nora hop right into the pool. There's another knock on the gate and this time Claire and Sean come in together.

That was a relationship I didn't see coming, considering Sean was the biggest manwhore, and Claire is, well she's the sweetest, most pure person in our friend group. They had a lot of ups and downs in the beginning, but they pushed through, and god, they're cute.

It might be the extra hormones, but thinking about all they went through and how they came out stronger in their love makes me want to weep.

Sean joins the others in the pool while Claire joins us at the table. We spent the afternoon lazing about in the pool, enjoying a BBQ. I love our weekly get-togethers, but carrying around a tiny human makes it more tiring, which is how I end up dozing off in the lounger by the pool after dinner.

I'm awoken by light kisses peppered on my swollen stomach, and baby Anderson flutters under his dad's touch.

I open my eyes to meet bright, blue-green ones smiling at me. "How long did I pass out?"

Miles shakes his head, kissing my stomach once more, "Not long, how are you and little man doing?"

I sigh, running a hand through his thick hair while he hums in response. "He likes to rile me up, just like his dad. He won't stop moving."

He rubs a palm gently across my stomach, the corners of his lips turning up at the movements. "Be nice to Mommy, little man, she's precious to us, okay?"

As if he's a goddamn baby whisperer, baby A ceases its attack on my belly.

"I'm not going to say it," I state.

"Say it," he hums, his arrogance still irritating yet charming.

"Nope."

"Riles, we made a bet, if I can get him to stop moving you–"

"Fine, you are a sex god, dad god, teacher god, and husband god. Are you happy?"

He smirks, a genuine smile unfolding after it. "Immensely, are you?"

I sit up and brush my lips against his. "I've got smiles for miles, love."

THE END!

Looking for more of Miles and Rylee?
Head over to my website to receive a bonus scene!

www.carliejean.ca

ACKNOWLEDGMENTS

I would like to start off by thanking you for reading this, it truly means the world to me to share my story and have it out in the world. It's scary but exciting. I hope you enjoyed the ride and are ready to hop on for more fun in the future.

First and foremost, I would like to thank my mom for always supporting me and encouraging me to follow my dreams. She's an avid reader as well, but I pray she does not read this book. Thank you for all that you've ever done for me.

I don't think there are enough words in the dictionary to describe how amazing my editor, Salma, is to work with and just in general as a human being. Her work ethic is top-tier, as well as her ideas for pushing the story in different directions to see what fits best. This book would not be getting published if it weren't for her, as I just wrote a book and had no idea what to do with it. She saw this book at its foundation and helped it grow into the book that it is. I am forever grateful to her for making this book the best it could be, for helping me as a writer, and for her long voice notes that would always bring a smile to my face. Thank you for putting up with my constant questions, and for allowing me to pick your brain and bother you will my neediness as we got closer to release day. Thank you for being not only the best editor but a friend too. I love you, and you deserve all the happiness in this world. Seriously, the best.

To my beta readers, Summer, Sabreena, and Christina thank you so much. You have no idea how important your words of encouragement were, as you were some of the first to read it and I was worried no one would enjoy it. You three proved that wrong, and your comments made my days brighter. A special shoutout goes to Summer, my best friend since birth, who dealt with my incessant messages about plot points and my need for validation regarding whether or not to publish this book. I appreciate all three of you for taking a chance on my book and loving it as much as I do.

To Cat, my cover designer. Thank you for working with me in a time crunch, I will forever be grateful to you. Your vision is untouched. The cover art is beyond what I ever imagined, and is simply stunning. Thank you for all your hard work.

To Nada, and the team at Qamber for formatting my book and being so easy to work with. The formatting process was simple and done so beautifully, thank you. I appreciate you all, and can't wait to work together again soon.

To Greys PR, for promoting my book and giving me the opportunity to share my story with readers. It is greatly appreciated.

And now, it's time to head to university. Sign up for my newsletter and stay in touch to hear about my next release coming this Fall.

ABOUT THE AUTHOR

Carlie is a romance author who loves all things swoon, sunshine, and spice. She lives in Canada. She has two brothers, and a dog named Milo. Carlie grew up watching her mom and dad play baseball and plays herself with her family. She loves to watch and play a variety of sports. When she's not teaching little ones, she loves reading, writing, going for walks, and traveling.

SOCIALS:

Check out my website for in-depth book information, what I'm currently writing, and bonus materials!
www.carliejean.ca

Tiktok and Insta for all book things,
snippets of my personal life and behind the scene writing
@carliejeanwrites

Printed in Great Britain
by Amazon

24760914R00166